Margot Justes

A Hotel in Paris

A Minola Grey Mystery

both
Enjoy Minola's
journey
Thank you so much
Margot
Justes

Echelon Press

Publishing

A HOTEL IN PARIS
An Echelon Press Book

First Echelon Press paperback printing / June 2008

ISBN 1-59080-534-8
978-1-59080-534-3

Library of Congress Control Number: 2007942956

Echelon Press, LLC
9735 Country Meadows Lane 1-D
Laurel, MD 20723
www.echelonpress.com

PRINTED IN THE UNITED STATES OF AMERICA

10 9 8 7 6 5 4 3 2 1

૭ৎ   ৎ৫

A loving dedication to Vic, whose total and complete support is cherished, my daughters Solonge and Dina for always being there, my son-in-law Bill for giving me Sydney and Anthony, and our wonderful friends, Michael Gaudry, Barbara and Richard Johnson, George Kotynek, Lillian and Nico Lalich, Lia Diniz Pocrnich, and Miriam and Dennis Robin.

૭ৎ   ৎ৫

Acknowledgements and thanks go to my 'at work' critique group, Diane Beninati, Pamela Gordon, Nusia Kushch, Judith Martin, and Marlene Skwarski. Ladies thank you for your support. Marlene who also happens to be my manager– her easy and flexible management style is greatly appreciated. To Gina Bogucki, who from the very beginning believed in me and planned my first book signing at work. Thanks go to Betsy Baird for her editing expertise, Kat Thompson for the fantastic final touches, and Karen Syed for giving me this incredible opportunity. To Sisters in Crime Chicago Chapter and Chicago North Romance Writers of America, an awesome and supportive group of writers and readers.

Every portrait that is painted with feeling is a portrait of the artist, not of the sitter.

Oscar Wilde

Chapter 1

Minola Grey was heading toward the elevator when she heard a shrill wail. She glanced to her left and saw the maid dart into the hallway in sheer panic. Minola reached her in a few brisk strides and asked, "Yvonne, what's the matter?" She didn't detect any sign of injury, just pure terror in her eyes. This type of behavior was unlike Yvonne, who was always steadfast. Nothing ever ruffled her.

"Mademoiselle Grey…body…blood…" she sobbed.

"Body? Blood? Whose body? Yvonne, please…please sit down." Minola led her to the plush oversized chair near the elevator. "Tell me what happened," Minola pleaded.

"Lord Yardleigh. In his room…dead…blood," Yvonne said, her voice shaking. Her weeping dwindled to a whimper.

"Yvonne, knock on Dr. LeBrun's door. See if he's there. I'll go to Lord Yardleigh's room. Use the phone in the hallway and call the front desk for help. Get Security up here, fast."

Since Lord Yardleigh's door had been left open, Minola walked in, and what she saw left no doubt in her mind. Lord Yardleigh was dead. The body lying splayed out on the floor did not diminish the quiet elegance of the room. Her stomach twisted in a knot, her muscles tightened, and nausea rose in her throat.

She had never seen a body in this state before. *Think! Don't touch anything.* She shook her head, as if to clear any lingering cobwebs. *Get hold of yourself. I don't see a gun. Was this murder?* Lord Yardleigh lay on his back in a big pool of blood, which had begun to darken. As a great fan of the mystery genre, she knew enough not to disturb anything in the room. The crime scene needed to be preserved.

Reluctantly, Minola looked at the body again and noted how impeccably dressed he had been–crisp white linen shirt, gold cuff links, and an expensive watch still on his wrist–impeccable except for the bloody stain that had spread beyond the hole in the shirt, creating a crimson river against the achromatic background. To relieve her queasiness, Minola swiftly glanced at the rest of the room. As an artist, she focused on the *de rigueur* hotel furniture, then on the few contemporary canvases displayed on the walls. She could tell they were not hotel issue.

The colors and textures of the paintings strangely complimented the hues of the grim, yet powerful, scene before her. Contemplating the pieces on the wall gave Minola a reprieve from the ghastly outline on the floor. Her hands clenched and she began to shake.

Nothing appeared to have been disturbed in the quiet, serene room. The curtains were open, and the sun filtered through to cast a warm dappled glow over the body. Minola shuddered. Trembling, she left the room untouched, went back out into the hallway, and patiently waited for what she knew would be a barrage of questions by hotel security and the Police Nationale de Paris.

This hotel is my home. What happened here? To give her an essential, although temporary, reprieve from the tragedy in the next room, she focused on yesterday's idyllic day sitting in a café, in a cozy secluded booth across the street from the Luxembourg Gardens. Through the gilded wrought-iron fence she gleaned the contemplative and everyday life of the *Parisiens.*

As she waited for the police, she relived the relaxed pace inside the gardens, so peaceful and calm. She remembered an old couple sitting and holding hands, a woman watching her child play, and on another bench, two women sitting and comfortably rolling prams containing their precious cargoes. Their hypnotic movements, back and forth, back and forth, helped lull Minola into utter contentment as the mesmerizing and soothing minutes flicked by.

The image of Lord Yardleigh's body intruded on her thoughts. So peaceful in repose...so still, except for the blood. *Go back to the gardens. Go back to the gardens.*

"Mademoiselle Grey...pardon, Mademoiselle," she faintly heard a voice calling her back to reality.

Art drew her to Paris, so well represented–not confined to museums, but present everywhere, and always in the gardens which peppered this amazing city.

"Mademoiselle Grey...Mademoiselle, *s'il vous plait.*" She heard the voice again, faintly and urgently calling her. Her serenity shattered, pulling her back to the reality of a gruesome murder in her quiet hotel. Slowly opening her eyes, she noticed that the hallway was now filled with police and crime investigators. She recognized what looked like a solitary pathologist carrying a black medical bag. The police did not block his entry.

"Mademoiselle Grey, are you alright? I need to ask you a few questions." The gentle yet insistent voice persisted through her hazy reality. "Yes, of course. I am sorry," she replied, and again clenched her hands to keep them from shaking.

"I'm Sergeant Luc Dubois with the Police Nationale. Mademoiselle, we already have a statement from the maid. She said that you went into the room. Did you touch the body?" he inquired politely.

"I didn't touch anything…no…nothing at all. I went in to see if I could help. Yvonne had said blood…I just wanted to make sure… I…"

The Sergeant nodded his head and continued, "Did you notice anything unusual? Did you see or hear anyone come up to this floor while you were waiting for the police?"

"The room appeared undisturbed. It was so clean. I didn't see or hear anyone, but I closed my eyes because I needed to escape the image. I am sorry, but I believe I drifted off a bit. Maybe Yvonne heard or saw something. Not a robbery…" Her calm voice belied her distress. She looked down and tried to still her quaking hands.

"Yes, I know. I had a difficult time bringing you out of your trance, Mademoiselle. The maid had gone downstairs to summon help; she could not get the phone to work. I believe she was too agitated. *Pour quoi*? Why are you so certain that it was not a robbery?" he queried.

"Sergeant, you must have noticed he was wearing a Rolex. There are also several very worthwhile contemporary art pieces on the wall. A thief would have certainly stolen these items. No self-respecting crook would leave a Rolex on his victim's wrist. The Luxembourg Gardens are a far more delightful escape than seeing a murder victim, Sergeant." She looked up at him expectantly. Her eyes shimmered, but she refused to let the tears fall.

"There I would agree with you, Mademoiselle. I am sorry you were a witness to such a tragedy."

"*Merci.* Thank you for understanding."

Minola glanced at her own watch and realized she was late for her class, an excuse to get away. She could still see the sun filtering through the pool of blood–a macabre scene, one that would stay with her forever. "Pardon, Sergeant Dubois, but I am already late for class. May I please go, unless you still need me for any reason? I will be back this afternoon. I can leave my passport at the front desk." As an afterthought she added, "If necessary."

"That will not be required, Mademoiselle. You may go. I understand this is difficult for you. There will be more questions for you this afternoon; please do make yourself available. *Merci*, Mademoiselle." He moved on to speak with another policeman.

Yves Lanier, of the Police Nationale, was a man with a mission. His dingy grey office with matching furniture was so littered with papers and books that he couldn't find the phone on his desk. It was here somewhere, he knew. *Damn it, I used it yesterday.* He momentarily stared at the mess…then, with quiet efficiency, slid everything off his desk to the floor, and heard the ping of the phone hitting the ground. He bent down, picked it up, and dialed a London number he knew well. A quiet voice answered, "Peter Riley."

"*Bonjour*, Peter. How are you, my friend?"

"I know that tone, Yves. Interpol at your service. What's going on?"

"Peter, Yardleigh was murdered sometime late last night or early this morning. I think your investigation into money laundering just veered off track."

The silence at the other end was palpable. "What the hell happened? He was cooperating. What do you have?"

"We have nothing, *mon ami*. He was shot once in the chest with a small-caliber gun. No exit wound–the lab's still working on that. Purely as an observation, it looks like he knew his killer. No surprise or fear…there's nothing reflected on his face. Nothing stolen. Everything, as you English say, was neat and tidy, save for the corpse on the floor. We secured the crime scene and did all the other things we are supposed to do. The bastard was not nice enough to leave any clues." Lanier spoke with the confidence of a seasoned cop.

"Let me talk to Clivers, my superior. Murder is out of our jurisdiction. I suppose that leaves Scotland Yard in the game."

"Peter, this started in England."

"Don't I know it. I will call you back." Lanier heard the phone click in his ear.

Peter Riley ran a hand through his hair and swore. As he reached for his phone, it rang. "Riley," he recognized the brooding voice, "what the hell is going on?"

"Sir, I just spoke with Lanier. I assume you know as much as I do."

"Scotland Yard just filled me in. As of right now you are on loan to Scotland Yard. Riley, get over there...yesterday."

"Sir, just what am I supposed to do? We can continue the internal investigation here..." Peter was cut off again.

"He was killed in Paris. You will go to Paris, do I make myself clear?" The voice at the other end softened perceptibly. "I can't think of a better man to handle this mess. Keep me posted."

"Yes, sir, I am on my way," Peter responded, and hung up the phone. "Bloody hell," he murmured to himself. He made a couple of phone calls and prepared to leave for Paris.

Chapter 2

It has been said that ignorance is bliss. Minola, on her way to the L'Écoles des Beaux Arts, returned once again to that innocent state. The murder had shaken her equilibrium. She tasted blood, and realized she had bitten her lip to keep it from quivering.

Her sudden perception of how fragile life was and how rapidly it could end brought her back to reality, as she contemplated her life. As an artist, she understood the intense and solitary process of creating a piece of art. She found solace in books, museums, and parks, but most of all in her painting. Paris offered her everything she needed. Even though the city was a living paradox…vibrant and busy, calm, old yet modern, solitary, and crowded…she could feel as alone as she wished, yet she was not lonely. At this moment, she longed for this reaffirmation of life.

Parisians seem to have a sense about others—respecting their desire for privacy yet eager to respond to animated, fiery conversation. Fully aware of the sights and sounds that swirled around her, it was oddly comforting. Today, she needed the chaos of the city streets as much as air.

Dickens was right: 'It was the best of times, it was the worst of times,' She felt the contradiction and needed to confront her future, the base of her discontent. Her time in

Paris was an interlude…however desirable, it must eventually end. Minola needed to decide what she wanted to do with her art, and with her life.

The fact that for the first time in her life she had seen a body lying in a pool of blood added an extra dimension to her bewildered state of mind. *Damn it, do something with your life. It is so short. It could end instantly.*

Instead of finding her way to class, she walked to her favorite café, across the street from the Luxembourg Gardens. As she hurried toward her own solitary therapy session, she reached for her cell phone, dialed, and asked her fellow art instructor to take her class.

Sitting in her favored spot, she looked out beyond the café windows to the beautiful landscapes before her. Despite her inner turmoil, or maybe because of it, being in the café calmed her spirit. It was a perfect day to reflect, to plan, to absorb. Trees lined the gravel paths in the park, and Minola imagined she heard the rustle of leaves beckoning her outside. The gardens always had the same serene effect on her; they placated her soul and stirred her imagination as an artist.

Amid the chaos in her soul, her morning suddenly improved. A well-dressed, middle-aged man strolled into the café with an air of sophistication, and sporting a quirky smile that lit his eyes. His presence seemed to light up the room. He put some coins in the jukebox and played her favorite songs–two oldies sung by Tom Jones. First she would hear 'Help Yourself', followed by 'Delilah'. So it was almost every morning…they would smile at each other, acknowledge their respective presence, listen to the music, and enjoy a morning coffee. Today the familiar action added an extra dimension of comfort and familiarity.

The routine with the gentleman had been established several months ago when Minola had first come to the café. She had ordered her coffee and played her favorite two songs. The man sat facing her, watching her intently. After a while he started to play the songs for her. She would acknowledge the gesture with a tentative smile. He responded in kind.

A very romantic and personal relationship developed wordlessly; yet neither party pursued it further. It remained a brief, wistful, intimate interlude, always kept at arm's length. This sense of romanticism was what had drawn Minola to Paris. Having read all the romantic poets, she appreciated the art movement and the history of the bohemian life so prevalent in 19th century Paris, the style that had allowed this romantic period to blossom and flourish. She felt a kinship and a sense that the artistic force was still there, still burgeoning with abandon and beckoning her forward.

Guilt suddenly overcame her. A man had been murdered, and here she was sitting in a café. Lord Yardleigh would never dream again, she thought. Somewhere, an idea lurked and she felt something had to be done. She was alive. He was dead. Suddenly the enchanting haven of the café lost all its appeal. Her innate strength took over, and she decided to teach her second class.

The Écoles des Beaux Arts was her base. She took a great deal of pleasure in teaching. Portrait painting to her was a study of stilled contemplation, a moment caught in eternity.

On her way to class, still seeking escape, she recollected that some critics had praised her work. Her canvases were real, the critics had said. The wisdom, good, bad, and indifferent choices made in life, were reflected in her paintings. She was good with faces, they stated. Minola possessed a romantic soul and, for her, despair was always countered with grace.

She thought about her work. The portraits were compelling works of art, not just photographs. Of all the passions, trials, and expectations she'd encountered, everything had been captured. Nothing was concealed, yet her portrayals were kind to her subjects–though life was hard, she made posterity a little kinder. *I have finally seized the day. I am alive.* That may be a temporary destination, her process of developing fully as an artist rather than just a commercial success, but to her it was most definitely a necessary one.

The gated entrance to the Écoles des Beaux Arts loomed ahead. Minola made her way through the courtyard and quickly stepped inside.

"*Bon jour, Jean Pierre. Ça vas?*" She acknowledged her fellow artist and instructor as he anxiously waited outside her classroom.

"*Ça vas*, Minola. I have been waiting for you. You never miss class. Something happened at your hotel…you hung up before I had a chance to ask, and I have a message for you." He spoke quickly. She heard a tinge of excitement in his voice.

"You have a message, and you are just going to leave

me hanging here? Come on, Jean Pierre...spill. Who called?" She was curious and a bit apprehensive; the calamity of what she had witnessed still very fresh in her mind.

"Bah. Oh, all right. Marie from your hotel called. Something terrible happened, and the English police are at the hotel."

"Marie called?" Minola had a close relationship with the hotel staff. Everyone went out of their way to make her feel like a member of the family–she was on first-name basis with everyone. Local hotel gossip was eagerly provided, and this case was no exception.

"There is a real mystery at your hotel. Someone has been murdered...on your floor, too," he pointed out. "She said it was a British Lord. If you are planning on leaving, I can come with you," Jean Pierre hopefully volunteered.

"Thanks, Jean Pierre. No, I will take the class. I need something to do, and I'm late. We'll talk later, I promise." Minola walked into her classroom, and her attention focused on the model in the center of the room. She was laying on her side on the floor, partially draped in a sheet of white silk. Minola felt the hair on her arms stand up. She excused herself and went in search of Jean Pierre.

"Jean Pierre, I thought I could stay, but I just can't. Can you take my second class as well? I need to get back to the hotel. I can't teach today. Please," she begged, "I will tell you everything tomorrow, I promise. Please don't give me a hard time. I know this is your free morning," Minola pleaded.

"*Moi*, give you a hard time? Minola, you do me a great

injustice. I have hoped to finish an assignment, but…what are you doing in your class?" He attempted to play the gallant Frenchman–one look at her determined and distraught face, and he relented. "Are you alright?"

"Yes. Thanks. Something right up your alley." Trying to sound normal, she explained enticingly, "They are currently studying the female form." As an afterthought, she added "From the neck up."

"Ahh…you just spoiled it. But you have twisted my arm, Mademoiselle Grey. *D'accord*, I will teach your class. But I want details–everything. By the way, when have I ever given you a hard time?" He grinned, turned, and headed for her classroom.

A brisk walk brought her to the hotel quickly. *Seems as though I've walked across half the city, this morning.* A large number of people were gathered outside the entrance.

Minola pushed her way through the crowd and entered the lobby. Hoping to see Marie, she was met by Jacques, the normally congenial porter who was always ready with a bit of gossip. Today, he looked positively deflated. "*Bonjour*, Jacques," she said. "Marie left a message for me. Is it Scotland Yard?"

"I do not know. I just heard that Scotland Yard and Interpol are involved. He must have been a very important man. Ohh, Mademoiselle, it is such a tragedy. I have heard that you saw the body. I hope you are alright." He heard a laugh and exclaimed, "Look at the young Roland. Nothing ever disturbs him," Jacques said with disdain.

Roland was working the guests who congregated in the

lobby. He had an easy wit and was attempting to lighten the now oppressive hotel atmosphere. Even today, his demeanor did not change.

Minola paid homage to youth and their irrepressible ability to assume that nothing would ever affect them. "He is young," she said quietly, as if that explained it all.

The police seemed to be everywhere. A man approached Minola as soon as she left Jacques' side. He identified himself as Officer Geneve,

"*Bonjour*, Mademoiselle. May I please have your name and room number?" He was polite and soft-spoken, but she knew he already possessed most of the answers. She had given the same information earlier that morning. He then inquired how long she was staying and asked for her permanent address.

Minola answered his queries as succinctly as she could. Asked if she had returned to the hotel for any period of time that day, she watched as he wrote everything down. As she glanced at his pad, she realized that her time of arrival was also noted.

"Monsieur," Minola queried, "would it be possible for me to go to my room?"

"Yes, of course, Mademoiselle. Please give the officer upstairs your name and room number. You should have no difficulties," he replied.

Minola thanked him politely and watched as he walked toward another guest who had just entered the hotel.

As always, the elevator groaned as it approached her floor. When she released the lever to open the door, a policeman immediately made his presence known. After repeating the necessary information, she was allowed to continue to her room. As she approached her door, she caught a glimpse of the police tape blocking the three-room suite that had been occupied by Lord Yardleigh.

Once inside her room, she wondered what on earth had possessed her to ditch her students. What could she do? The fact that mere curiosity had brought her back to the hotel upset her even further. *I am no better than the most common voyeur.* No help that she could have provided to the dead man, nothing, would have made a difference. She tried to grapple with her feelings.

Past impressions of the victim floated before her eyes. His distinguished looks and impeccable grooming revealed his autocratic bearing. Not a hair ever out of place, perfection right down to his Ferragamo loafers. Minola had a thing for shoes and always checked to see what others wore.

She pictured the vitally alive Lord Yardleigh. He had been of average height, with a slight physique, piercing blue eyes, and a fixed smile that never seemed to reach them. A face she would not want to paint. An instant later she recalled his body on the floor lying in a pool of congealing blood. The gruesome image persisted. *Think of something else.* She settled for the second member of the Yardleigh entourage–Edwards, the victim's secretary, who had a pinched and sunken face that normally sported a grimace instead of a smile. The same height as Lord Yardleigh, he was gaunt and therefore seemed taller. Well taken care of, he was *prêt-a-porter*, whereas Lord Yardleigh was *haute couture*. Vividly, she recalled memories of their sporadic encounters.

At some point she sat down at her desk, a pad in hand, to sketch the layout of the hallway as well as Lord Yardleigh's suite. There were eight rooms on this floor. Across the hall from her, three rooms belonged to Yardleigh. The only other guest on that side was Dr. LeBrun, a retired physician who occasionally helped in cases of emergency. She believed he was still affiliated with the American Hospital. On her side of the hall, it was hotel business as usual–here today, gone tomorrow. The two rooms currently occupied there seemed normal. She remembered one family and a businessman traveling alone.

Minola loved mysteries, but a life had been taken. She shivered. *I need to do something.* Once her sketch was finished, she rose and entered the bathroom to wash her face. Refreshed, she went downstairs and stepped out the door into the life and vitality of Paris. The police were discreetly observing everyone's activities, but they did not detain her.

Notre Dame soared ahead, providing spiritual solace as she walked to the little café that offered a spectacular setting for the glorious cathedral. It was a proverbial tourist trap, but the view was like none other, the coffee good, and the noise level from all the tourists abundant–a perfect Parisian site for all to indulge.

As always, the café was crowded. Minola watched the mesmerizing effect Notre Dame had on those tourists who viewed it for the first time. The immense structure demanded homage; man was infinitesimal in comparison. This was a heroic piece of architecture to reflect the glory of

God. However one looked at this breathtaking edifice, Minola as an artist was struck by its magnificence. She realized she needed this reaffirmation of artistic and individual survival. At the same time, she felt slightly guilty because of the quick revival of her spirits…life overtaking death, such a basic human concept.

She finished her coffee and walked toward the Cathedral. The interior was as incredible as the exterior, monumental, yet intimate. She found an empty pew, sat down, and paid homage to the men who built such a remarkable structure hundreds of years ago. The sheer joy of watching the tourists respond to the Gothic glory alleviated some of her sorrow and restored her peace of mind. Minola looked down at her wristwatch. It was getting late, she had spent the better part of the day brooding. The Metro took her back to the hotel.

With a sense of foreboding, she realized she made a viable suspect in the investigation.

Jacques, usually long gone by now, guarded the hotel entrance. He greeted her at the door, a wan smile reflected on his pale face. He moved slowly.

"Jacques, you look exhausted," she said gently.

"*Oui*, Mademoiselle. It has been a long day, and it will never be the same. A new man from England has arrived."

"I am sorry, Jacques." She could think of nothing else to say. "I am going up. Take care."

Even the elevator seemed to creep up at a slower pace than usual. She exited, started down the hall toward her room. While looking in her purse for her key, she came up against a solid mass.

She looked up to meet a pair of emerald green eyes in an uncommon face. Breathless, Minola stared. That face had lines placed in such a way as to give what would have been an ordinary face one of extraordinary character. There were slight creases around the eyes, and the lean, rather scraggly beard told her he hadn't shaved recently. His gaze, still locked to hers, deepened to a forest green hue. The change in color captivated her. She looked down, saw he wore a well-cut dark blue suit that looked like it had been slept in. Worn, comfortable Italian loafers completed the ensemble.

Minola immediately wanted to sketch him, though it would be a challenge since at the moment his features didn't seem to give away much. The man had wavy hair that could never possibly remain in place, yet it suited his face, a remarkable face–perfect, although not handsome. His powerful countenance was intimidating, leaving Minola at a loss for words. *Okay, what do I do now?*

She took a deep breath and regained her composure, and said, "Excuse me I need to get to my room. It is just down the hall." His gaze didn't relent.

Peter Riley was totally aware of her presence. "I know exactly where your rooms are, Miss Grey. Who else is staying with you?" As he spoke, he noticed her eyes, which were big, deep brown with a tinge of gold. Her hair was windblown, auburn with specks of red and honey gold. Her body was voluptuous, and lips were full and rounded. She wore a loose brown tunic that did nothing to hide her ample breasts. His hands clenched at his sides...he wanted to reach out and touch her. *What the hell is the matter with me? She is a suspect.*

"You obviously know my name. I can only assume that you are with the police. I need to see some identification, please." She waited while he took out his badge. Taking a closer look at the picture, she thanked him. "No one is staying with me, Chief Inspector Riley," she replied.

He didn't take his eyes off her face. "Is there a reason you need two rooms, Miss Grey?"

"I have two rooms because I require two rooms. Surely that is not a matter for the police."

"Miss Grey, I will be staying in this hotel on this floor for an indefinite time," he replied. "This is Sergeant Welsey." He motioned to the man standing next to him.

"Since the incident occurred in Paris, why is Interpol involved? Does a murder fall under the jurisdiction of Interpol, Chief Inspector?"

"No, it does not, Miss Grey." He continued to glare, certainly not giving any information away. "Did you hear anything at all last night–any noise, voices, anything out of the ordinary?" he persisted.

Undaunted, she looked straight at him and replied, "No, I did not hear anything. My rooms are at the other end of the corridor. The hallway is heavily carpeted, and therefore very quiet." She continued without pause, "Chief Inspector, I am expecting a guest tonight. Will he be allowed to come up here without difficulty?"

"What is the name of your guest?" he asked gratingly.

"His name is Robert Jones, Chief Inspector."

At hearing that common name, she sensed his distain and understood what the good Chief Inspector was thinking. The look on his face reflected it exactly, hard and grim. The tension between them was palpable.

Minola wondered if the hotel staff had told him she had frequent guests at odd hours of the day and evening without explaining why the visitors were there. Should she tell him the truth? She was a painter, and these were lucrative commissions. Or should she let him think the worst? Surely he must know what she did. Minola looked up at his face, saw the same disapproving, withering scowl, and made her decision.

"Chief Inspector, you have not responded to my request. Will my guest be admitted to my room?"

"I will need a list of all the guests that seem to visit you rather frequently, Miss Grey." His voice was as cold as ice.

Minola found it amusing that he'd done his homework, found out she was a Miss, had frequent guests, and nothing beyond that. The hotel staff must have given just enough information to mislead. What about the other police reports? Didn't he have those?

She met the glaring scowl of the Chief Inspector. He had apparently made his decision about her activities. *For God's sake do I look like a prostitute? This is a reputable hotel. What is the matter with him? More to the point, why do I care?* At that moment, she decided to let him believe what he would. He could dig up all the information he needed about her on his own.

"Chief Inspector, the list changes frequently. I'll keep you posted on all my guests. Now I really must get back to my room. I shall expect no difficulties for my guest tonight. Good evening, Chief Inspector Riley."

She did nothing to dispel the thoughts plainly reflected

on his face. She recognized his quandary: she didn't fit the profile he had selected for her, a battle reflected in his eyes. With one final nod and a tight smile on her face, she quietly turned and went to her room.

He watched her walk away. He found her intriguing. Her supposed activities belied her serene composure, self-assurance, poise, and that damned twinkle in her eyes. Maybe the fact that he had not slept in twenty-four hours had something to do with it. Damn it…Robert Jones. Who, what is he to her? He thought about her full mouth. No lipstick…those eyes…those big, beautiful brown eyes.

Peter turned and, with the Sergeant, walked back into the victim's room. "Sergeant, we'll need the names of those who frequently met with Lord Yardleigh. Check with the staff and see if any strangers have been present recently; maybe something was missed by the local gendarmes. Right now, we have nothing–no weapon, no break-in–and yet he is dead. I am betting it was an inside job. Let's meet with the investigating officer from the Police Nationale, and get the crime scene reports. This is too clean."

"Yes, sir. Shall I check on all guests staying in the hotel? Your friend Inspector Lanier is handling the investigation; the reports should be easy to get."

"Good. I'll meet with him tonight, if he is available. In the meantime, have absolutely everything that you can get ready for me tonight. Sergeant, investigate everyone except Miss Grey. I'll do that myself."

"Yes, sir," the sergeant replied, grinning.

"Wipe that smile off your face. In fact, Sergeant, stay behind the scenes. Blend in with the guests and the staff.

For the time being, it would be best if you were not too easily recognized. I have taken the room that Yardleigh used as an office."

"Sir, I will also check in with our office to see if anything new has developed."

"We are the misfits here, Sergeant. The local police are investigating the murder; we are investigating Yardleigh Enterprises. I know we will overlap. Now, concerning the murder, it would do well to go over everything again. Please be sure to listen to everything that is said…hotels are notoriously rife with gossip."

"Yes sir, understood." Sergeant Welsey acknowledged his instructions, and left.

Peter did not like neat and tidy murders. The investigations invariably dragged on and almost always led back to the closest source to the victim. It just took longer. Here, the original case was complicated enough without the added crime of murder. Peter took out his notebook, jotted down what little information he had, then looked down at his pad and saw the possible time of death and two suspects–the secretary and the wife. It wasn't much to go on.

What gave this case an added element of bizarre intervention was the request for the original investigation. The request for Peter's help had come from Lord and Lady Yardleigh. Peter had had a relationship with Lady Yardleigh prior to her marriage.

The pad still in his hand, Peter thought about that relationship. He had been engaged to be married to Alexis until she suddenly announced she was going to marry an English Peer for a title and financial security. That had been five years ago. They had parted somewhat amicably, and Peter had come to learn the difference between lust and love. He had long since realized he was thankful for his escape.

Peter knew that in this investigation he would have to move with extreme caution. He, along with his Sergeant, would have to interview the grieving widow and, even though Interpol was aware of their prior relationship, nothing must be compromised.

He had brought with him all details of the ongoing investigation of Yardleigh Enterprises, including all accounting reports from the reliable and respectable accounting firm that Yardleigh used. Till recently that is–the firm no longer represented Yardleigh Enterprises. They had been unceremoniously fired and no information was currently available on their replacement, at least not yet.

His head beginning to swim, he reached for his cell phone and called Lanier to make immediate plans for Peter to visit that evening. Peter was grateful that the accounting reports would have to wait–always a headache, these were a migraine.

During the short walk down St. Germain des Pres to the Police Station, Peter's thoughts reverted back to Minola Grey. That full, sensuous mouth, those incredible eyes. In his mind, he slowly caressed her body and felt himself tense perceptibly. *What the hell is the matter with me? She is a potential suspect, and more.* He could not bring himself to call her anything else. His pace increased.

As if in a stupor, he found himself on the steps of the

old Police Nationale building. He walked up, and met Inspector Lanier at the door. His entry would not have been that easy had Peter not been expected–security in Paris was tight.

"*Bonsoir, Pierre. Ça va?*" Lanier spoke English beautifully, but always greeted Peter in French, just to hear Peter respond in kind.

"*Bonsoir*, Yves. *Oui, ça va. Pas mal, alors, Anglais s'il vous plaît.*" Peter's French was practiced, courtesy of Yves Lanier.

"All right, old friend, let's sit down in my office and discuss the murder of Lord Yardleigh. You are lucky to find me in this evening." They walked down a narrow bleak hallway into a room with a drab, gray motif. The paint on the walls appeared ageless. The windowless office was cluttered with papers, books, notes, and various mugs filled with stale, unfinished coffee. Peter, eager to get started, made himself comfortable. "I see your décor has not changed," he grinned.

"Can I offer you some coffee?" Lanier asked, ignoring the jibe.

Looking at the cups covered with thick, dried residue, his mouth curved in a smile. "Thanks, Lanier, I think I will pass."

"Good decision. All right, business it is. There's not much new since the last time we spoke. All the prints we were able to identify so far belong in the room, and that includes hotel staff. No obvious uninvited guests. We have photographs of the body from all angles. Nothing. We are still waiting for reports from the lab."

"Yves, do you have a numbers man in your organization? Someone who can manipulate the numbers, look at the ledgers, and recognize any ambiguities that may exist? Interpol is evaluating absolutely everything that is available. I am waiting for a response, but it never hurts to have a fresh pair of eyes."

The conversation continued for another twenty minutes, Peter trying to ascertain if he had all the information, and where it would lead.

"I will see what I can do, but Interpol is the leader worldwide. Your labs are the best." Lanier slouched in his chair.

"I know. We are good, but I am grasping at straws. Yves, you look as tired as I feel. Let's call it a night. Sorry I took your time, but it is nice to see you." Peter got up, shook Lanier's hand, and left. He was tired and hungry, and the walk back to the hotel did nothing to lift his spirits. Again, he pondered how he had gotten immersed in this murder. A murder was investigated by the local police–if Interpol got involved, it was only to offer assistance to local authorities. He kept reminding himself that he was here more or less as an observer. He was conducting an investigation already in progress.

Chapter 3

In her room Minola tried to plan her week; instead, her mind kept working overtime as she thought about the murder. The colorful image on the floor played havoc with her artistic sensibilities–she kept seeing beautiful tints of magenta, deep red shadows, and ashen gray colors as well as the quiet repose of the body.

Famished, Minola picked up the book she was reading and took the stairs down to the hotel restaurant.

She said hi to Jeannine, the woman at the front desk. As she nodded toward the clerk, she was suddenly stopped by a strong grip on her arms. Glancing up, her gaze collided with the Chief Inspector's. The physical contact shook her, not in fear, but something totally different–a reaction she did not want to define nor think about. She started to apologize, but he interrupted her.

"Miss Grey, you should really watch your step." His eyes blazed into hers. His body tensed in acute awareness. He was reluctant to let go. "You might hurt yourself and not be able to meet your guest tonight," he said savagely. He could not explain his brittle attitude, even to himself.

"Chief Inspector, it would take a lot more than bumping into you to cancel my appointment. Now, if you would be so gracious as to move out of my way. You seem to have blocked the entire entrance, and I am hungry." She waited for him to release her, which he did abruptly. She rubbed her arms. Smiling blithely, she moved away from him and walked toward the restaurant.

As he watched her retreat, his mouth curved in a tentative smile. He still felt her skin on his hands.

Minola went to her usual spot, sat down, and opened her book. She glanced up and realized Chief Inspector Riley still watched her. As their eyes met again for a brief moment, her temperature rose a few degrees. The man did have a strange effect on her. Minola watched as he abruptly turned and walked away. She took a long, haggard breath and returned to her book.

The service in the hotel restaurant was impeccable as always; Minola had only a short wait before being served with the salad and coffee she ordered. She ate in solitude, her book her only companion. Once finished, she went upstairs to wait for Robert Jones, her appointment, her dear friend.

Robert was already comfortably seated on a chair near the elevator, reading a magazine. He greeted her with a bear hug, which Minola promptly returned. As she looked up, she saw the Chief Inspector come out of Yardleigh's room. He glared at her, evaluated the scene, jumped to the wrong conclusion, and promptly stormed back, slamming the door behind.

Robert Jones was married to Minola's best friend, Sally Rander, who was to join her husband in a couple of days. They planned on staying in Paris for a few weeks. "Robert, how are you? I am so happy to see a friendly face," Minola gushed.

"So I gather. I heard you had some excitement here, a murder no less. What happened?" Robert was as curious as everyone else.

"Honestly, I know very little. An English Peer down the hall was murdered, and somehow Interpol is involved. It seems so unreal," Minola said quietly. She wanted to get a sense of normalcy back, so she changed the course of the conversation as they entered her room.

"Did you remember to bring pictures? It will help me." Robert had asked her to paint a portrait for their anniversary, as a surprise for Sally.

"I have pictures. Did you by any chance forget what Sally looks like?" He said, trying to bring Minola out of her somber mood. Robert had come armed with various pictures of them together so Minola could prepare and draw the initial sketch.

"I'm going to have to work hard to keep this from Sally. Maybe I'll ask if I can have some storage space somewhere around here."

"She does have a way of snooping. Always wants to see your next project. God, I miss her," he sighed.

"She'll be here soon enough," Minola replied casually. She started to outline the canvas to frame the portrait, to see how she wanted to lay it out.

"Yes, that's it," she muttered. A simple portrait of them together, holding hands and looking out to their future would be the best reflection of the couple. The charcoal drawing developed quickly; it helped that she had Robert there. Half a pair was better than none. She showed her outline to Robert, he made some comments, and they agreed to meet again before Sally's arrival. Robert left with a glowing smile on his face.

Finally Minola was able to relax, shower, and get some much-needed sleep, although a certain English Chief Inspector kept interfering with her peace of mind.

Peter sat on the couch in his room to reflect on the muddled case in front of him, but instead thought about the woman. His reaction to her had been intense. She couldn't be...the innocence in her eyes, the impish smile, the full mouth. *I want to taste that mouth.* Gripping a file in his hand, he got down to business.

It's all here. John Yardleigh was no stranger to violence, albeit it was all beneath the surface. He was the perfect picture of a successful businessman. Very generous with his pet charities, he was front-page fodder for Fleet Street. He had a high-maintenance wife who always managed to snag a headline in the society pages.

Because of the ongoing investigation, Peter knew his man. Always superior in dealings with others and with a vile temper, Yardleigh was not liked by his peers, but he appeared to have too much money and power for anyone to stand in his way. He ruled with arrogance and intimidation. In essence, he was feared in all business circles in which he traveled, above and below ground.

The below-ground activities interested Interpol the most. Yardleigh had the appearance of being exceedingly successful in the business of import and export, as well as trading in foreign currencies. It was a ready-made setup for dirty money.

Somehow Lord Yardleigh knew the avalanche was about to envelop him, and he had been ready to strike a deal with Interpol. He had chosen to cooperate rather than face a humiliating court case. Peter couldn't remember how many times he had gone over the case in his head. He could hardly keep his eyes open; bone-weary, he shook his head and decided to call it a night.

The next morning, refreshed, he woke up wondering if Minola was up–if, in fact she ever went to bed. *Bloody hell.* He got dressed quickly and went to pay a visit to Mr. Edwards. The scrawny secretary seemed surprised at the intrusion, and for a moment looked panic-stricken, but quickly recovered. He seemed to personify the condescending style that had served Lord Yardleigh so well right up to the time of his murder. Then again, maybe it had not served him so well after all.

"Yes?" Edwards demanded.

"I gather that you were his Lordship's secretary, Mr. Edwards, am I correct?" Peter inquired after introducing himself.

"I was and still am his assistant. The business continues and I will do my best to make sure it will succeed until new leadership is established. How may I help you?" he said importantly.

Peter gave the appearance of being somewhat apologetic, "Mr. Edwards, where were you the night before last? We checked this room, and the maid said it had not been slept in. She also indicated that this was unusual for you."

"I was working in the Champs Élysée office, the one on Avenue Foch. By the time I realized how late it was, I decided to just sleep on the couch in the office," Edwards replied.

"Can anyone verify your whereabouts? What was so important to keep you there that late?"

"That is confidential information I cannot release to the public, and no, I cannot verify my whereabouts. I did work with Madame Armand till late; however, she left and I finished the report myself."

"Mr. Edwards, you'll find nothing remains confidential in a murder investigation, nor will you find I am the public. Please make yourself accessible to me and any other police officers."

"I will not leave this hotel room, except to go to the office," Edwards agreed amiably.

"Mr. Edwards, did Lord Yardleigh have any enemies, in business, or in his personal life? Did he have any financial difficulties?"

"Certainly not. He was a respected businessman, very charitable and greatly admired," Edwards answered briskly, not looking directly at Peter.

"That will be all, Mr. Edwards. Oh, and please make sure I get a copy of whatever it was you were working on so diligently. Good morning."

"Inspector, you did not ask about Madame Armand, she—"

"I know who Madame Armand is. Good morning, Mr. Edwards," Peter answered briskly, purposefully cutting Edwards off. He wanted him edgy. He knew his alibi had been checked, but it was always a good idea to make suspects a little nervous.

Chapter 4

Minola stretched luxuriously in her bed. The curtains, partially open, gave her a glimpse of daylight. It was Saturday. The day of Sally's arrival, even the lack of sunshine did not mar her morning. She was going to meet Robert downstairs for breakfast, and both were going to pick up Sally at the airport. Robert had insisted; the two friends had not seen each other for several months.

Progress on the portrait was considerable–Robert's and Sally's likenesses had been drawn on the white canvas and the background filled in. Minola's familiarity with their facial expressions, mannerisms, and characteristics made the process easier, yet she found it more difficult to capture their essence on canvas. She thought that perhaps she was too close to her subjects, too afraid to show more than was needed. In her friends' case, she didn't want to reveal too much.

Robert and Sally were very private people; Minola did not want to diminish this sense of privacy nor did she want to trivialize the emotional attachment they had for each other. At the same time, those qualities were precisely what she wanted to capture. These thoughts went through her head as she took care of her morning routine. One last look in the mirror, and she was satisfied.

Margot Justes

On her way to the restaurant, she spotted Peter Riley coming her way. She acknowledged his presence by a cheerful "Good morning." After all, she didn't want to be rude, she told herself.

"Miss Grey," he replied curtly.

Well, so much for morning courtesy Minola continued on to where Robert was already waiting. The Inspector, not far behind her, nodded as he passed their table and sat right across from them. Minola felt awkward. She wasn't sure why, but she inherently knew it was a calculated move on his part.

She and Robert discussed the painting and its progress; He wanted to make sure it would be ready on time. The conversation then drifted toward the recent murder at the hotel.

"Minola, have you heard anything more?"

"No," she replied, "but I aim to try. I've been so busy that I haven't snooped at all. You do know the man from Interpol is sitting across from us?"

Robert instantly turned and faced the Chief Inspector head-on. Peter had been watching them intently.

Minola looked up and smiled. Surprised, he returned the smile. She turned back to Robert and chose an alternate path of discussion, talking about Sally and their plans for her stay in Paris. "After we pick Sally up, drop me off at the hotel. That way, you will have some time alone with your wife. We can meet at the Luxembourg Café. You can call me and let me know what time."

"Sounds like a plan. I miss her." He sounded wistful.

"You sound positively romantic. That is so unlike you,"

she teased. They finished breakfast, and together left for the airport.

Peter's eyes smoldered. *Damn it, I am jealous. She looked too comfortable with that man. Stop being such an idiot. You have access to any and all information...so use it, you bloody fool, before you are in too deep.* The rest of Peter's musings drifted toward the investigation and Alexis Yardleigh.

Alexis Yardleigh practically lived in Paris. Haute couture was her mainstay, and what better place than Paris? He needed information from her. She was a suspect. With her help he could also check on the last two weeks of Yardleigh's life.

Peter reached for his cell phone and dialed Lanier's office. "Yves, Good morning, I have a favor to ask. Do you, by any chance, have the telephone number for Lady Yardleigh? Address too, if possible?"

Lanier responded. "Wait a moment, let me check the file. Ah, here it is. Are you ready?" Peter had his notebook out, and jotted down the number. "Peter, take Welsey with you. Be careful."

"I'm not doing this alone, Yves." He thanked Lanier, and called Alexis Yardleigh.

The phone rang, and a breathless voice answered, "Yes, hello."

Peter recognized the wispy voice immediately. "Alexis, Peter Riley here. My sympathies on your recent loss." His voice sounded flat. He felt nothing, not even a twinge of regret.

"Thank you, Peter. It is lovely to hear from you," she responded in the same panting voice.

"I am in Paris, continuing the investigation. I should like to meet with you, if possible."

"I happen to be free for a couple of hours. How about the Luxembourg Café, say in an hour? It is such a charming place. I have a meeting nearby this afternoon. Does that suit?" she whispered.

"That is perfect. I shall see you there," Peter responded. He dialed Sergeant Welsey and asked him to be at the café. This interrogation had to go by the book, and a witness was needed.

He spent the hours before his appointment organizing his schedule. With time to spare before the appointment, he decided to walk to the café. The street was filled with students and tourists alike, and the stroll provided an extra jolt of energy. He found it oddly refreshing. His thoughts strayed to Minola Grey–he wondered if she liked walking in this city. Invariably he was working when in Paris, but today he acknowledged the essence of the city.

He had been here several times. He worked well with the French police, and frequently their cases overlapped. Peter had investigated some very interesting and politically charged cases. He had been chosen for the high-profile cases because of his background, and because he got the job done with minimum fuss and publicity.

Educated at Cambridge, he had access to the privileged side of English life, and an added bonus of an advanced degree from an American university. He found psychology interesting, and had a Master's degree from Yale in that discipline. It augmented his acceptance in social circles, but it also allowed him to study his potential suspects in depth. Due to his background, Peter was often underestimated by suspects. He had authority, but rarely used it, preferring to be totally unassuming. That approach served him well.

His early arrival at the café gave him an opportunity to have a relaxing cup of coffee. As he walked in, he noticed Minola sitting near a window. She sat alone listening to music from the jukebox. Her head was bent, and she had a pad in front of her. She looked like she was either writing or drawing.

He found a table facing her at the opposite end of the café. Suddenly, she looked up. Their eyes met. Peter sat and watched. She acknowledged his presence by a nod and a hesitant smile, then bent her head down to continue her work, totally oblivious of her surroundings. He ordered his coffee and found that he couldn't take his eyes off her. Her hair escaped from the tuck behind her ears, and she frequently pushed it back in place. His stomach tightened as he watched the color change perceptibly, from auburn to red streaks when light hit it just right.

Minola had become so intent on her work that she didn't notice Robert Jones until he jostled her shoulder, she looked up and smiled as she got up to give him a hug. Seconds later a young woman walked in, ran to Minola, and more hugs were exchanged.

They all sat down, ordered coffee, and began an animated conversation. Eager to talk to Sally, who was also a nut about mysteries, Minola realized she would have a willing partner in the snooping business. While Robert, hard at work, would not interfere, they would be free to do their thing. Neither had a clue how to proceed–someone should write a manual for beginners in the 'amateur detecting business', they decided.

Sally was ready to detect. "Okay, Robert has filled me in on the murder. Well, not really, he didn't know much. So what's going on? Tell me everything, I want all the details."

"What details? I don't know anything." Minola quipped. "Aren't you tired, jet lag, and all that?"

"Nope. So what's going on?" Once on a mission, Sally became relentless.

"Okay, if you insist," replied Minola. "A man was murdered on my floor. I know as much as Robert does; which is to say, not much."

"Well, you're right, that is certainly not much." Sally sounded deflated. Looking around the café she suddenly exclaimed, "Why is that man staring at you, Minola? Do you think we should call the police? He could be dangerous."

Minola looked in the direction of Peter Riley, and laughed out loud. "He's dangerous, all right. He *is* the police. That's Peter Riley from Interpol."

"My first question still stands. Why is he staring at you?" Sally persisted.

"I have no clue. Presumably, he thinks I had something to do with the murder. It happened on my floor, so the assumption is that I was somehow involved. We do seem to run into each other frequently enough. He's staying in Yardleigh's suite. I assume he's there to keep a close watch on everything. Now, you really do know as much as I do."

"I know what I would like to do," Sally piped in, beaming. "I think we should try to talk to the hotel staff. They always know what goes on. We have an adventure on our hands."

"By 'we,' you mean me, don't you?"

"Well, of course. They don't know me," Sally stating the obvious.

Robert looked from one to the other, but knew better than to try to dissuade them. Still, he had to make an attempt. "You two had better be careful. This was a murder, serious stuff, and dangerous. Leave it to the police. That Interpol man looks capable enough," Robert said, looking in Peter's direction. He said his goodbyes, told them he would meet up with them in the hotel for dinner, and warned them again not to meddle, even though he knew it was a wasted effort.

The Inspector was obviously watching them, and it made Minola uncomfortable. "Sally, he just keeps staring here. What should I do?"

"Well, go over there. Ask him what progress he has made."

"Yup, great idea, and you really think he will tell me all about it? We barely exchange civil banalities. He suspects I have a very active night life."

"What night life? How come you never told me about it? Just go over there. What better way to get him going? Ask about progress in the investigation. It'll be worth it just to see his reaction."

"If I get arrested, you will have to bail me out. Don't come without coffee." Minola paid for their coffees, packed her drawing pad, and went to wish Peter a good day.

Peter sat and watched Minola make her way through the café towards him. He knew the Jones couple since routine police surveillance provided names and relationships. Curiosity had gotten the better of him, and he had checked everything out that morning. He needed to know. He had taken a deep breath when he discovered Minola was not involved with Robert Jones. There was something primal about his thoughts as he watched her approach his table.

"Chief Inspector, what brings you here?" Minola inquired, her eyes bright and alert.

"I'm meeting someone, and I'm early," he responded simply. "What brings you here, Miss Grey?"

"I love coming here. It is one of my favorite cafés. It is a reasonable walking distance from the hotel, the view is spectacular and very peaceful, the Luxembourg Gardens are amazing, and the coffee is terrific. One could not ask for more." Minola realized she was babbling, but had difficulty controlling herself. She knew that was something she did when stressed and nervous.

"No indeed, one could not," he responded in kind as his gaze softened and lingered on her full mouth. He raised his eyes to directly meet hers. *Why, she is blushing. How rare.*

Embarrassed by his intense scrutiny, she firmly responded, "Isn't it somewhat off the beaten path for a murder investigation that was committed in the hotel? Are the suspects so far-reaching?" *Why am I still babbling? He does not need to hear all that, what is the matter with me?*

"They are indeed, Miss Grey. You are here, are you

not?" He gazed at her face, his lips creased in a smile.

"Touché, Chief Inspector. I am indeed here. Have you made any progress in the murder investigation?"

"Miss Grey," he almost shouted, but controlled himself. "Stay out of this." His face dramatically changed. His eyes flashing a darker green and his mouth tightening, making him look grim and furious.

"I just wondered," she hastened to reassure him, "since there has been very little publicity, and the hotel on the surface seems back to normal."

"What do you mean, 'on the surface'?" Now he glared at her–gone was the gentle approach. She acknowledged the toughness in his bearing. Not a subtle change, but a primal shift in his attitude. "It's just that new staff at the hotel appeared almost overnight, more obvious attention to arrivals is being paid, and your continuous presence in the hotel is an indication as well that things are not really back to normal."

"Pray continue, Miss Grey," he commanded quietly, his stance visibly softening.

"I had also observed a new face. I assume it is a policeman. He is keeping track of arrivals." She looked back at him and now saw a twinkle in his eyes, but his face remained somber.

"We have to track your visitors somehow, Miss Grey."

"Was that a joke, Chief Inspector?" Minola hoped he was kidding. "Please, Inspector, just ask. I'll be more than happy to give you an updated guest list every day. If that is the reason for the extra help, you are wasting your time. My visitors are work-related and I can assure you murder is the last thing on their minds." She smiled impishly. *What on earth did I do? I just fed him more ammunition.*

His expression was tight, again, with strain. Carelessly he looked her over, and returning to her face, held her gaze. "One more time, Miss Grey–stay out of this."

Minola smiled tentatively, nodded her head, and turned back toward the table where Sally sat waiting for her.

"I thought we were going. You are behaving strangely, even for you," Sally quipped.

"I just think we should stay. He said he was meeting someone; I'll bet it's related to the murder. We can order more coffee. We want information, right? Well, this is as good a start as any."

"What are we going to do with the information once we get it?"

"I have no idea," Minola replied.

"Minola, are you interested in the Inspector? I have never seen you so disjointed. I don't even know how to define it."

"Well, for the time being let's not define anything. I can't explain. I am confused."

"Yes, I can see that. He certainly has gotten your attention. Are you going to sketch his face? It is rather interesting, in a brooding sort of way." One look at Minola's blazing eyes, and Sally switched gears. "What are we going to do with the information, once we get it?"

"I have no idea. Maybe we could find out what the victim was like. What he did. How he treated his employees. If we do a character study, maybe we could learn who had a motive. Sort of when I paint a portrait, I observe body language, facial expressions, anything at all, no matter how trivial. I try to see everything I can. I either study photographs or the real subject, or preferably both; in that way I gain an objective point of view. I think we can build a written portrait by studying the impact he had on people. What do you think?"

"What a terrific idea. We can start by waiting to see who meets the Chief Inspector. In the meantime, tell me about your gallery opening. It's coming up, isn't it? Robert told me everything, at least everything he actually remembered."

Sally had never been to Paris before, and expressed her delight with the adventure so far. They talked about the work Minola was doing, the gallery opening night, which was quickly approaching, all the preparations that were still needed, and the help Jean Pierre had provided.

While Minola and Sally waited patiently, Peter watched. They were curious, and he was furious. He did not want some interfering women making a mess of his investigation, which he would then have to clean up. He did not want Minola to get hurt. He wanted to protect her. As to why…he could not answer. He didn't want to look too closely at his motives. He just knew he wanted her safe, and safe she was not going to be if she interfered in this investigation.

An incredibly alluring woman walked into the café. She was poised, self-assured, and dressed to the nines in the latest high fashion, wearing an elegant dark burgundy silk sheath that looked like it had been painted on her. A matching belt with a gold intertwined clasp completed the simple yet stunning outfit. Her shoes were the same color as the dress. Like radar, her gaze focused on Peter and they greeted each other as old friends.

Minola was sure this woman would be comfortable in any situation.

Sally, patient no longer, wanted to leave. "We can't hear anything. All we can do is figure out who she is. I know you can't read lips. We are wasting our time."

"Let's wait a while. Her face is very familiar. I want to know who she is. Anyway, we have a bit of time."

Occasionally Minola glanced in the direction of the other table-another man had arrived. Minola recognized the Sergeant, but her concentration stayed on the woman. Minola was sure she had seen her somewhere. Maybe it was a recent photo in the newspaper. Of course! Her picture was plastered all over the paper. The bereaved widow. Minola knew for sure the Inspector was working. She was equally sure he knew the woman. The ease with which he greeted her was evident, and her interest in him was equally obvious. *He knows this woman, intimately.* Astounded, Minola realized jealousy sizzled through her veins. Her spirits plummeted.

Chapter 5

Peter scrutinized Alexis as she walked toward him. He assumed she would be uneasy about being considered a suspect. She had been instrumental in her recommendation that Yardleigh visit Peter to discuss his deteriorating business and money-laundering schemes. She had stopped short of finding out exactly what was going on. She liked her creature comforts, which was why she had thrown Peter over and married for money. She had tried to help Yardleigh out of his financial debacle, whether it was to retain her financial security or to really help Yardleigh, Peter didn't know and didn't care.

"Peter, it is so good to see you even under these circumstances," Alexis purred in her soft, silky voice.

"I am sorry, Alexis. I know it is difficult for you, but we must ask some questions," Peter replied noncommittally as he introduced his Sergeant to Alexis Yardleigh.

Sergeant Welsey was all set, pad and pen ready to take down the conversation.

"Couldn't it be just the two of us? It is, after all, a personal matter."

Peter noticed she stopped short of batting her eyelashes. "Alexis, murder is never personal. It is as public as it gets. Since we do have a past together, we must have a witness to this interrogation. Sergeant Welsey is very capable. You and Yardleigh officially requested my help, and that is why I am allowed this extraordinary leeway. This has to go by the book, Alexis. This interview cannot be compromised." He wanted to make sure she understood the ground rules.

"When was the last time you saw your husband?" Peter kept his tone professional and impersonal. He was amazed at how easy it was.

"I saw him last week…Monday, I believe. I have my own apartment. I did not like living in the hotel. It was too confined. Peter, honestly, what do you want from me?" She still played the part of the innocent ingénue.

Peter's memories flooded back. He remembered how sweetly she had told him she was going to marry for money; he did not earn enough to make her happy. All this while still engaged to him. He realized, once again, how easily he had been deceived.

"What I want from you, Lady Yardleigh, are some honest and forthcoming answers. Now, other than living apart, were there any problems in your relationship? Did he discuss his business in detail with you, after our meeting?"

"No, Peter, he didn't talk about business at all. But then I didn't ask, either. I did notice that he had become withdrawn lately. I know we discussed the original problem when we visited Interpol, but nothing since. He felt he was being watched. I thought it was just paranoia. We were not close. I was a trophy wife for him; he was my financial backer. That was it, nothing else," Alexis admitted candidly.

Peter thought he heard a note of regret in her voice. "Alexis, I have to ask, and you have to be honest. You know everything will come out eventually. Did you at any time during your marriage have an affair with someone?"

"No, of course not. I was married." She sounded very indignant.

Peter remembered she had that uncanny way of looking someone in the eye when she fibbed. Things had not changed. "Are you sure?"

"Yes, Peter." She wrung her hands nervously, and instinctively he knew that she was lying. He also knew he would need to get the answers from a different source, if it became necessary. She was not going to admit to adultery. "All right, I will accept that for now. Do you know if your husband was having an affair?"

"Well, I had heard a rumor that Giselle Armand was his current mistress, but really, I did not pay attention to such gossip."

Another fib, Peter thought. "Was it fact or rumor, Alexis?"

"All right, fact. He did have a relationship with Giselle. I really did try to help him. Who would do such a thing? Was it because we went to the police?" Beseechingly, she looked directly at Peter.

Peter tried to offer some comfort–part of his job, nothing more. "Alexis, this was not your fault. Yardleigh was in over his head. He underestimated his enemies and, ultimately, his greed paved the way for his death." As they talked and more memories surfaced, Peter felt eternally grateful for his escape.

"Did he talk to you about his business associates? Did he give you any papers or reports to keep safe? Anything at all?" he continued

"Why would he do that? I told you we were not close," she snapped coldly.

"Maybe because you were there during the first initial visit, he might have trusted you with some information."

The sergeant quietly writing everything down saw Alexis Yardleigh was beginning to get irritated, and intervened. He had a couple questions of his own. "I beg your pardon, sir." Welsey looked up at Peter.

"Of course. What is it?" Peter replied, grateful for the interruption.

"May I ask a question, sir? Just to clear up a point or two."

"Of course, please continue." Familiar with his sergeant's tactics, Peter knew he was attempting to diffuse her temper. Welsey looked at Alexis Yardleigh in his deprecating, worshipping style, and she immediately warmed to him.

"Lady Yardleigh, I know this is most difficult for you. I offer my deepest sympathies for your loss. But perhaps his Lordship said something that you did not realize was important? Perhaps he may have mentioned some names that were not familiar to you? Anything at all would be of great assistance, Lady Yardleigh." He looked at Alexis with what appeared to be great admiration.

"Well," Alexis responded with new warmth in her voice. "He did mention a new accounting firm–LeClerque, I think. He mentioned something about a joint venture. Honestly, I didn't pay any attention. It really didn't affect me at all. It was his business, but now I guess it is my business.

I need to find out what shape the company is in. I will work closely with Edwards. He has assumed greater responsibility in running the office on Avenue Foch. I wish I had more to give you, Sergeant." She sounded coy.

"Thank you, Lady Yardleigh," the Sergeant resumed his previous duties.

"So, you have been keeping tabs on the business. Is there anything else that you can tell us?" Peter interjected.

"No, Peter. But if I find out anything, I will let you know."

Peter knew she would do her damnedest to hear everything. There might be a fortune at stake, and Alexis was not one to miss out on any opportunity. Peter asked for her whereabouts on the night of the murder.

"Am I a suspect?" she demanded, scowling.

"Alexis, everyone closely associated with a murder is a suspect. The police investigate and weed out potential suspects. My abject apologies, Alexis, but yes, you are a suspect."

"Peter, I have already told the police everything, and my alibi checks out. I was attending a benefit for something or other. Many socially prominent people were there."

"I assume you were photographed with all of them," he quipped.

"Yes, of course. One must do what one can to promote oneself," she stated simply.

"How quaintly put, Alexis. Please, if you hear anything let me know."

"Peter, I count you as my old friend. If I need anything, may I call upon you?" she asked, with mock sincerity.

"Alexis, our history is such that it would preclude…I am only investigating the corruption aspect of this case. The Police Nationale are handling the murder. I know it overlaps, but I…"

Peter did not know how to finish. He could not, and more to the point, did not want to get sucked in to Alexis' personal issues. Once was more than enough. Welsey again came to the rescue.

"Lady Yardleigh," Welsey spoke. "If you need any assistance, please do not hesitate to call." He took out his business card and graciously handed it to Alexis.

If Alexis expected anything more from Peter, or was disappointed in his reaction, she did not let on. With an elegant nod of her head, she rose and made a swift departure.

"Sir, she didn't give away anything. This was a waste of time," the sergeant commented.

"You are right in that she did not give much away," Peter replied. "She gave us the new accounting firm; that's something. Lanier will keep an eye on her. She will get involved in the business to protect her assets and lead us to his associates. Have no fear, Sergeant, we got her thinking today."

"I will go back to the hotel and continue. Is there anything else?"

"No. This was a bit awkward. Thank you for your help. I will see you this afternoon."

Welsey left. Peter decided to finish his coffee and observe Minola's attempt at subterfuge. *Hell, she was made for love and seduction, not murder.* Somehow, in a short period of time, she had become firmly entrenched in his mind. Peter's thoughts were going in the wrong direction. He shook his head as if to clear his mind.

Observing Alexis' exit, Sally and Minola decided to go back to the hotel and try to find out just what kind of business resulted in Lord Yardleigh's murder. The list of motives included personal reasons, greed, hate, or simply bad business practices. Minola glanced at Peter's table, and was surprised to see the Inspector notice their departure. She nodded her head, and he responded in kind.

The realization that they'd spent so much time in the café came as a shock. It was late afternoon already; they had achieved no more than finding Lady Yardleigh. Beyond that, Minola had no clue how to continue. The list of suspects was short. So far they had two names, the wife and the secretary. Minola had seen Mr. Edwards quite a few times. They had always acknowledged one another with a brief greeting or simple nods. Marie had told her that Mr. Edwards worked for a very demanding boss, but not much else. It was a start. What they needed now was the address of the office.

Minola had decided on a plan. "Yardleigh divided his time between England and France. It has to be here, right here in Paris. This is where he was killed, and this is as good a start as any. What do you say?"

"Okay. A good start for what? Even if we get some information, then what? What do we do with it? Surely the Inspector will have the same thing, plus more."

"Look, we will have limited information. We have the Internet and something more. There had to be financial aspects to his business that may not have been above board. We have Robert, on the inside, as it were. Finance is his business. He knows the right people, he hears rumors, he can help. At least I hope he will help. We can start with the Internet."

"Great. If we get a lot of information on the net, what then? Do you really think Robert will want to help, considering how he feels about our snooping? Besides, what can he do that the police can't? They have access to the Internet and experts in finance too, you know." Sally did not sound hopeful at all.

"Well, for starters he can check out the company for us. He can also find out whether Yardleigh was financially sound. What kind of investors there were. How much of the investment belonged to the victim? We can get all sorts of information. Robert has access to business gossip, and he can find out the reputation of the company. You just have to convince him to do it. "

"That won't be easy. I'll work on him. We really don't need to do anything with the information. As you said, this could just be an interesting character study."

Computer access had been easy. Back at the hotel, they went to the business center and used a computer there to check the Internet. It appeared that Lord Yardleigh had just one company–a financial company involved in the import/export business–with multiple offices in three locations. One was in Paris itself; the other two were at opposite ends of suburban Paris. Not too many assets to worry about, and they were highly disposable. How convenient. Now all they had to do was convince Robert to do his part.

"We have the information. Tonight, you need to talk to Robert."

"Do we know what we are doing?"

"No, we'll figure that out later. But listen to this. I just had an incredible idea. I can tell Mr. Edwards that I want to paint a portrait of the late Lord Yardleigh and I need to see his offices, to get a better idea of what he was like. What do you think?"

"It is a great idea, except for one tiny little problem. Who wants the portrait painted, and why, for what reason? He's dead, how are you going to explain that?"

"I have that covered. He was an English Peer, right? I'll get in touch with Ian Stoddard at the *London Sentinel* and ask him for a favor. We're old friends. I'll ask him to request an official portrait for his publication. No cost to him, of course. Edwards may buy it."

"That is so farfetched that it may just work. I will talk to Robert tonight, and we'll meet you for breakfast tomorrow morning here in the hotel. I do want to do some sightseeing too. You need to include that in your plans. So, in the morning we can check out the Parisian location–kill two birds with one stone, as it were."

"Tomorrow it is. While you are charming your husband, I can work out a chart. I will need to record all the information we have to date. That should cover the first two lines on the page," Minola said good-naturedly. She gave Sally a hug, and set the breakfast time for eight in the morning.

Sally got a copy of the reports, just in case Robert agreed to help, which Minola was sure he would do. He never could say no to his wife–good thing, too. Minola gathered her copies and went into the little café located just to the right of the restaurant. It was a quiet, delightful little place. While not very hungry, she did want a bite to eat, a cup of coffee, and a chance to relax. Needing to feel as if in some way she was helping, she studied the paltry information in her hands.

Time passed quickly as she concentrated on her itinerary. She had no idea how late it was, but noticed the restaurant had filled with diners. It must have been at least seven or eight o'clock in the evening. Extremely tired, she stopped daydreaming, finished her cold coffee, packed up her papers, and went to her room.

Exhaustion crept up on Minola. Detecting, which was proving quite difficult, drained her and she still needed to finish Robert and Sally's anniversary portrait. So far she had captured them beautifully–their independence, passion, and companionship. Minola had shown that comfort and love with each brush stroke, yet a sense of privacy came through. Only so far was one permitted to look. Immense pride shone in this work, and she couldn't wait for them to see the final product. Even Robert was not allowed to see the practically finished portrait; the completed canvas was to be a surprise for them both.

Minola had worked out an arrangement with Jean Pierre at the school–for the duration of Sally's stay, he would take her classes. A curriculum had been worked out and copious notes written for him to follow, or not. Minola was now free to pursue her own ideas of detecting. Although admittedly missing the daily contact with her students, this new challenge intrigued her. It eased her guilt and she felt alive, loving her art and life.

Chapter 6

Minola woke up rested, refreshed, and eager to explore and investigate something. Last night she had finished the portrait and had it taken to storage, just in case Sally got curious, which she invariably did. Now, amidst everything else, Minola had to prepare for her gallery opening. She was behind schedule and that meant at least a couple of sleepless nights, but she was so energized she was sure she wouldn't miss the sleep.

While gathering her portfolio for the opening, she realized her work had gained an added quality of realism, sometimes even harshness, since for the first time she had allowed real life to intrude on her painting. Her colors were bolder, more vibrant, and the canvas as a whole more dynamic. It was a marked improvement in her style.

The police, by now familiar with Minola's daily routine, acknowledged her briefly as she went downstairs to the restaurant Sally was not there yet, but Minola seated herself and got a jump-start on today's first cup of coffee and the pursuit of potential suspects. *Hmm, there's no better way to start the morning in Paris than with a great cup of coffee.* She was engrossed in reading the notes she had brought with her when she suddenly sensed the approach of the Chief Inspector and glanced up right into his scowling face.

He stood in front of her table, tall and foreboding, but did not utter a word–just waited and watched.

"Good morning, Chief Inspector. How are you?" She gave him her brightest smile.

"What are you up to, Miss Grey? You look guilty of something," he brusquely responded. He made her feel like a little girl who got caught with her hands in the cookie jar.

She tried to look shocked and pretend she didn't understand his comment; but alas, she was not good at subterfuge. He continued scolding, "This is not a silly joke, this is deadly serious." *I want you safe. Damn it to hell. I want you, period.*

"I'm fully aware that this is serious. A man has been killed, killed on the same floor where I live. I know this is serious–I saw his body, and the crimson blanket of blood...the lifeless eyes. I..." She realized that she was shaking.

To cover her jittery hands, she put them on her lap, but not before Peter noticed her distress. His stance abated perceptibly, and he prodded more gently: "You are putting yourself at risk. Don't get involved. I have this horrible feeling that you are playing at being a detective, a young Miss Marple. Please stop. Leave it to the police. We do know what we are doing."

"Chief Inspector, I do not doubt your ability, although I do not have a basis for comparison." She quickly continued, "A young Miss Marple? At least you said young, and I will take that as a compliment. Are you a fan of the mystery genre, Chief Inspector?"

"I read books, Miss Grey." He continued looking at her.

She considered asking him to sit down, but the whole thing seemed a little awkward and surreal. Minola felt uncomfortable under his steady gaze. This was their strangest meeting yet. What was he after? He kept staring at her and he seemed angry, yet he was reluctant to let go of this little tete-a-tete.

Minola felt oddly excited. They were actually having a conversation—a strange conversation, but a conversation nevertheless. "Inspector, I might as well tell you that Sally and I are planning on doing a bit of research on Lord Yardleigh."

"Miss Grey, please stay out of it. This is dangerous. Whatever was at stake, someone was willing to kill for it. I do not want you to get hurt in the process of your snooping, and I certainly do not want to have to investigate your murder as well. I much prefer that you remain intact," he said quietly.

"Thank you, Chief Inspector. I will be careful; I will not interfere with your work."

"See that you don't. If you do, I will have you arrested." He looked like he meant business.

Just as Minola searched for a swift comeback, Sally appeared at the table.

"Good morning. It's a beautiful day," she chirped.

Minola and the Chief Inspector both stared at her as she continued, "Well, it looked a little tense in here so I thought I'd break the ice."

"Thank you. I guess you could say it was tense," replied Minola. "I was just threatened by the Inspector. He is going to have me arrested if I interfere with his investigation. By the way, Sally Jones, may I introduce you to Chief Inspector, Peter Riley?"

"Good morning Chief Inspector. Don't worry, I will come visit you, and bring cigarettes," replied Sally with a straight face. She knew Minola detested cigarettes.

"Thank you. You forgot the good coffee," Minola replied.

"Mrs. Jones. Do you smoke, Miss Grey?" he demanded.

"No, Chief Inspector, I do not smoke, but I do like good coffee. Sally was just trying to lighten the mood."

"Inspector, I've asked my husband to do some checking into the financial affairs of the late Lord Yardleigh." Sally took some of the pressure off Minola.

"I know I am wasting my time, telling you to stop this nonsense. Since I now know better, you must pass on any information to me immediately. I am stating again, please be careful. This person has killed once–in my experience, he will kill again if threatened."

As Minola sat and listened to the Inspector, an incredible idea took hold. The surprise anniversary dinner which had been planned for Sally and Robert could still take place, except now it wasn't going to be a surprise, and it would be held at the hotel restaurant.

The portrait would still be kept under wraps, but dinner would not. Besides, Sally would enjoy the intrigue. She was already heavily invested in the sleuthing business. Sally would ask Robert to invite all his friends in the financial district, and Minola would invite the Inspector. Minola, Robert, and Sally would mingle and gather as much gossip as possible; the conversation should be easy. After all,

Robert understood money matters and traveled in lofty financial circles, a rather small community. It seemed a perfect way to try to pump the guests for details about Lord Yardleigh–an ideal way to gather information.

"Inspector, I've just had a wonderful idea. Please don't scowl, it does not become you." Minola looked straight up at him, their eyes met, and for a brief second Minola thought she saw a glint of desire. Just as quickly it disappeared, and his frown returned.

Peter knew he was fighting a losing battle. He had to confess he quite enjoyed looking at her, but he was taken aback by her directness and the mischievous glint in her eyes. Her face was very expressive. *What is it about this infuriating woman? What makes me lose control of the situation? I don't just want her safe, I want her in my bed.* He had never before felt such an incredible pull.

"Inspector, please sit down and join us for a few moments. We are about to have breakfast, and I have a proposition for you."

"A proposition? Indeed, how can I refuse a proposition?" His reply was swift, with a hint of a provocative smile. "Thank you, I have already eaten, but I will join you. I suspect this will be the only way I will find out what's going on."

"Robert is in his element in financial circles. I was planning on having a surprise anniversary party for Sally and Robert."

Sally chimed in. "Minola, that's wonderful. Thank you. I thought you had forgotten, with the murder and everything. A surprise party! I didn't know anything about a party. I love parties." Sally's excitement percolated.

"I know you love parties. Of course, I haven't forgotten. You are my best friend, and you didn't know about the party because it was to be a surprise,"

The Inspector looked from one to the other and noticed, not for the first time, that a very close and honest relationship existed between the two women. They must have known each other a long time to develop a bond like that. His thoughts drifted back to Minola Grey. What an unusual name. She was definitely worth a private, intimate investigation.

Minola cut in on his reverie. "Inspector, Sally is going to ask Robert to invite all his colleagues to this dinner party. Before you get upset, I plan to invite you as my guest so you can mingle and casually talk to everyone."

"I see that you have completely disregarded my warning. That was to be expected. You are asking me to join you for dinner, Miss Grey?" His eyes brightened with pleasure, surprised and delighted at the same time. No matter what the reason, he would be with her, needed to be with her.

"Yes, Inspector, I am inviting you to join me for dinner. Will you be my guest? We will see if there is a flicker of suspicion about the financial status of Lord Yardleigh. I will check with the hotel, set up a menu, and make all the arrangements. How does next Saturday evening sound?"

"That is a task I won't mind you undertaking; you will be reasonably protected. I cannot stress enough, though, do be careful. I want you safe." He realized he wanted more, much more from her. She was in his blood. "Once you have your guest list, please give me an advance copy. I will have the police check out all the invitees." He found Minola's suggestion to be an excellent idea, since little progress had been made in the financial circles and he would be able to keep his eyes on both of them. "What will be on the menu, Miss Grey?"

"What do you like, Inspector?" she replied.

"I am open to suggestions, Miss Grey." He smiled easily.

"Well then, in that case, you will be surprised," she replied in kind.

With a wide grin on his face, he said, "I am looking forward to the dinner, Miss Grey, Mrs. Jones." He gave Minola an ardent glance, turned and walked out of the restaurant.

Minola watched him leave. He had a clean, elegant gait that suited him. She decided to add a few more sketches of his face to her collection–she had now memorized his angular face and mannerisms.

"Sally, can you get all the names from Robert? I will talk to the hotel chef, using the excuse that you are here only for a little while and that's why we have to rush and schedule the party quickly." Minola continued on her quest. "I will send out the invitations as soon as I have names and addresses. I've some invitations upstairs–scenes from the Luxembourg Gardens–which I had drawn specifically for your party. I just hope I have enough; this was to be a small gathering. Each one is a little different. I thought that might be an original approach. What do you think? Sally, say something. Stop me. I am babbling, and have no clue as to why."

"You don't, do you? I can tell you why. His name is Chief Inspector Peter Riley, and he has an interesting way of looking at you, too. Don't tell me you haven't noticed. Did you really draw individual invitations to the party? Can I have one? I am now really excited. What do you want me to do?"

"Well for one, you can address the invitations once we get that list from Robert."

"I can do that. I also want to remind Robert about the financial reports. I just really don't know what we are looking for, but hopefully it will all make sense to him. They should be ready this evening. What else do you need from me?" Sally asked.

"You can help me with the menu. First, let's have breakfast. Afterward we can talk to the manager and make all the arrangements." She felt inner turmoil as she thought about spending an evening with Peter. Somehow, he had managed to reach her both physically and emotionally in a short period of time.

"Don't forget we are also going to check out Lord Yardleigh's office. It looks like a busy day. Who would have thought my trip to Paris would be this exciting?"

Sally had never seen Minola so animated before. She was sure it was the fascinating Inspector–he was most definitely charismatic and, more to the point, Sally was sure he was profoundly affected by Minola.

Over breakfast, they discussed how to approach the office visit. The idea that Minola was going to paint the portrait of Lord Yardleigh gained in appeal.

The day would have to include some sightseeing. A visit to the Rodin museum was a must.

Minola thought about the gardens and their beauty. The intimacy of the grounds made it her most favorite museum. It had been Rodin's home, and his presence, passion, and the sheer magnetism of his work still lingered. Minola's artistic force reached new heights every time she visited this shrine.

The plan for the day progressed rapidly. After talking to the manager at the restaurant, the little café area had been reserved for Saturday evening. It was going to be a dinner with a delicious dual purpose.

Minola and Sally worked closely with the restaurant staff. Minola welcomed Sally's input; Robert, on the other hand, gave them the information they needed and then stayed out of their way. The final head count would determine how many tables would be necessary. Minola felt that eight people per table would be a good number.

Each table would be set with crisp linen tablecloths, flowers, and of course candles. Candles were *de rigueur* for any dinner party she planned. Original hand-drawn place cards would address the issue of food and serve as a souvenir of the evening. Hopefully, it would be a memorable dinner and a very good information-gathering tool.

Minola wanted Peter to appreciate her efforts. *When did he become Peter to me?* During the flurry of activity, the Chief Inspector kept creeping into her thoughts. She even wanted to take him to the Rodin Museum, and Minola did not like to share her time there with just anyone. No man had ever before affected her in such a way.

Shopping also made it to the top of the chart for the day's activities. Minola had to find something elegant to wear. It was true, the common highly overused phrase, 'so much to do, so little time', was very apropos for this occasion.

Chef Etienne was superb, and his judgment in food trusted. Minola knew that, with Robert and Sally's favorite dishes included in the dinner menu, the meal would be ambrosial. She was very excited about Saturday and instinctively knew why–the Chief Inspector had accepted her invitation with alacrity. Whether it was professional or personal, she was not sure, but it was a step in the right direction. Minola wanted to get to know him better, much better. This would be a perfect opportunity for her to do so.

With Saturday's arrangements made, they could now do some sleuthing. When Sally and Minola left the hotel, the city was awake and vibrant. It smelled of spices, perfumes, and car fumes; a delectable conglomerate aroma indeed. The morning bustle of the city was in full gear–this was Minola's Paris. "Sally, take a moment, listen to the city. It is awake."

Her favorite time, however, was in the very early dawn, before the city awoke. "Listen. One morning, we will have to get out at dawn, just as Paris begins to stir, the air is fresh, and the sun is slowly rising. It is quiet and subdued then, and the city is covered by a blanket of hushed introspection. Soon the streets will be cleaned, the cafés will open, and the city will come to life. But not yet, not yet, early morning is breakfast-for-the-soul time. You have to feel it."

Sally replied in hushed tones, "I would love to do that. Your description is incredible. Are you alright?" She broke in on Minola's reverie. "Where are we going–do you have the address?"

"Sorry. Yes, I'm fine. We will head out to Lord Yardleigh's office, right off the Champs Élysée. It is on Avenue Foch, next to the Arc de Triomphe, expensive location."

When the Metro reached the Place de la Concorde, Sally and Minola walked out of the station and were awed by the spectacular view of the Arc de Triomphe as well as the busiest street in Paris, the Champs Élysée. This wide, tree-lined boulevard is the vibrating pulse of the city, filled by tourists, restaurants, exclusive boutiques, cafés, and anything else one desired–a place to see and be seen. The street traffic, culminating at the Arc de Triomphe where one could conceivably drive around in an endless circle for an indefinite time, can give inexperienced drivers nightmares.

The address off the boulevard was so central to Paris that Minola assumed it to be the office headquarters, or at least the center of the business.

"This is incredible. On the way back, could we stop at a café? Maybe do a little shopping? After all, I need a new dress for the party," Sally asked.

"Yes, of course, that was the plan. I don't know what we'll find. I will identify myself, let them know my reason for being there, and ask for Edwards. I forgot to tell you last night, I received a pass from the *Sentinel*. I have been officially commissioned to do the portrait. As a matter of fact, Ian thought it was an excellent idea."

"Okay, so once you identify yourself, what then?"

"Well, I will ask to see the office, sort of get acquainted with the personality, look at everything, check out photographs, if there are any. I'll try to do a quick sketch of the individuals in the photographs. You will take copious notes and just generally snoop."

"What else do you want me to do?" Sally was all ready for action.

"You can try to create a diversion so I can go beyond the obvious. You will be the reporter. Ask about Yardleigh's personal habits, idiosyncrasies, and anything else that comes to mind so that we can gain a better understanding. You know what? This really will be a character study. I will finish the portrait," Minola said with conviction.

"That sounds absolutely terrific. I can ask how he spent his time, what he liked to do. Did he meet anyone here? Who were the people closest to him? What he liked to eat, his favorite restaurants. Is that what you had in mind? My God, that is a long list, it just flowed." Sally was amazed. "We will improvise once we case the joint."

"'Case the joint'? You sound like a thug. The Chief Inspector would not approve of our plan."

Minola grinned and replied, "Which is precisely why he knows nothing about it. We will tell him later tonight. It will be nice to see him scowl again. Do you know that Ian hopes we succeed? He couldn't think of a better headline than 'Artist and Pal Solve High-Profile Murder.' He wants details as soon as possible; in the meantime, all will be quiet."

Walking slowly as they talked, they soon arrived at their destination.

Sally had folded and unfolded the map in her hands several times. "I think we are here. This is it. According to the map, it is the next right turn." Sally exclaimed, "Wow, what a location. I think it is a couple of buildings down on the left hand side. I am having a wonderful time, and this city is glorious."

Chapter 7

While the ladies were getting ready to meddle, the Inspector was otherwise engaged. He visited the Jurac firm, and found they had been fired by Yardleigh a month ago. They were above reproach and promised to produce any necessary files at their earliest convenience. He also decided to visit the major newspapers in the city, the intellectual *Le Monde* and *Le Figaro*. He needed to see just what kind of press Lord Yardleigh had received in the financial as well as the society pages.

Looking forward to the dinner on Saturday night, he realized that a woman had never affected him so much. His reaction to Minola was physical and heated, Alexis not withstanding. This was different, very different, on a much higher plane and it unsettled him to be so vulnerable. He still knew very little about Minola Grey. He needed to stop thinking about her, but he could not. He imagined that full, ripe mouth against his, her body against his, and his insides jangled with desire.

The first rule of an investigation is to check out the people with closest proximity to the victim...that would certainly include Minola Grey. He had not done so, nor would he let anyone give him any information that involved Minola. He had no idea what she did, although he knew she had frequent visitors in her suite.

He recalled the first evening when she returned to her room and Robert Jones was waiting for her. Peter had been angry and jealous that she was so at ease with the man. He distinctly remembered his gut tightening. He had just met her, yet he didn't want any man touching her–only *his* hands and mouth on her body. *Damn it to hell, she isn't even here and I am becoming aroused. Why is she living in the hotel?* He knew she was American, and yet her name was not an American name. It was unique, and it suited her so well. He could not imagine another name for her. She was simply Minola Grey. She was the woman who consumed a great deal of his thoughts, day and night.

He felt a passion and an awareness he had never felt before and he was curious, but hesitated to investigate further. He did not want to be disillusioned. She could *not* be a prostitute, he refused to believe that. Surely, the hotel would not risk its fine reputation on such nefarious goings on. She was simply and elegantly dressed. His first impression just didn't fit.

Once a policeman, always a policeman and Peter had learned to pay attention to the most insignificant details of an individual, all information could be useful in an investigation. That ability served him well in the past, although he had never ignored a background check on a potential suspect before.

He rationalized absolutely everything where Minola Grey was concerned, admitting that he was growing attached to a woman he barely knew. Not for the first time since meeting her, he realized that what he had felt for

Alexis had been a passing, lustful infatuation.

He knew that Minola was observant, paid attention to detail, and seemed organized. He had observed her treatment of the hotel staff–she was kind, not demanding, and they adored her. They accepted her various guests with equanimity and delight.

Peter found himself at the offices of *Le Monde* without realizing how he got there. Most assuredly not a good sign. He needed to focus back on the case. He entered the old building and asked to speak to the person in charge of the 'morgue'.

A bookish-looking young man appeared, looking as though he hadn't slept for weeks. Both his facial expression and his clothes had seen better days–the shabby polyester suit looked quite dingy and definitely had not been to the cleaners in a long time. When he saw the smartly dressed man standing in front of him, however, his harried expression softened perceptibly.

"Can I help you?"

"I hope you can. I am with Interpol." Peter showed his identification. "I need to see any news articles that were printed about Lord John Yardleigh in the last five years. I am investigating his murder." Peter felt that was close enough to the truth.

"You are an Englishman. He was killed in Paris. Surely the Police Nationale are handling the investigation," the polyester-clad man said.

Peter assumed the young man just did not want to dig in the files if he could help it. "The Police Nationale is investigating, but so am I. The victim was, after all, a

British Peer. Now that we have established the logistics, I need to see everything–business, social events he may have attended. I am especially interested in any gossip."

"*Le Monde* does not deal in gossip," replied the young man with bare civility.

"I see. Then, let us find anything at all that mentioned Lord Yardleigh. If I can help, I would be very pleased to do so. How shall we proceed?"

"I will take you to the dungeon; everything is kept there. You can see the hard copies, since you are looking only for the last five years. We can also access the information by computer simply by using his last name. Some of the older files are kept on the microfiche. It might take a while," he replied tersely.

"Well, in that case, let us not delay." Peter mentally prepared himself for a long and tedious morning. He was not sure exactly what he was looking for, but he would know once he saw it. Normally Welsey would do the job, but today Peter felt restless and he needed the mundane activity.

As he searched through the records, he noticed a camera occasionally captured something that could be incriminating. His efforts might prove profitable–a convoluted hierarchy existed, and he began to know who the victim's associates were. It would take time and an expert, maybe an expert like Robert. Through him, he would be one step closer to Minola.

Peter hated to admit it, but Minola had the right approach to the investigation. Instead of *'cherchez la femme,'* it was *'cherchez l'Euro'*.

* * *

While the Inspector dug through papers at *Le Monde*, the ladies were digging for information at the victim's office, located in an impeccably kept building. It had an exceptional view of the 'Place de Charles de Gaulle', formerly known as the 'Place de L'Étoile'. An easy translation of 'the place of stars', the name still stuck because the circle around the Arc de Triomphe created a star-like effect and played havoc with the awe-inspiring Parisian traffic.

They entered the venerable old building and searched for the office listing on the wall plaque. An old elevator with polished brass doors took them to their destination on the third floor.

Entry to the Yardleigh office presented an abrupt contrast to the old building, and the sudden transition was eye-popping. The reception area was subdued, elegant, and spoke of old money. The area was full of light, focusing the eye on the geometric patterned carpet. Rich burgundy, ivory, and plum colors were woven into a lopsided angular pattern. It appealed to Minola instantly. The furniture was modern, understated, and looked comfortable. The office exuded muted elegance. It was a perfect location for a financial institution.

A middle-aged receptionist, dressed in a subdued, severely cut blue suit sat behind the elegant desk. Minola introduced Sally and herself, and enquired, "*Bonjour Madame, parlez-vous Anglais*?"

"*Bonjour, Mademoiselle. Oui*, I speak English. Can I help you?" she replied effortlessly.

"*Bon*…Good, thank you, Madame. My name is Minola Grey. I was asked by the *London Sentinel* to do a portrait of the late Lord Yardleigh. I would like to see his office, see his surroundings; it would help me to understand and give me a sense of the person." Minola began feeling like a fortuneteller.

The receptionist eyed Minola carefully and said, "There is no one here today, Mademoiselle. Lord Yardleigh's secretary, Mr. Edwards, will be in later this morning, but until he arrives I cannot allow you access to his office. You have no appointment."

Minola thought quickly. "I am staying in the same hotel as Mr. Edwards. I really am an artist, and I have met Mr. Edwards briefly. Perhaps you can get in touch with him. I can talk to him, explain my commission. I would hate to have wasted my trip out here." Minola sounded as if she could not afford to lose the income such a commission would provide. Further encroaching on the subtle working-class environment, this was money, and she was working for a living.

The secretary looked Minola over again, hesitated, then made her decision. "I suppose you can go and look, no harm can be done."

"Thank you." Minola was surprised at the quick acquiescence and, without delay, walked into the office. It was impressive. The modern décor continued uninterrupted, right down to the wild and bold facets of the carpeting. Nothing broke the eye appeal. The modern, massive glass doors gave it a much grander appearance; however, they did not diminish the old Romanesque style of the building.

The desk was a beautiful rosewood piece, accompanied by a high, comfortable chair. Minola observed that the two chairs facing the desk were considerably less comfortable looking, and much smaller. It was obvious who was in charge here.

Sally, meanwhile, worked the receptionist. She plied her with questions about Lord Yardleigh–his business, his visitors, how often Mr. Edwards worked in this office, what other offices were part of the business, and so forth. The receptionist must have been lonely. It was as if floodgates opened up, and she couldn't talk fast enough.

Minola took out her pad and quickly sketched the office floor plan. This effort would not be wasted–she would use it as a backdrop for the portrait. At the same time, Minola glanced around, looking for any kind of information, anything at all that would give her insight into the business at hand.

While Sally kept the receptionist occupied, Minola sat in the comfy chair, making a pretense of drawing while she quickly and quietly checked the drawers in the desk. She found a small leather black book in the center drawer containing some numbers–maybe phone numbers–and alphabetic characters. She removed it and copied all the information into the back of her sketchpad, then did a quick but thorough sketch of the office and carefully returned the little book to its rightful place.

Minola looked around, got up from the desk, and walked over to the bookcase. The selection there obviously displayed to impress–interesting and discerning choices were flaunted, with business, fiction, and a bit of science proudly exhibited. All were well known, almost as if they were trophies. Minola was not sure if it was truly an intellectual pursuit, or if the books were simply there to impress.

She reasoned that if Lord Yardleigh really did read them, he was a thinker and a sharp, ruthless businessman. Given that *The Prince* and *The Art of War* were prominently displayed in the center of the case, whether for display purposes or actual reading material, he was a force to be reckoned with. Either way, it was a warning to his guests and business associates alike.

The large bookcase, desk and chairs, a couch that matched the burgundy color in the rug, and two pieces of art completed the office. The decor was sparse in its simplicity, although one painting depicted an intricate pastel flower garden scene which seemed totally out of place for an office of this caliber. The other was an abstract oil painting that used the same colors and wild geometric pattern that set in the astonishing carpet. The frame matched the desk, the effect quite pleasing. She did not recognize the artist, but she was sure it had been commissioned specifically for this office.

She glanced over to the reception area and saw that Sally was done. Minola walked out of the office and showed her sketch to the receptionist. It was a way to validate and appease any lingering doubts that the receptionist might have had.

"I noticed that quaint pastel painting hanging on the wall. Was it commissioned for this office?" Minola was quite curious about that painting. It just did not belong.

"No, Mademoiselle. It was given to his Lordship by a friend. He was quite fond of it, yet he changed the hanging location frequently. He just could not decide where he wanted it."

Minola found that to be very interesting, but decided for the time being not to dwell on it. "Do you have a name for this friend? I should like to find the artist. It is quite lovely."

"Yes, I have it. Madame was a frequent visitor to this office. Her name is Giselle Armand. Even now she comes and spends much time with Mr. Edwards. Together, they are keeping the office open."

"Thank you so much. You have been of great assistance. Please tell Mr. Edwards that I have been here. I would like to meet with him, preferably at the hotel. Thank you again." Minola quickly packed her things, and wished the assistant a good day.

Sally was puzzled at the reaction to the painting. Once outside she asked, "What caught your attention about that particular painting?"

"It doesn't belong in that office. You saw the décor. Everything fit like a glove, right down to the abstract painting that matched the colors and patterns in the carpet. He believed in a minimal effect, everything coordinated to the max. Yet that little pastel came out of nowhere. Some people enjoy art and coordinate nothing–they hang a piece because they enjoy looking at it. In this office, everything was paired to perfection in color, pattern, period, and style. Except for that little pastel..." Minola was clearly puzzled.

"So, you think this woman had some special friendship

with him?" Sally was curious.

"Yes, that is exactly what I think. You and I are going to visit her. I was also lucky in my snooping–I found a little black book. Why does it always have to be a black book? Anyway, I copied all the numbers and letters listed. I think Robert and the Inspector will be busy."

"Why did you mention that you would like to see Edwards?"

"Didn't it strike you as odd that Edwards and Giselle Armand are working in the office together? She is not listed anywhere as an officer of the company. The few things we gathered from the website mentioned his most visible and prominent associates quite openly. She was not mentioned once. I find that interesting."

"Who is actually running the company? The offices are open, at least this one is, but no one seems to be at the helm."

"That caught my attention too. Hey, are we a good team, or what? Tonight, over dinner, we can discuss our findings. Should we invite the Chief Inspector? Right now, a bit of lunch on the Champs would be lovely. We will call Madame Armand, see if she is home, and we'll arrange a meeting. In the meantime, we can do some shopping, then go back to the hotel. Sounds like a full day to me."

"I am looking forward to lunch, shopping, and a run-in with Peter Riley this evening. I don't think the Chief Inspector will be happy with us; in fact, he will be furious. I had better call Robert and have him meet us for dinner. What time?"

"I'm sure Peter won't be pleased, but we will cross that

bridge later. Let's have our lunch. Plan dinner for seven. We can shop and it will give us enough time to freshen up and change."

Their walk on the Champs Élysée was leisurely. Their first stop was a café filled with tourists. They ordered coffee to tide them over till lunch arrived, while a spectacular view of the Arc de Triomphe provided visual appeal.

The boulevard is the best place to people-watch. They say that if you sit in a café long enough, you will eventually meet someone you know. Minola did not want to sit there that long, but the respite was extremely satisfying.

Painting Lord Yardleigh's portrait was not going to be an emotional experience on her part. She was beginning to know him a little, and realized the initial coldness she had felt was real. *How does that explain the little landscape?* It was a soft, gentle painting. That pastel told her much. He obviously enjoyed it and had found room for it in a professionally decorated office, yet he appeared to be neither a docile nor a kind man. Still, he must have found that painting pleasing. He could always see it from any angle, and the abstract piece was permanently hung behind his desk.

Minola felt she had some good information, although some aspects of the victim's character had seemed to be outside the box. Why was he killed? There were some rumors about unsavory business dealings, but then what powerful businessman did not face those on a daily basis? Was it greed, passion, or something else that got him killed?

Sally broke in on Minola's thoughts. "Hey, come back to earth. Lunch has arrived." Their salad and a scrumptious ham sandwich on a baguette arrived with a flourish. They placed a call to Madame Armand, leaving a message that they would call again.

After lunch, strolling down the boulevard they shopped at every opportunity and there were many.

Finally, Minola found her dress. It was basic black, her favorite choice, with sheer sleeves, low-cut front and back, and scalloped edges outlined in the same lovely material that covered the sleeves. Perfect, thought Minola. High-heeled black sandals and her pair of ruby earrings would complete the look. She wanted to keep it simple, elegant, and stunning. She refused to contemplate why it mattered so much.

Sally found a lovely peach dress, her favorite color. The dress had an embroidered neckline, very feminine, just like her. They were now all set for the party on Saturday.

Late afternoon seemed to arrive in the blink of an eye. They placed another call to Madame Armand. The lady was in, but unable to see them today. "Perhaps another day," she suggested. Minola introduced herself as an artist, and suggested a meeting tomorrow morning at the café across from Notre Dame. The Latin Quarter was, after all, suitable for artists. Madame Armand agreed to meet them there the following morning.

Once the meeting had been arranged, Minola and Sally were free to do anything else that appealed. Minola decided that, if the Inspector might be coming to dinner tonight, she would wear her new black dress. Of course, she would need something else for the Saturday dinner, so the shopping spree continued full force. Progress to the hotel may have been slow, but shopping was not.

Chapter 8

Once inside the hotel, Minola spotted Peter. He and Robert were sitting on a lobby sofa, drinking wine and looking downright chummy.

Sally ran up and affectionately greeted Robert with a kiss. "We had a wonderful, productive day. Wait till you hear about our adventure." Robert looked at her packages and wondered if anything had been left in the stores.

Peter's attention focused on Minola's face. He found himself staring at her like a young schoolboy. "Miss Grey," he muttered.

She greeted him apprehensively and spoke quickly to hide her flustered emotions. "Good afternoon. Could we possibly meet for dinner? I am starving, and we do have some news." Peter smiled at her and quietly replied, "An invitation has already been extended, as Robert put it, to get better acquainted."

"So, where are we going?"

"We are going to a Mediterranean restaurant on Rue de La Huchette. If you both go dump the bags, we can get a move on. Did you clean out all the boutiques?"

Sally, who up to now had been quiet, addressed herself to Robert. "This is Paris," as if that explained everything. "One goes to museums in Paris. One shops in Paris." She gave him a peck on the cheek, and pushed Minola toward the elevator.

Minola knew Sally needed no excuse to go shopping, but somehow she had always managed to find one and this time was no exception. She waited while Sally showered, and thought about the evening with Peter Riley.

When her turn came, Minola moved swiftly. She got dressed in record time, pulled up her thick hair in the back and secured it with a glittering pin, then changed into a stark white silk blouse and black silk pants. A pair of black Prada sandals completed her outfit. After all the shopping, she decided to wear something old and comfortable.

Even though Minola liked jewelry, she chose not to wear any tonight–the only thing that glittered was the hairpin. Looking at herself in the mirror, she decided she had somewhat achieved the look she was aiming for…simple, yet elegant. She was ready to face the Inspector, feeling like a high school girl on her first date, only this wasn't a date. It was a murder investigation, one she had chosen to get involved in despite Interpol's objections.

Peter Riley was an enigma to Minola. He had an easy, elegant style, an intimidating presence, and he seemed to possess a keen awareness of human nature. She wondered what it would feel like to be loved by him. Her thoughts became more erotic by the minute. He had a full, generous mouth, and his hands were lean and powerful. How would they feel on her body? Minola shook her head to bring herself back to reality, but thoughts of him remained in the back of her mind.

He had never treated her, Sally, or Robert, for that matter, as suspects. Given what he must have witnessed in his career as a policeman that in itself was a feat. He was curt at times, but courteous, and above all concerned for their safety. *I don't know him, but he moves me.*

Ready at last, the two women left Minola's rooms. As they neared the elevator, Edwards came out of his room. Sally quickly nudged Minola. She intercepted his path and introduced herself. "Mr. Edwards, my name is Minola Grey, and this is my friend, Sally Jones. You were Lord Yardleigh's secretary?"

"Good evening. Yes, I was. Is there anything I can do for you? I have been told that you visited our office this afternoon."

"Yes, I was there. I am a painter and I was commissioned by the *London Sentinel* to paint a memorial portrait of his Lordship," Minola replied demurely.

"I know who you are, Miss Grey. In fact, Lord Yardleigh was familiar with your work. Why do you need access to his offices? Who exactly commissioned you?"

"He was? I am so pleased to hear that. I am sorry I did not get a chance to meet him. Actually, it was Ian Stoddard who asked me to do the portrait. Are you familiar with his writing?"

"Yes, of course I am. He is rather well known, just as you appear to be," was the terse reply. He was not quite rude, but seemed reluctant to continue the conversation.

"I was not aware I had fans across the Atlantic. That's gratifying to hear." Minola was not sure how to proceed.

"Miss Grey needs to see the environment in which her

subject lived and worked." Sally had quietly watched the exchange and quickly came to Minola's rescue.

Turning to Minola she said, "I'll go downstairs and tell Robert we will be leaving shortly." Sally did not mention the fact that they were also dining with the Chief Inspector. "Good night, Mr. Edwards."

"Thanks, Sally. I won't be long. I just need a few more minutes of Mr. Edward's time." Minola now addressed herself to him.

"Mr. Edwards, I really would like to visit his office here at the hotel. If you would allow it, that is. All I need to do is to sketch his surroundings, get a feel for his lifestyle, if you will."

He hesitated, but finally relented. "That can be arranged. Please let me know when it would be convenient for you. I will be here."

"Thank you. Once I check my schedule, I will leave a message for you downstairs. Good evening, Mr. Edwards."

"Good evening, Miss Grey." With that acknowledgement, he turned and walked back to his room.

As she watched him retreat, Minola remembered he had originally been coming from his room when they met. Had he been watching for her?

When she arrived in the lobby, Robert and Peter quickly stood up to greet her. Peter's eyes lingered on her face, and she felt herself blushing. Minola was the first to look away, quickly acknowledging everyone.

They meandered toward Blvd. St. Michel. Strolling alongside Peter, she asked, "Can we make this less formal? May I call you Peter? You do know my name."

"Yes, I do. That would suit me very well."

She found it strange how quickly he became Peter to her. She smiled and decided to start the conversation, since she noticed he had not used her first name.

"Sally and I met the secretary on our way down this evening. He seemed a bit abrupt, decidedly in control, and not pleased with our interference. Is he a suspect, Peter?"

"Yes, he is a very viable suspect." Peter liked his name on her lips.

Sally and Robert, walking ahead, turned left, on to the Rue de La Huchette. The narrow side streets seemed to blend together. They were cobbled and uneven, but a haven of bustling activity. One was never sure where one street ended and another began. The city, as usual, was vibrant with evening strollers. Like an illuminated beacon, Notre Dame stood guard.

The meandering little streets led them to the restaurant. It was not a Grand Michelin-rated eatery, but a normal everyday place for normal everyday people, a sheer delight for all the senses.

Walking together, Minola gently took Peter's hand so he would not miss the turn. She felt him tense. She tried to withdraw her hand, but his grip tightened. His touch was electric. It felt good, solid and safe, Minola thought ruefully. He continued to hold her hand until they were seated.

The back corner of the restaurant guaranteed them some privacy. The table was old and scuffed, with two red and white candles accenting a well-used, threadbare red tablecloth. It was a casual, warm place.

It occurred to Minola that Peter might be involved with

someone; maybe she was making it uncomfortable for him by taking his hand. She suddenly remembered Lady Yardleigh.

Robert, who knew Minola almost as well as Sally did, noticed she was a bit uncomfortable, so he took the initiative. "Peter, did the ladies tell you what they did today?"

Peter looked at Sally, then his attention centered on Minola and he replied, "I am almost afraid to ask, but I will nevertheless. What did the ladies do today?"

"They visited Lord Yardleigh's Avenue Foch office," Robert said succinctly.

Peter looked stunned. "Minola, there was more to Lord Yardleigh than the consummate businessman. He was, after all, a murder victim. That office might be a dangerous place. I cannot stress enough–please, please be careful."

Hearing her name softly spoken by him was enchanting–it came so easily to him. He did not hesitate and, as silly as it sounded, it thrilled Minola.

"We just went to his office to check it out. I had a perfectly good excuse, a really good one if I do say so myself. The receptionist was very helpful. Sally kept her occupied; she really has a way with people. At any rate, I snooped in his office while Sally talked to the receptionist. It's a stately office, by the way, well lit and elegantly decorated. Some discrepancies, but the overall effect was exquisite. Oh, I almost forgot, I have a list of some letters and numbers; at least I think that is what I found. There was this black book in his desk, and I copied all the information in it." Breathless, she finished her narrative.

Speechless, Robert and Peter listened. Sally, on the other hand, enjoyed the effect Minola had on Peter. That Peter was deeply affected by Minola, Sally was sure. That Peter would act on his feelings, Sally was not so sure. She would have to figure something out. Her best friend needed to find the same happiness she found with Robert. Minola had been alone far too long.

"Where did you say you found this book?" Peter demanded. He was back on the job, full force. "Everything was checked and I have a list of everything that was found. No mention was made of a book."

"It was actually quite easy. I just sat at his desk and pretended to do a sketch of his office. Well, not really pretend, I sketched while Sally kept the receptionist occupied with questions. I opened the center drawer." She recapped her adventure. "It's probably nothing," Minola added.

While they talked, the waiter brought their drinks and took their orders. Peter kept the interrogation going.

"Please, whatever you do, no one, absolutely *no one* must know that you even saw a list, much less that you actually have the list."

Minola quickly reassured him that she would tell no one. "Peter, I didn't keep the list, I simply copied the information onto my sketch pad, then put it back in the drawer. I have not told anyone. Sally has not said a word either. I will give you the information this evening, then I will be rid of it. It may not even be significant, it was easily accessible."

Peter reaffirmed that the office had been searched, but

nothing was found, certainly not a black book, which meant that it had been put there after the search, and after the murder.

Concerned, Peter told Minola not to interfere again. He emphasized point blank that she could be risking her life, since obviously it appeared to be business as usual with or without Lord Yardleigh. Sally came to Minola's defense. She reminded Peter exactly how the information was retrieved. "She went to the receptionist and showed her the sketch, so it looked legitimate. The receptionist could see that Minola was not carrying anything but what she came with."

Robert listened to Sally's explanation and became quite concerned for their safety. "Peter, I know you cannot share all your information, but just how far has the investigation progressed? I worry about them. I've had a chance to look at some of the reports the ladies have unearthed on the Internet–it's amazing the kind of information that is available. On the surface, the financials look good. Upon deeper digging, and using some information from friends, a lot of money was going through the company; however, there is no record where the money came from. Something decidedly foul was, and most likely is still, going on. I assume you had someone look at the less public numbers?"

Peter, a tentative look on his face, briefly debated how much information to share. "Yes, we had an accounting firm look at the books, and they so far have come up with nothing concrete. The company was in a financial shortfall, and last year there was a large influx of money. It is not a hard goods company per se; it is a service company–an import and export business working in multiple currencies, soft goods. He traded a great deal in European currencies, and it is much easier to launder money in those circumstances. The quid pro quo is easier to manipulate. Your analysis, as far as it goes, is correct."

"Please explain." Minola said. "I don't understand how this money laundering works. I know it is easier to peddle soft goods, because there is no inventory to account for. What really happens?"

"You are right, Minola, there is very little hard-core accountability in the soft goods area. Trade in the European currencies makes it difficult to account for each transaction. If you use a certain amount of cash, and go through the various currencies, it is difficult to account precisely. It is a very handy way to launder money. With the introduction of the Euro, however, this sort of trading has become a bit more difficult. I assume that is when problems started."

Peter was filling in the missing pieces of the financial puzzle, at least the pieces that were available. He trusted them implicitly. Call it instinct, a professional hunch, or whatever it was, Peter was comfortable in disclosing the information.

"Lord Yardleigh was suspected of laundering drug money. He was going to testify against some of his associates, and that is how I came to be involved."

"At least now I know what to look for," Robert said.

Their appetizers arrived and the conversation became more cheerful. The upcoming Saturday dinner came up for discussion, as did their shopping adventure, the tourist sights that Sally still wanted to see, and Minola's promise to continue playing tour guide.

Robert and Peter listened attentively while everyone ate their Mediterranean feast of couscous, falafel, assorted salads, and freshly baked pita bread. For the moment even Peter's concern for their safety abated, albeit briefly.

Discreetly observing Minola, Peter again wondered what she was doing in Paris. She was very familiar with the city, and he wanted to see Paris through her eyes. She had an intoxicating affect on him. He certainly did not need wine with dinner, he had Minola. He still knew nothing about her, not one single iota. He had broken all the rules in his approach to her. He was keenly aware of her and thought she appeared at ease in his company–more relaxed than she had been earlier.

Robert brought Peter out of his reverie by asking some questions about his work and his background.

"Living in London is convenient. It makes my commute minimal, but I do enjoy the countryside. I try to get away as often as I can." He did not discuss his personal background any further.

Conversation flowed smoothly and the food was admirable–the wine was a typical *vin* ordinaire, but was nevertheless fruity and full-bodied. The evening so far had been perfect.

Peter continued to reflect on his life. He felt he could get used to this lifestyle, and he was tired of being alone. *Hell, I want her in my bed, in my life. I am repeating myself.* Her effect on him was shattering. He had not realized the extent of his desire until earlier today when he saw her coming toward him in the hotel lobby.

What an extraordinary situation to be in. He barely knew her, and yet he trusted her. He felt the whole concept was absurd. What was he thinking? He was a cop, he should know better. He thought back to when he first met her, and his suspicions now seemed incongruous to him. He stopped musing and asked, "Minola, you mentioned that you were sketching the office. Whatever for?"

Caught off guard by Peter's question, she now must tell him about the concocted scheme. She did not want to spoil the camaraderie that existed, and spoil it she would. "Peter, it is rather a long story." She was going to let it go for now.

However, Peter had other ideas. "We have a whole evening for long stories. I am sure Robert will not mind hearing it, will you?" Peter asked.

"No, I certainly won't," came the prompt response. "Sally has had a very smug look on her face all evening. Let's hear the story."

"Thank you, Robert…you are *so* helpful," Minola said waspishly.

"I aim to please. Do continue. I am sure Peter wants a thorough explanation," He continued, unabashed.

Minola gave Robert a cross look and continued with her story. "Okay, here it goes. I have a journalist friend, Ian Stoddard, who works for the *London Sentinel*. I called and asked him to commission me to paint Lord Yardleigh's portrait, as sort of a memorial tribute. His paper will print the portrait along with an eloquent editorial about Lord Yardleigh's charitable works. Ian thought it was a wonderful idea, provided, of course, that his paper really got the portrait and a possible scoop. There, that's the short and sweet of it, and actually not very long at all."

"What do you mean, a portrait? How are you going to get a portrait of Yardleigh?" Peter at this point was very confused.

She thought back and remembered his original suspicions. "Why, I am going to paint it, of course," Minola replied. She looked at Peter, saw the disbelief on his face, and realized that he really hadn't investigated her background at all. *Perhaps he is too afraid of what he would find.* She really was letting her overactive imagination run away with her.

Peter, reluctant to let go of this conversation and terrified that if she got into trouble he wouldn't be there to protect her, continued. "Minola, you cannot pretend to paint a portrait. Someone will get suspicious."

"I won't get caught. I've done it before," she quipped impishly.

"Done what, snoop or pretend to paint?"

Minola decided that she wasn't going to tell Peter that she was an artist. He would find out soon enough–Saturday, to be precise–but for now she was going to evade the whole subject. Maybe she was apprehensive he wouldn't like her work. It mattered a great deal what he thought of her.

Sally and Robert noticed her reticence, and kept quiet about Minola's profession. Sally tried to get the conversation back to a more congenial topic and brought up the office décor. She seemed to think that merited more discussion.

Minola decided to share some of her impressions. "The office is elegant, very simple, with sleek lines and rosewood office furniture. Contemporary carpet in the reception area carries through to the office and a beautiful abstract painting that had to have been commissioned was hanging behind the desk. Something else rather odd..."

Peter noticed her omission and postponed the obvious questions to pursue her observations on the office décor. "Why did it have to be commissioned?"

"Well," Minola replied, "either the carpet or the painting, or both, were commissioned. The colors and shapes are a perfect match, sort of a variation on a theme. It is a set, of that I am sure."

Peter listened intently. "I will have to pay a visit to this office again. I ventured to his other two lesser known locations, assuming there would be more activity in the outlying areas, but there was nothing out of the ordinary in the suburbs. Mr. Edwards seems to have consolidated, so the main office in Paris now appears to be the hub."

Robert was curious. "Peter, why in the suburbs and not in Paris?"

"I wanted to quickly check the other less obvious locations. Paris was central and too exposed. Lord Yardleigh had indicated the actual business was conducted outside of Paris, so we had been watching the suburbs. There were no receptionists, just occasionally Edwards and of course standard mail delivery. It was all very neat and portable."

"One more question. If you knew who went in and out, were there any suspicious characters that you or the French police could identify?"

"No, that was the interesting part. There were legitimate

mail deliveries and pick-ups, but nothing out of the ordinary. It all seemed quite innocent. I don't even know at this point if Yardleigh was being candid about the business, but he is the one who contacted Interpol, so we assumed he told the truth. Maybe everything went through the local office here. The Police Nationale had been watching the Avenue Foch office, and they couldn't find anything suspicious."

"I am glad you've told us that the other offices are basically shut down. Sally and I were going to go and visit them. You saved us some time," Minola responded.

Again, Peter expressed his concern about their safety. He seemed to be doing that rather frequently. "You do not want to be seen anywhere near those offices, just in case anyone other than us is watching them. You mentioned something that stood out in his Avenue Foch office, what was it?"

Minola, listening to Peter, was glad they had not ventured out beyond Paris. She looked up and found him patiently waiting for her answer. A gentle smile softened his face, although his eyes reflected his deep concern for them. Minola returned the smile and said, "There was a lovely pastel landscape facing his desk. It was painted by a Giselle Armand; I am not familiar with her work." Looking at Peter, she knew at once by his lifted eyebrows that he was familiar with the name. "The painting was totally outside the decor's style. It was a personal decision to hang that particular painting in the office." She waited for a response that did not come.

Minola plunged ahead. "Peter, who is Giselle Armand?

When I mentioned her name, it seemed familiar to you." He broke eye contact and hesitated. She quickly continued, "Sally and I are having an early meeting with her at the little café across from Notre Dame tomorrow morning."

Peter, although not one to restate the obvious, did so at this very moment. "What do you mean, you are having a meeting with her?"

"I am interested in the pastel painting. It is out of place in the office, and I want to know its significance. I told the receptionist I liked it and asked who the artist was. She promptly provided the artist's name, so we telephoned Madame Armand and made arrangements to meet."

Peter remained silent for a second, staring at Minola. He knew he needed to answer the unasked question that was so apparent on her face and said, "I know Giselle Armand. We have met a few times."

Minola kept looking at Peter, and waited.

His glance never wavered. "She is a rather well-known painter in the Parisian Bohemian circles, something of a bon vivant, likes to have a good time. She was also Lord Yardleigh's mistress. It was Giselle, along with Lady Yardleigh, who convinced him to seek help from Interpol."

"But Peter," exclaimed Minola, "she has been working in the Avenue Foch office with Mr. Edwards. The receptionist said they worked together frequently. Surely she knew the business was in trouble? Why continue, especially since Lord Yardleigh was murdered? How could she not be aware of the shenanigans, and yet continue to work there? Don't you think this is strange?"

"That is decidedly strange. However, there is more than

an artistic side to Giselle Armand–she is also an accountant by profession. She must have seen or heard something to convince Yardleigh to seek help. She is, by far, more streetwise than Yardleigh ever was. She must have realized he was in over his head, and I think she really tried to help him out of this quagmire. Well, I think I have answered all your questions. Would you care to share your suspicions? What are you two planning to do when you visit Giselle?" Peter gently, but firmly, inquired.

"We will discuss the painting and also try to get information about her current employment with Mr. Edwards. Art should be a good icebreaker. Peter, maybe you could offer professional guidance in interviewing techniques before we meet with Giselle." Minola said.

Sally wondered if it would be a good idea to invite Peter to join them. She was curious to see what Peter would do with the invitation, so she took the proverbial bull by the horn and asked him.

He was surprised at the offer. "I should really like to come along; however, my going would signal that you two are involved in the investigation. Giselle will be more forthcoming without me there. And last, and most important of all, I do not want anyone tipped off that you are somehow connected in this business beyond painting a portrait commissioned by your journalist friend. It will be safer for you. Do not offer too much information–she is connected and might inadvertently let something slip."

Minola sensed that Peter trusted them, but he was also walking a tightrope between being a cop, a friend, and allowing civilians to get involved. "So, what do we do?"

"Keep the conversation impersonal. Hold a general discussion. Avoid anything that might arouse suspicion. Keep to the roles that were created in the Avenue Foch office; namely, Minola is to paint the portrait, and you, Sally, are the journalist. Discuss the pastel, it would be a good time to bring out Giselle's involvement in the office: what she did there, who visited. This would be done through you, Sally, as the journalist. You could explain that it is necessary to get to know the subject. At some point in time, the conversation could become broader, which will allow you to bring up Mr. Edwards, his duties, and his relationship with Lord Yardleigh. Keep it natural, and follow the flow of the conversation."

Minola, still puzzling over the pastel, as she listened to Peter and Sally, decided that most likely Yardleigh enjoyed the painting since it was from his mistress. But why not hang it the bedroom, which was more private and certainly more intimate.

The dinner ended on a positive note. Peter seemed satisfied they would be careful. Outside, the conversation changed to lighter topics. Peter said he had never relaxed more than he had tonight. Robert was quick to agree. Sally confirmed that she would see Minola and Peter in the hotel lobby at eight the next morning. Robert and Sally said their goodbyes, and Robert hailed a waiting taxi to take them back to their apartment.

It appeared as if the evening on Blvd St. Michel had just started. Minola and Peter decided to wander along the boulevard for a while before returning to the hotel. They strolled together in total contentment. The air was crisp, with that wonderful smell that only Paris offers. Minola took a deep breath and savored the essence.

Peter looked at her curiously and asked if she was alright. She replied that she was splendid.

Peter wholeheartedly concurred with that statement. "Yes, you are, Miss Grey."

Minola started laughing, "I'm not splendid, the city is. Are we back to 'Miss Grey'?"

"Only occasionally…"

"You must think me a strange creature, but I really enjoy the fragrance of this city. It is unique; it has a signature all its own."

Peter did not think that she was a strange creature at all; in fact, he found her downright captivating. She was sophisticated, shy, reticent, and worldly all at the same time. She comprised quite a package. He needed to touch her. Unable to stop himself, he put his arm around her waist and pulled her closer to him.

She did not resist. "Peter, how often do you get away from London?" She felt the heat from his hand raise her body temperature.

"Not as often as I would like. My parents still live in the countryside, in what was always my family home. Work has been demanding lately, and I am long overdue for some time off. Maybe, once this is finished."

"Do you often get involved in murder cases?"

"Generally, Interpol gets involved in money laundering, international drug trafficking, crimes along those lines. We basically help police departments around the world. We have facilities beyond the scope of most agencies. This case is unique."

"Why did Yardleigh request you, specifically?" She felt his hand tighten on her waist.

"Alexis Yardleigh requested my services," he said abruptly. "Now, Miss Grey, how about a café stop to finish the evening?"

"That sounds delightful. Your choice, Chief Inspector." Minola listened to what wasn't being said. He didn't discuss his personal relationships. Alexis Yardleigh was in his past, she would bet anything on it. She could also be his future. The woman was now free, rich, and drop-dead gorgeous. Minola felt a stab of jealousy at the thought.

"Do you have sisters or brothers?" she went back to a comfortable topic.

"I have a younger sister, Mary. Her family lives just down the street from my parents, in Slough. I have twin nephews, age seven, and a five-year-old niece. Let's see, it is William, Jonathan, and Katherine. Do not ever call her Kate. I still have a hard time telling the twins apart. What about you, Minola? Family? Anyone special in your life?"

"You mean other than all my guests at the hotel?" She did not smile; it still rankled. "I have no one. Robert and Sally are my immediate family." Minola's eyes clouded with memories of loneliness. She continued walking alongside Peter in silence.

"I'm sorry, I-" his hold on her tightened.

She cut him off. "That's all right, Peter. It really doesn't matter."

Amid all the chaos that is Blvd. St. Michel, Peter gazed at Minola. He noticed the change in her demeanor. *What is it? Has she been hurt?* She quickly snapped out of it and seemed again to revel in the atmosphere.

People mingled in the cafés and sidewalks. It seemed the street never shut down, always alive with activity. Of course it helped that at all hours students from the university abounded. Gilbert Jeune, a Parisian institution, was still open for business. People sat in the cafés, bought books, listened to music, and talked, enjoying the camaraderie. One could hear the clinking glasses as various aperitifs were poured and served outside. The waiters could be heard jingling coins in their pockets. The sheer pleasure of just being out and about was a delight to the senses. As he watched, Minola's face mirrored the vitality of the city.

"Are you ready for coffee? We can stop right here." Peter selected the lively café right next to the bookstore.

"I am always ready for coffee. This is perfect. Why would someone resort to murder? What makes a person cross the line and take a life?"

He didn't expect the question. "I have never been able to understand any reason for that course of action, but we have had people rationalize many things. It all narrows down to greed, passion, hate, and, believe it or not, love. At least a very narrow definition of love, one even I as a cop cannot comprehend. Greed and discovery are very strong factors and, in cases like this, if discovery is eminent a second murder is not out of the question. In fact, it is a distinct possibility," he said quietly.

"I know where you are going with this. I will be careful, I promise. I just don't believe that anyone should get away with killing another human being."

"Minola, what are you doing in Paris?" he asked suddenly while sipping his coffee.

"That was out of the blue–I almost forgot that you are a policeman. It's my turn, is it? Hmm…I just needed a change, to prove to myself that I could. Peter, I am not a… Could we table this for right now? It is late; I think we should head back. Thank you for the coffee." She gulped her coffee.

From the first moment he met her, he had noticed a certain taciturn quality about her. Even sensing her withdrawal, he trusted her. He felt comfortable and at peace. For a jaded cop who has seen it all, this was a blessing indeed. He would do anything to protect and keep her safe. Anything. His other feelings were too new and raw to even consider–he needed to move slowly.

They strolled back to the peculiar little streets off the beaten path away from Blvd. St. Michel, and were besieged by smiling innkeepers asking them to come and eat in their establishment.

Their feet beginning to ache from the quaint, yet difficult to walk on cobblestones, they found themselves back in front of Notre Dame. Minola never missed an opportunity to view this incredible structure. She asked Peter if he wouldn't mind taking a few minutes to enjoy the breathtaking sight.

Notre Dame was lit up for the night. Minola pointed out how the shining lights created shadows and how, at various perspectives, it changed the perception of the cathedral. They sat on a bench and watched as the cameras held by tourists seemed to swirl around them, adding to the blaze of light.

Peter, enthralled, could not take his eyes off her animated face. Finally they decided it was time to go back home, but they were too tired to make the walk, deciding to take the Metro from the St. Michel stop to St. Sulpice, a short way from the hotel.

During the evening Peter got a sense of her Paris. He paid attention to the smells and the sounds; he listened to the waiters in the open-air cafés clanking glasses, and noticed that a quiet game of chess has its own peculiar sound.

She had an inebriating effect on him. He would never look at Paris the same way again. All this in one evening. It had been momentous, indeed. Once back at the hotel, Peter walked her up to her room and wished her goodnight. He noted that her face was flushed from the brisk air and the wind had blown her hair partially over her face, the clip no longer effective. He gently pushed her hair back in place, his hand trembling and lingering on her cheek for just a brief moment. She did not draw back, just stood and smiled at him. Shyly, she reached up and brushed her lips against his.

His response was instantaneous, devastating. He put his arms around her, and deepened the kiss. Her arms reached around his neck as she pressed herself closer. It was a drugging and lingering kiss. Peter finally released her mouth, but did not let her go. He gently caressed her face, then trailed his fingers down her neck and up again. He felt her shiver, tangled his fingers in her thick hair, and again lowered his head to kiss her.

The kiss was an explosion of senses; he couldn't get enough of her.

"I want to make love to you, with you," he groaned into her mouth. His hands possessively caressed her back.

"Why?" she asked, her voice not quite steady. She tried to move out of his reach, but felt his grip on her tighten.

"Because I want you. Because I think you want me. Because there is something between us," he whispered into her hair.

She tried to free herself again. "Peter, I don't have casual sex. I'm sorry if I started something–I normally don't behave this way. I'm sorry." *My damn stupid hang-ups… He's got Alexis. I am not going to be second best, not ever again.*

"Shhh. You didn't start anything. We'll take it slow. I want to get to know you. This isn't just sex." Peter released her, waited till she opened the door and walked in, then quietly walked down the hallway to his own room. He felt elated that she had responded to him, but she was terrified. Why? Sleep did not come easily to him.

Minola entered her room and leaned against the closed door. Shaken by her reaction to Peter's kiss, she brought her hands to her face. The taste of his kiss still lingered on her mouth. She showered, and got ready for bed. Her last thoughts of the evening were of Peter and the impact he had had in her life in such a short period of time.

Chapter 9

She didn't move fast in relationships. She hadn't had many, and her approach was very contrary to the prevailing attitude. *This is so Jane Austen.* She believed in getting to know the person intellectually and emotionally before the physical aspects of a relationship took over. She bluntly believed in making love, not having sex, and the fact that she was even thinking along those lines frightened her immensely.

By the time she was finished with her toilette, it was seven thirty. Minola planned to go downstairs for a cup of morning coffee, her answer to everything. Before leaving, she took one last look in the mirror and decided she liked what she saw. Minola was always glad to work with what she had. She never pined for the perfect face or the perfect body. She knew who she was, and that would have to suffice. If she was down at any time, she had coffee and went shoe shopping–she had always found that to be a perfect panacea for whatever ailed her.

On her way, she heard what had quickly become a very dear and familiar voice.

"Good morning, Minola." Peter waited for her to turn, looking for any sign of distress.

She faced him and joyfully replied, "Peter, good

morning." She recognized his look of concern and set out to put him at ease. "I am all right, Peter, really. I was just going for coffee before Sally gets here and we have our meeting with you."

"Well, since I am here, let us have that cup of coffee and wait together." He realized she looked absolutely radiant this morning. She was simply dressed, as usual, so that wasn't it. Was it her beaming smile? He tried not to stare. She made him feel like a callow youth in his twenties. At his age, he was not sure that was a good thing.

Minola, on the other hand, had no such scruples. She was glad to see him, and let him know it. Her greeting was heartfelt and genuine. "That sounds delightful, Peter. I really don't know what I am looking for in this meeting with Giselle. I just don't think that landscape belonged in that office; it was the only piece out of sync. If he had been a sentimental man, there would have been other personal items on his desk, pictures, anything."

While Peter listened to Minola, he reached into his pocket, took out a business card, and quickly jotted down his private cell phone number. "I will leave my cell on all day. Call me immediately with a report, or if there are any problems."

Minola took the card and put it in her purse. The elevator arrived and took them down.

As they enjoyed their coffee, Mr. Edwards walked by. He seemed surprised to see them together. He acknowledged them, curtly offered a greeting, and briskly walked on.

"Peter, do you think he suspects something? He

certainly doesn't seem to be very friendly. I guess he has a reason to be cautious and nervous."

"He is careful. I don't believe he takes anything for granted. Now, since we are both staying on the same floor, he may think that I consider you a suspect, or maybe he does believe we are working together." Peter grinned.

"Are we working together?"

"Let me ask you. Will you stop snooping right now if I ask you to?"

Minola looked at Peter, and her expression decidedly told him no, she would not. She was going to continue to the end, just hopefully not to her end. Minola smiled, and looked at him sheepishly.

"I do believe the look on your face gave me your answer, Miss Grey. Since you will continue to put yourself at risk, I might as well be there to make sure that risk is minimal."

More coffee was delivered, along with a wonderful fresh, flaky croissant and a piece of brie. It was Minola's favorite morning start. Peter was surprised that it arrived along with the coffee, when all she had ordered was coffee.

A few minutes later, Sally appeared. "Good morning, Peter, Minola. I knew if I found good coffee, you would not be far behind, and I was right. Minola cannot live without her morning cup, mid-morning, afternoon...you get the drift. This looks yummy!" Sally sat down and almost immediately her coffee and breakfast appeared. She was positively famished–the truth be told, she was also nervous.

Peter was thoroughly enjoying his morning; however, the business at hand was important. He had earlier called his

Sergeant and asked him to inconspicuously follow the ladies. He did not want them any more nervous than they already were.

"Let's cover the meeting with Giselle Armand. Minola, you apparently are well versed in the art world. She is an artist, so chat about art. Mention what you are working on. Discuss the painting in the office, her connection to Yardleigh, and the office décor. As an artist she probably has made the same connection, so you can ask her why her painting was hanging in the office. Above all, let *her* talk."

While Peter talked, they listened. Sally was ready to tell Peter that Minola was an artist too, a damned good one, but one look at Minola's face deterred Sally from disclosing that bit of information.

Peter continued the lesson in interviewing a potential suspect. "Do not lie to her too much, keep it as honest as you can. If she is involved in this mess, everything you tell her can be easily checked and confirmed. Sally, you are a freelance journalist. Stay with that story, if it comes up. Hopefully, she won't verify anything, since you are Americans, and it is a vast place, but remember that Internet access is easy. Minola is showing you around. You are friends and do things together; it may explain why you're working jointly on this project. Be aware of everything you see–something may strike you as odd. And remember, she can authenticate everything if she wants to. Take nothing for granted and pay attention to everything. If you have any questions or problems, I shall be available to you immediately. Make sure you have your cell phones with you."

Minola listened intently. "Peter, if we hit it off, do you think I should invite Madame Armand to dinner Saturday? It could be an impromptu gesture of friendship, for lack of a better definition."

"That is a possibility. You can decide on the spot. Some of the guests on Saturday also happen to be on the board at Yardleigh Enterprises. It might make for more interesting dinner conversation. Just be careful. And remember that she could be very involved in the organization. Please keep in touch." With that statement, Peter excused himself. He gave Minola one last lingering look, and left.

Minola watched him walk away. She realized she and Sally were on their own, fortified with coffee, and hopefully full of useful information on how to proceed.

Peter reached into his pocket to make sure his cell phone was on. He made a quick call to his Sergeant to let him know the ladies were leaving the hotel. Now he could concentrate on the group of suspects attending the dinner Minola had arranged.

As he set out to meet with the Police Nationale, he went through the investigation in his head. The French police had been busy, checking alibis, and backgrounds of everyone connected to Yardleigh. Checking and rechecking everything was the dismal and tedious side of police work, and so it is with every case.

As usual, the pile of information seemed insurmountable. It was a gigantic puzzle that seemed to grow each day, but would ultimately show patterns until everything fit and revealed the truth.

Past investigations had helped create camaraderie

among Interpol, Scotland Yard, and the Police Nationale that Peter used to the fullest extent. With the three organizations working together, it was likely one office would catch anything missed by the others.

In this case, the Police Nationale did the background checks in France, Scotland Yard pursued the same process in England, and Interpol collated all the data. It was Peter's job to collect all the pieces of the puzzle. As yet he had no idea where everything fit.

Hopefully, the Saturday dinner would give him more resources from which to gather additional information, however unimportant, and create his charts. Peter knew that his most valuable asset was his uncanny ability to understand the motives of others, particularly the criminal mind, which gave him an added edge in dealing with the element. It made him a commendable adversary.

Peter considered that the board of directors at Yardleigh Enterprises may not have been aware of the insidious infiltration that had occurred in the company—on the other hand, how could they not know? There were blatant financial difficulties. How could they not be aware of systematic problems?

Yardleigh had not implicated anyone on the board. By the same token, he had been still waiting for the deal, granting him partial immunity if he cooperated with the police, to be closed. As a shrewd businessman, he had not planned to give his trump card away.

The board members had met right after the murder, and Peter had had a chance to interview each individual. All seemed stunned and saddened by the death of the man they had considered a trusted colleague and friend. There did not seem to be any connection between the board and money laundering. Lord Yardleigh had hinted there was a formula being followed for the money laundering, but again he had been reticent about providing information till his deal was secured.

Peter somberly reflected that Yardleigh had not lived to see that happen. He had refused a safe harbor, stating it would alert the people he did not want alerted; however, someone had guessed what he was up to. Otherwise, why kill him? It had to be someone close to him. Peter suspected more than one proverbial bad apple in the bushel.

The set of numbers that Minola had found in the desk so far had proven useless. Hopefully, the Saturday dinner would provide some gossip, if nothing else. This kind of operation was not a one-man effort, someone had to know something.

Peter knew that once he figured out *how*, he would know *who*. The *why* had already been established by Yardleigh. Not for the first time Peter wondered about the greed of the species. When business slowed, rather than cut back and change his opulent lifestyle, Yardleigh found another way. It cost him his good name, his reputation, and finally his life–a high price to pay, indeed.

Chapter 10

Once Peter reached the Police offices, he planned to go over all the names associated with the murder and their business affiliation with Yardleigh, leaving no one out, absolutely no one, right down to the delivery people. He was convinced that whatever was going on was directed from the Avenue Foch location. The office had been somewhat ignored because of its high-profile location. *Maybe Minola was right about the movement of that little landscape and the black book. What changed hands, and how?*

As absorbed as he was in his thoughts, he also paid attention to the people and sounds of the city. She had taught him that. They had a number of important things in common, he realized, as he thought about his penchant for modern art. Art was not a dot in the middle of a blank canvas. He liked early Picasso, he loved the Art Deco period, and Erte was his favorite. Having Minola in his life was like a salve for all things wrong in his line of work. She tempered the greed, the virulent human nature he had seen, with her idealism and kindness. *I need her. Not just in my bed, but in my life. I need her gentleness, sweetness, innocence.* He simply could not believe he had thought her to be a prostitute. *I am a bloody idiot.*

Arriving at the police station, he walked up the steps and was greeted as he entered. All formalities had been eliminated–Peter was one of them, he had been accepted, he played fair, and he didn't seek publicity. He treated all gendarmes equally. All were eager to offer any gossip, any rumors heard on the streets. Peter had made that his first request. "You are out in the streets–listen and pay attention to any deviation in behavior from the usual culprits. Ask the informers what is going on in their sectors. The bottom dwellers are involved; let us look to them for information. We must exclude no one. A Peer was killed, but he had been connected to them. He, in fact, was one of them. He just had a better tailor."

That had been his war cry from the beginning, and was starting to pay off. All sorts of rumors had been reported, even that Yardleigh was hooked on drugs. Nothing in the autopsy showed he had ever been a user, but other gossip warranted investigation. Rumors substantiated the theory that Yardleigh had started dealing drugs to offset heavy trading losses.

Earlier in the investigation, before the murder, some well-connected hoodlums had paid visits to the outlying offices under the guise of seeking financial investments. Money was coming in. A great deal of money was also going out. Those investors were making a lot of money along with Yardleigh. Peter began to form an image of the kind of business being conducted. Just how it was done was the big question. Who stood to lose the most?

Sally and Minola arrived at their destination. Minola

pulled a small pad from her purse to pay homage to the magnificent structure through a quick sketch.

Sally briefly caught sight of Peter as Minola flipped the pages of her sketchpad. The pad was filled with random drawings. Finding a blank page, Minola quickly sketched the scene before them. Sally was charmed by the drawing and awed, again, by Minola's artistic abilities. The light was just behind the gothic marvel, the Seine smoothly flowed downstream, and people strolled arm in arm. Minola, with a few strokes, captured it all. Sally wanted to ask for the sketch, but kept silent. She also wanted a closer look at Peter's profile, but hesitated to invade Minola's privacy.

Without saying a word, Minola signed the drawing, tore out the sheet, and handed it to her.

"Minola, I…you are going to make me cry. I just love it. This is such a perfect memory. I have never had a better vacation."

The vague description of Giselle Armand did not begin to do her justice. Minola expected an elegant, middle-aged Parisian woman. Instead, walking toward them was one of the most colorful and flamboyant women she had ever seen.

Madame Armand wore a huge hat with feathers that nearly covered her face and seemed to contain every single color in an artist's palette–a peacock would have been proud. She wore vibrant stiletto heels that matched the hat, and a vivid caftan reflecting a double rainbow of color. The outlandish outfit was complemented by a large brown *sac* under her arm, and huge round gold earrings finished her ensemble. Strangely enough, no other jewelry was visible;

not even a watch adorned her wrist. She looked like a dazzling gypsy, ready to tell anyone their fortune.

Minola walked up to the woman, extended her hand, and introduced herself. Madame Armand greeted her effusively, "I am delighted to meet you, Mademoiselle Grey."

Minola acknowledged the greeting, quickly led her back to their table, and introduced Sally.

After taking her seat, Giselle Armand caught the attention of their waiter. Coffee was ordered all around; Madame Armand ordered a cognac to go with hers. "I prefer to start my day with gusto," she said with a grin. "Mademoiselle, why is it important for you to meet me? There are many artists in Paris."

"Madame Armand, it may sound strange, but as an artist you will understand. I visited Lord Yardleigh's office in Paris. I saw your painting. I admired it very much, but it didn't belong in that environment. When I asked the receptionist who the artist was, she told me, and I wanted to meet you," Minola replied.

Weariness appeared to surround Giselle Armand like a cloak. She looked first at Minola and then at Sally, seemingly puzzled why they were meeting with her in the first place. "Why is that so important?"

Sally spoke quickly, "I can answer that, Madame. As an artist herself, Minola was given a commission by a British reporter to do a portrait of Lord Yardleigh." Sally decided to stop there. She remembered Peter telling them not to give away too much. *Let her ask the questions, this way the conversation can be prolonged, and more information might be forthcoming.*

Madame Armand wanted to know why a British paper would pay for such a commission. Minola had a ready answer. "Lord Yardleigh was a large charitable benefactor. Since I happened to be staying at the hotel where the murder took place, the editor believes the portrait will increase circulation. I certainly had no objection to the commission," Minola said with a twinkle in her eye. "Madame Armand, surely no sane artist would refuse such a commission."

"Yes, of course," she readily agreed. "Please, call me Giselle. All my friends do." The ladies happily complied, and the atmosphere became less guarded. To explain her presence, Sally told Giselle she was a freelance journalist working with Minola.

Over coffee the conversation centered on the different styles of the two artists. Sally listened and loved hearing about the technical aspects of producing a work of art. She enjoyed looking at art, but had never really thought about the work in progress. She knew it took Minola a long time to finish a piece. She had never really grasped the total effort it required.

Minola finally felt enough time had been spent in getting acquainted. It was time to get back to business. "Giselle, why was the painting hanging in the office? Why not in the hotel room?"

"I really don't know. I have no answer for you. He just couldn't find the right space for it. He kept rotating it, and every month it hung on a different wall. As far as I know, he never took it to the hotel. I agree with you, the office was not the place for it. It was where we first met, and it was a silly, sentimental thing for me to do. He was not sentimental, and it wasn't his usual style. But a man will do much to keep his mistress happy." She admitted with a chuckle.

It would have been a more intimate gesture to hang it in the bedroom, Minola thought, but said nothing. Changing the location made no sense. He either liked it or not. She suspected there was more to the painting, but she couldn't reason it out. Paintings didn't change locations on a monthly basis; maybe in the home, but office décor was more permanent. Once something was hung on the wall, it usually stayed there.

Giselle discussed the work she had been doing with Edwards. She was very familiar with the office in Paris, and further explained that Edwards had tapped her to go over the books. "I am an accountant by profession," she pragmatically put it. "Art does not always put food on the table."

Minola wondered if Edwards was trying to protect himself, or if he was trying to show a clean front. How much did Giselle know? Was she safe, since she had encouraged Yardleigh to seek help? Minola extended an invitation to the dinner, which Giselle accepted with delight.

The realization that she probably was lonely and missed Yardleigh made Minola feel guilty. Giselle, in her own way, must have loved him, but was there a more sinister reason for the quick acceptance? Was she hoping to gain some information from Minola?

Minola noticed Giselle's curiosity quickly assert itself. She wanted to know who was going to be at the party, and

Sally responded that some friends from her husband's office would be attending. Among them would be some members of the Yardleigh board, since her husband traveled in those circles.

Minola watched for a reaction, and found none. "Giselle, are you involved in the business? It seems so strange that the Paris office is open. Who is at the helm?"

Although Giselle did not appear surprised by the question, she looked as if she groped for an answer. "Minola, I am not sure what will happen now. I was a consultant. There were rumors. I have since helped Edwards do an audit. He asked me to help, and I agreed. I do not think I have seen all there is–the books seemed incomplete, transactions seemed misapplied. But I could not, with the information available to me, decipher where the problems were, so when Edwards asked me to stop, I did."

Minola's tenacious streak suddenly awoke and she could not resist asking, "Rumors? What kind of rumors? You must admit this is most interesting. The murder happened right across the hall from where I am staying. It must sound ghoulish to you, but it is such an interesting case. My commission has allowed me more access to Lord Yardleigh's history. How can the company function without the man in charge?"

"Edwards is there. He understands the business and is good at it. The board gave credence to the operation, they and Yardleigh were friends, and the board existed in name only. They didn't really serve a purpose, but they collected nice fees. Yardleigh had total control and power. He needed the…the aura of big success, all the accoutrements that came with business success," Giselle said. "He was making connections with people who were bad for business, and was trapped."

"Giselle, I am sorry you lost a friend."

There was a sad, faraway look in Giselle's eyes, but she responded quietly. "He was knighted by the Queen. He didn't inherit the title, and he craved social acceptance. He came from a very poor background. His father worked on a farm. He always wanted to break away and become somebody. When he became successful and married the extravagant Alexis, his image of himself was complete and he would do anything to keep that image alive, anything," she whispered.

"What are you saying, Giselle? What did Lord Yardleigh do that would get him killed?" Minola was sympathetic to Giselle's loss, but she had to understand this side of life. She suddenly thought of Peter. *He sees this routinely, how can he bear it? Where does he escape? Who is there to help him?*

"I suspect something did happen to his financial stability. I helped him many times. He had the Jurac firm working for him, too. They were good, but I was asked not to do any additional audits last year. He told me he had hired a new firm, LeClerque Accounting, to do his books. At best, they have a shady reputation and I asked him what he was doing. He never responded. He simply indicated he no longer wanted me involved and that he was in some kind of trouble. I think I have said enough. Nothing will help him now. Thank you for the invitation," she said wistfully.

Minola did not want to push any further, nor give an

impression of anything other than idle curiosity. Their conversation returned to normal topics for two artists discussing their profession.

Giselle looked at her wrist, realized she wasn't wearing a watch, stood up, and said, "I have another appointment, but I will be at the dinner. Thank you again. Goodbye." She waved and briskly walked away.

"If Giselle knew of LeClerque's reputation, Robert probably would too," Sally suggested.

"I think you are right. We have a basic idea why Giselle was helping Edwards, but why did he ask her to stop? Robert needs to look into the rumors surrounding the firm." After a pause, Minola added, "I feel sorry for her, she seemed so lonely."

"I know. I do too. She was so colorfully dressed, and so sad. I think she picked her outfit to show bravado she didn't feel."

Per instructions from Peter, Sergeant Welsey had been sitting a few seats behind them, sipping coffee and apparently enjoying the moment. He called Peter and told him that everything was fine. Minola and Sally were safe; Giselle Armand had left, and was being followed by a *gendarme*.

Peter was immensely relieved Minola and Sally had finished their meeting Thoughts of Minola disturbed the rest his day. *Bloody hell*! Peter left a message with the concierge to let him know the minute she returned to her room. Her report could alter the guest list slightly, and he wanted to see her.

* * *

The ringing phone told Peter Minola was back. He thought about putting his jacket on, but decided against it–long sleeve shirt, no tie–he did not want to appear too formal. He walked down the hall and lightly knocked on Minola's door. Sally let him in.

Peter looked around, and noticed the connecting door. He had never been in Minola's room before. It was neat, yet looked lived in. She had made it her own. There were big, bold, colorful bouquets of flowers in vases, one on the table and another on the desk, and personal items that added warmth, and looked comfortable and intimate.

A few photographs hung on the wall. Peter thought if they were hers, she had a good eye for composition. He recognized a charcoal sketch of the Luxembourg Gardens, hanging on the wall along with a couple of unframed prints. The artist had used limited strokes, yet got the idea across. The prints looked somewhat Oriental in their beauty and simplicity, with vivid, brilliant colors, probably the Tuillerie Gardens. None of the pieces were signed, yet they looked original. Without a longer look, he couldn't tell for sure.

Sally watched and waited as Peter looked around, tempted to tell Peter it was all Minola's work. She finally broke the silence, "Hello, Peter, you certainly did not waste any time."

"Good afternoon, Sally. My apologies, I became distracted. We need to discuss the dinner guests for Saturday as well as your morning meeting," he replied.

"I agree there is food for thought after meeting Giselle. She is flamboyant, delightful, and appears to really adhere to the Bohemian lifestyle, but she also seemed very isolated.

Minola is changing, she will be right out."

"Changing? It is early afternoon. Changing to what?" he inquired laconically.

Sally was not about to tell him Minola was planning to paint. She needed to finish Peter's invitation. She shouldn't have said anything. Now it was too late. "Let me just tell her you are here. Please make yourself comfortable." Sally quickly knocked and walked into the oversized European bathroom.

Minola was in the process of putting on her colorful, paint spattered painting shirt. She totally concentrated on the work in progress, and her clothes reflected her chosen profession.

Familiar with Minola's routine, Sally remembered one day she had interrupted Minola, while wearing a wonderful crisp white cotton blouse. She had caught Minola off guard, and wound up with a beautiful wide cobalt blue streak right on the front of her blouse…a Minola Grey original because, when painting, Minola talked with her brush. She had apologized profusely, but Sally had never washed the blouse. It still hung in her closet, well preserved. Some day she would ask Minola to sign it.

Her shirt showed all imaginable colors–some washed out, others imposed on existing stains. This was her 'creative shirt, in which she did her best work

"Peter is here."

"Stall him. I'll change back and be there in seconds. What does he want? Never mind, that was a silly question."

Sally returned to the room, "Minola will be right out."

Peter stood by the window. When he heard the door

open again, his attention shifted to Minola. She wore the same thing she had that morning. The only difference, her hair was pulled up, and off her face.

"Hello, Peter. I'm just taking a wild guess here, you would like to know what we found out?"

"You are becoming very good at this detecting business. You read my mind." Peter smiled.

"Please sit down. That couch is quite comfortable. I have coffee or, since it is afternoon and you are British, I can order tea. Your choice," she offered as she sat down.

"Coffee would be delightful, thank you." Peter sat down next to her. He didn't want her to move.

"I don't think we got much; I do think Giselle is very lonely. The one decidedly odd thing we found out is that Yardleigh kept changing the location of Giselle's painting for no apparent reason. Remember that landscape that seemed so out of character? Even Giselle couldn't explain it. At some point in time it has hung on every wall in the office, somewhat bizarre behavior. What do you make of it?"

"At the moment, absolutely nothing. Maybe, somehow, the painting was a signal. We will check and see if Mr. Edwards has moved it since you were there last. Do you remember where it hung?" he asked.

"Yes, it was right across from his desk. Peter, we also found out that Yardleigh had hired an accounting firm by the name of LeClerque. Giselle doesn't believe them to be reputable. More to the point, when they took over, Yardleigh specifically told her he didn't need her help anymore. Her last comment to us was that 'nothing would help him now'."

"The meeting was profitable." Peter sipped his coffee. He knew the LeClerque accounting firm, but nothing about them had been found in the files he had collected, no indication that they were involved except that alexis mentioned them. Someone must have cleaned house quickly. Maybe a visit to the 'esteemed' firm was in order.

Sally, by now, felt like a third wheel. She played hostess by pouring, since Minola's cup was already empty. "Okay, there must be a coffee drinker's anonymous organization somewhere that treats people like you. I am going to go and see my husband. Call you later." She bent down, gave Minola a hug, and let herself out.

Peter continued to gaze at Minola's face. He, too, had noticed her pleasure in the coffee. "Do you think you should take Sally's advice?" His smile sent her pulse racing.

"Certainly not! Coffee is the only vice I will admit to, publicly, that is."

"I see," he drawled.

"Once and for all, Peter, I am not a prostitute and have never been one." Her eyes blazed in anger.

"Oh, I know that. I knew that the first time I kissed you. The first time I touched you." He leaned over and caressed her cheek. He felt her shudder.

"So, what you are telling me is that you are an expert with hookers."

"No, I didn't say that. I said I knew you weren't one." He leaned a little closer, took her mouth in a gentle, lingering kiss, and felt her body melt to his. She offered no resistance. He ran his hand over her breast and lightly caressed her nipples, first one, then the other. He felt a shiver of desire run through her, making his heart pound erratically. He slowly moved his hands up to her face, their eyes locking for a second. He bent his head to recapture her lips. He was lost in this woman.

"Peter, please," she moaned against his mouth, trying to free herself from his grip.

Slowly, as if coming out of a trance, Peter lifted his head, kissed her forehead, and whispered, "What would you like me to do?" as he continued his light kisses.

"I want you to stop," she murmured. The sound of his voice disturbed her deeply. "I don't take sex casually. You are very good, and very dangerous." She moved out of his reach to pour more coffee.

"You want me to stop, and I want you in my arms, in my bed. You won't be able to run forever. Whatever it is holding you back, we need to talk about it." The huskiness in his tone lingered.

"Peter, right now we have other issues. The dinner is coming up, for example. How is that going to work?" She refused to be number two in Peter's life. There was Alexis Yardleigh, the woman with everything. *Remember her. Sex for men is just...sex.*

"You drive a hard bargain, Miss Grey. All right, back to business. I'll have the final guest list for you by tomorrow. Some of the police will be acting as waiters. If you don't mind, I will arrange the seating chart. I think the best thing to do would be to place the board members, along with Giselle Armand, at one table, which will be serviced by the police. The second table will seat Sally's and Robert's friends, and ours will be the third table. Since I'm your guest, I'll need to be at your table and by your side." He moved closer, letting his fingers play with her hair.

"Peter, you make it sound so dutiful…'by my side'. I can be a decent companion, really, and I know for a fact that Sally is a hoot. Wasn't the whole idea to be circumspect? Not to arouse any suspicion? It would look peculiar for you to sit at another table. I promise you the dinner will be delicious and the conversation tantalizing." Minola cheerfully winked at Peter, then remembered Alexis Yardleigh and the intimacy with which she had greeted Peter in the café.

"That is not what I meant, you know that. There is no place I would rather be. What are you afraid of? Talk to me." There was a note of pleading in his voice.

The ringing phone broke the tension. Minola quickly answered, "Sally? What's going on?"

Peter stood up and reached for Minola. He softly brushed her cheek with his hand, gave her a quick, possessive kiss, and left.

"My God, Minola, with all the excitement I completely forgot to tell you that James and Samantha are flying in for the dinner. It's to be a surprise for Robert."

"How on earth could you forget something like that? How are you going to pull it off? Where are they going to stay? Do you want me to do anything? Sally, for God's sake, how could you forget? The dinner is this Saturday." Minola sounded drained. She was beginning to look forward to some time alone, some peace of mind. In fact, what she wanted most was to go to her studio and paint. The world is too much with us, she poetically thought.

Sally heard Minola's weary voice, and knew to cut it short. "You don't need to do anything, I have it all covered. I hope. We just need to remember two more people at our table. The concierge here at your hotel made all the arrangements–booked a room for them, arranged transportation from the airport, any and all tours they may want to take, everything. It's certainly handy, this living in a hotel," Sally exclaimed. "I had better get everything settled. I will see you tomorrow morning."

"You are the proverbial hurricane when you get going. Tomorrow."

Grateful for the respite, Minola changed and quickly settled down to paint. She picked up a pad and worked on her sketch of Peter's face, altering the shading and making his face a bit more angular. Unruly and wavy, his hair was just right. She had caught various aspects of Peter's personality well, but decided to keep them a secret even from Sally. This was too personal, too new for Minola. Peter had a connection to Alexis; whatever she felt for Peter had to stay hidden from everyone. *I respond physically to him. He thinks it is just sex. He will not know there is more, much more.*

She worked all afternoon until dusk, recharging her energy. She decided to take a walk to the little garden just a few blocks down the street. Wrapped up in her thoughts, she didn't know her departure was observed by Peter, who was talking to his Sergeant nearby.

He decided to follow her.

She wandered up the boulevard, enjoying the evening

commotion as she crossed the street and found her own little paradise, totally oblivious to everything and everyone. She sat on a bench and pondered her current predicament.

What am I doing in Paris? She had come here to be an artist and to teach, but she had given up the teaching. Now, involved in a murder investigation, she had met an Englishmen who, in such a short period of time, had turned her life upside down and he didn't even know it. An Interpol man, no less, and probably involved with another woman.

She had come here to paint, not to see people get murdered. She seemed to have muddled her life and it was too late to back out now. *Carpe diem*...she seized the day, more like a lifetime. In retrospect, getting involved in the investigation was a silly thing to do, yet she had been taken seriously. Peter agreed to it all. What was she thinking? Obviously, she wasn't. What to do now? She heard a familiar voice call out her name.

Jean Pierre seemed to appear out of nowhere. "I went to your hotel; they said you were out. I took a chance on your penchant for gardens, and here you are," he smiled.

"What are you doing here? What's wrong?" was her immediate response.

"I have a favor to ask of you. We are doing a series on Botticelli, and we need a model."

"So, go to Ada's, she'll provide you with one. Why are you telling me this? All right, just why are you here?" Minola was in no mood to humor Jean Pierre.

"I had this idea," he continued.

"Am I going to want to know about this idea of yours?"

"Hear me out," he insisted. "You have the perfect

Botticelli body–all the curves, in all the right places. Ada will send me a board–a flat-chested model who could pass for a man. You know Botticelli's style. You have a body a man could get lost in–that is Botticelli!" He smacked his lips.

"You have got to be kidding. You are positively insane. You have lost your mind. Have I missed anything?" she demanded. Her eyes were blazing.

"It would give you publicity," he continued impishly.

Minola interrupted him. "Publicity? I don't want that kind of publicity. Jean Pierre, this crazy idea of yours stops right here…you are insane. Publicity!"

Peter, watching from a discreet distance, heard everything. Instantly jealous, he seethed. This man talking to Minola obviously knew her well, maybe too well. He felt as if someone had punched him in the stomach. Hands clenched, he stepped out of the shadows. "Am I interrupting?" he asked quietly. Much too quietly.

Minola was startled by his presence and his calm, deceptive voice. She knew immediately that he had heard everything. She wrapped her sweater tightly around her.

Peter noticed her reaction and asked, mockingly: "Are you cold, Miss Grey?"

"No, Chief Inspector, I am not."

Jean Pierre watched with fascination. "Chief Inspector, my name is Jean Pierre Gravis. Are you investigating the murder at the hotel?"

Peter stared at the man and demanded, "Who are you?"

"I am a friend of Minola's. We are in school together. I just came to ask a favor."

"I heard the favor you requested. Perhaps you had better say goodnight to Miss Grey. I need to speak with her privately," Peter replied coldly, his intense gaze centered on Minola.

Jean Pierre, uncertain how to proceed, decided that his departure would be the better part of valor. He said goodnight to both and left, but not before adding to Minola, "Think about it."

"Goodnight, Jean Pierre," Minola replied firmly.

Peter walked up to Minola and extended his hand. She took it and rose from her bench. In the process of getting up, her sweater unwrapped and revealed her light V-neck top. Peter looked at her in the dim light, his eyes blazing. He honed in on her exposed skin as his fingers sensually ran over her cleavage. She shivered at his touch.

"He is right, you know. A man could lose himself in your body," he whispered, as he took her mouth in fiery possession. The kiss was explosive. Minola responded to him immediately. Her heart hammered in her chest and her mouth opened to accept his tongue. Peter played havoc with her senses. She felt her knees buckle.

He heard a groan, realized it came from him, and tightened his hold on her. She had a remarkable effect on him. He felt her tremble and loosened his grip on her, but still held her in his arms.

"Peter," she whispered softly.

"Do you see what you do to me, Minola?" he said, caressing her cheek.

"Are you implying that I need to lose weight, Chief Inspector? Botticelli used full-figured women as his models." Minola tried to diffuse the sexual tension.

"No, I am simply stating that I want to make love to you. I want to lose myself in you," he whispered hoarsely.

Reason began to return to her senses. "Peter, why are you here? Is something wrong?"

He continued to hold her as his hands moved up her arms, and he drew her closer. "Nothing is wrong. I saw you leave the hotel and followed you. Would you care to explain the conversation I just overheard?" Peter's eyes glistened in the shadows.

"No."

"Try, Miss Grey," he demanded.

"We are both affiliated with the *Écoles des Beaux Arts*. You heard the rest."

"Have you been intimate with him? He seems to know you rather well," he inquired harshly. He didn't want to think about other men touching her–a bitter jealousy stirred inside him.

"Is this a professional inquiry, or a personal one?"

"A very personal inquiry," he said. He held himself tensely in check while waiting for an answer he did not want to hear. *Why the hell should the answer matter. I am no innocent.* Just the thought that another man loved her, held her, sent tremors through his body.

"I assume you are asking if we had made love. The answer, Peter, is no, we have not. He is a friend, nothing more." Minola watched as he visibly relaxed. "Just why did you follow me?"

"I was concerned for your safety, I apologize for the intrusion," he said quietly. "I feel better having you within my sight."

"Peter, you were not intruding. I am trying to come to terms with my life in Paris, and I needed to clear my head. This place always helps put things in perspective, Jean Pierre not withstanding."

"Minola, just why *are* you living in Paris? Why Paris? You obviously love the city, but what are you running away from? What is your affiliation with the school? Are you a student?" He wanted to know everything, but from her.

"I am running to, not from, or at least I thought I was." She looked at him, then quickly down to avoid the eyes that blazed into hers.

"If I asked what you are running to, would you answer? Sometimes it helps to talk to a friend."

Minola held fast to the friendship that was offered, although she was not quite sure how far it extended. There is always Alexis, she thought sadly.

"We are friends, aren't we? I am pleased you feel that way. Is it the murder that is the basis of our friendship?" She realized she might give away too much, and quickly added, "Sorry, I am tired. I don't make much sense when I am tired."

"Would you like me to answer that? No, I will answer. Yes, it started with the murder, but we have gone far beyond that. We share a bond beyond the crime–surely you must know that by now."

Minola did not know how to answer, afraid she was reading way too much into his statement. As she looked at Peter, however, she realized he was in earnest. His gaze lingered on her face, never faltering. Inexperienced, Minola decided she had imagined it all, better this way.

"Peter, it's getting late and tomorrow is a busy day. Why don't we walk back to our hotel, but first let's have a crepe Grand Marnier and a coffee."

Peter's eyes were understanding. He knew something was wrong, but she wouldn't let him in yet. He needed patience. This woman was worth everything to him. "Yes, let's. That sounds delightful. So far you have avoided mentioning the school. Why?"

"You have access to everything. Why don't you use it?"

"Because I want you to tell me about yourself. I want the process to be between us."

"Why?"

"Under the circumstances, this is the only way I can show you that I trust you completely," he said.

"Thank you, Chief Inspector. Obviously, since you are an intelligent man, you have figured out that I can paint. Somewhat. Can we for the time being leave it at that?"

"So be it. Whenever, you are ready."

They walked on in silence. Peter reflected that this woman had entered his soul and would stay there. A nearby street vendor provided the crepes, and the café across the street sustained them with coffee.

Minola finally relaxed as coffee came to her rescue. They talked about literature, especially the mystery genre, which both enjoyed. They discussed art. Minola was surprised at the depth of Peter's knowledge of good modern art. He specified "*good* modern art, not this 'black dot in the middle of a white canvas' art," which made Minola laugh. He enjoyed the resonance her voice held. She needed to laugh more. He loved hearing it.

He told her he loved the pieces that hung in her room. She pointedly ignored the comment. He noticed the omission. Again, he decided not to pressure her. Asked if the photographs were hers, she replied yes, they were. She enjoyed photography a great deal. Both were well read, enjoyed the theater, and loved to travel. They had so many common interests, but the one binding them was murder.

Minola had queries for him as well. "How do you handle what you see in your job? How do you escape?"

If he was surprised by her question, he didn't show it. "I have my family. Often, I just hope to make a difference somewhere, and that holds me for a while."

"Is this case particularly difficult for you?"

"I was asked to help, and I agreed," his voice was distant.

"Peter, are you alright? Can I help? You seem far away." She felt his withdrawal.

"What did you have in mind?" His lips curved up. His slow smile was as erotic as his kisses.

"I was offering comfort, friendship, I don't know." She flushed under his scrutiny.

"I'm fine. I enjoy your company, and at this point, I will take anything you offer," he said quietly.

"At this point—what does that mean?"

"Simply stated, it means anything you are ready for, as long as it includes me in your life. I feel your physical response to me, but I also feel your reticence." He looked at her face, saw fear reflected in her eyes, and asked her again. "What are you afraid of?"

"Betrayal," she replied.

"What happened? Do you want to talk about it?"

"No. At least not yet. I know this is absurd. It is already Wednesday night, but on Friday morning would you care to visit the Rodin Museum with me? Tomorrow will be busy with last-minute details, but I need to get away. The museum provides incredible solace for me."

As usual, she caught him by surprise–she was good at changing subjects she wanted to avoid. He answered quickly lest she think he didn't want to go with her. "I haven't been there in years. It will be wonderful to see it through your eyes. That, in case you haven't noticed, is a resounding yes. What time would you like me to have the car ready?"

"Actually, I was looking forward to walking. It's only a short stroll from the hotel."

"A walk it is, Miss Grey."

"Chief Inspector, I didn't know you were so compliant."

"It's not difficult to be compliant with easy requests, and I have a feeling I'll learn a great deal about Rodin." Minola smiled and assured him she wouldn't lecture.

The rest of their walk passed quickly. Back at the hotel, Peter walked her to her room, asked for her key, and opened the door for her. She smiled up at him. He cupped her face in his hands, and kissed her with a longing that continued to shock him–he just couldn't get enough of her. "Open your mouth for me," he whispered and deepened the kiss as he felt her respond. She caressed his back, pressing herself closer, her erect nipples thrusting against him, and her pulse pounding. She felt his hands tremble on her face.

He released her only to stare at her passion-filled eyes, then once again he lowered his mouth to hers. This time, his tongue ruthlessly invaded her mouth.

She was shaking. She was so close to him, she could feel the effect she had on him. He didn't try to hide his response, she felt him. The drugging assault on her mouth left Minola totally vulnerable and terrified.

Peter released her mouth, but not his hold on her. Her head was buried in his shoulder. He wanted to possess her completely, totally. He wanted her to be his, only his.

This was not temporary, it was permanent, and not a new sensation for him since he had met her. He finally raised her head, looked into her eyes, saw passion and raw fear reflected, and knew he had to stop. He softly wished her good night, and tenderly pushed her inside, then closed her door. Drawing a long breath, he swiftly went to his room. A cold shower was definitely in order.

Once inside, Peter briefly glanced at his desk full of reports, then paced the floor, trying to get his equilibrium back. In such a short time the woman had completely shattered his peace of mind.

The reports on his desk would have to wait. He showered, sat down, and glanced at the dossier on the LeClerque accounting firm left for him by Sergeant Welsey. It appeared that Lord Yardleigh was a personal friend of the most senior partner of the firm. Wasn't that a coincidence? The firm certainly had a checkered history. After a cursory look at the packet, Peter got up from his chair and headed for bed. *Tomorrow should prove rather interesting.*

Chapter 11

Minola decided to sketch Peter again. She wanted to capture his expressions now so familiar to her, especially the passion-filled, smoldering gaze she'd witnessed after she'd returned his kiss and molded her body to his. That particular sketch would remain very private indeed. *How can he respond to me this way, and still love Alexis?* She couldn't push the thought from her mind. *I can't compete...she's perfect.*

Saturday loomed as Wednesday slipped into Thursday, and Minola was preoccupied with last-minute details. A sense of foreboding overshadowed her tranquility. Haunted by the murder, her serenity had vanished long ago and she looked forward to the break tomorrow and the visit to the Rodin museum. Rodin had a way of bringing her back to reality in spite of his more tormented pieces.

Sally suggested Minola's favorite café for an evening outing to settle everyone's nerves. Minola had been working like a demon to finish the place cards, as well as Peter's invitation. Saturday would be exceedingly busy with final details. At least the anniversary portrait was done and safely tucked away.

Minola called the restaurant and spoke with Chef Etienne. He had chosen a fresh asparagus salad with his own vinaigrette dressing, followed by warm seasonal fruit compote. Since Robert loved meat, steak au poivre would be the main entrée, with young red potatoes roasted with scallions and fresh spring vegetables to round it off. The dessert would include a lovely chocolate mousse cake, Sally's favorite, and French vanilla crème brulée for Robert. A great selection of cheeses and cognac would end the feast. Quite pleased with the final result, she graciously thanked him.

Minola arranged for a coffee bar. Any type of coffee would be available, along with an assortment of biscotti. She decided to present the portrait before dinner.

The day had simply vanished. Starving, Minola looked at the clock and realized it was nearly six, time for a quick bite to eat.

She knew the hotel restaurant served a delicious *Croque Monsieur*, a gooey melted cheese and ham sandwich prepared to perfection. She was leaving the restaurant when she saw Peter coming in. Like radar, he noticed her immediately, and with quick strides she met him halfway.

She looked at ease, yet he knew she had had a busy day. *It must be her damned coffee addiction. Most people became frazzled, but she just becomes more relaxed.*

"Good evening, Minola. Ready for yet another meeting?" He reached out as if to touch her, then quickly dropped his hand to his side. She noticed, but said nothing.

"I just had a sandwich and a good cup of coffee. I am ready for about anything, especially more coffee," she responded.

"In that case, you are ready." Peter, in a very good

mood, guided her out of the hotel. He had missed her all day, and was elated to be with her.

He talked about his day and his meeting with the accounting firm. He did not get much information, but the receptionist had been very accommodating. Peter was pleased that the two senior partners had been invited to the dinner Saturday.

Peter's visit with LeClerque Accounting had brought him nothing but platitudes. He would have to meet with LeClerque again after the Saturday dinner. He needed one more informal get-together with Minola, Sally, and Robert before the party. Peter wanted to discuss everything right down to the security detail–for example, how many officers would be in the hotel, how many were going to be waiting tables, and what would be the final seating arrangements. He was taking this dinner very seriously. No one had declined the invitation.

"I told them I was your guest."

"That was positively Machiavellian. Oh, Peter, with all the commotion I forgot to mention that Robert's brother and sister-in-law arrived late last night. It's to be a surprise; Sally made all the arrangements. They are staying in the hotel. I think Sally is planning to take them around Paris tomorrow."

"Is she going to be able to keep it from Robert?"

"Yes. Believe it or not, she can keep a secret." Minola hesitated then asked, "Peter, do your parents mind that you are a policeman? They must worry about your safety."

"Yes, probably sometimes they worry, but my choice of career was my own. They would never try to interfere."

"Your family seems very loving and supportive. Are you close to your sister and her family?"

"Yes to that too. We have always protected each other. My brother-in-law comes from a large family, so during the holidays it gets a bit rowdy."

"I can't imagine how difficult it must be to love someone who is on the front line, as it were."

"You can't help who you fall in love with. You learn to adjust. How about you, Miss Grey? Would you not love someone simply because of a dangerous career?" Peter prepared himself for the blow.

"I suspect that is something you learn to live with, if you love well."

He didn't realize he had been holding his breath until he released a deep sigh. "A good answer." He held her hand as they walked in companionable silence. He realized just how comforting her presence was–she was not put off by his chosen profession and she listened.

Inside the café, Minola was startled to see her early morning friend, sitting where he always sat, enjoying a cup of coffee. He acknowledged Minola with that same smile and a raised cup. She responded, and he walked over to the jukebox to play her favorite songs.

Baffled by this exchange, Peter wondered if she had someone in her life, although her physical response to him and her reticence clearly seemed to preclude another man. He felt his fists clench at his sides. What an odd and familiar greeting.

Meanwhile, the jukebox started playing the old Tom Jones song, 'Help Yourself'. Peter watched Minola's face light with pleasure. She turned toward the man, nodded her head, and smiled briefly.

Peter's jaw clenched as he extended a chair to Minola. She sat down, quite aware that both Peter and her silent friend were watching her. Peter took a keen interest in the man who apparently knew Minola–knew her well enough to play songs she liked, and to greet her with such familiarity.

Minola registered Peter's reaction to this exchange. He appeared to be interested in her, yet the stunning Alexis was his past and, she was convinced, his future. Minola certainly did not possess the physical attributes that were *de rigueur*, nor was she very well versed in picking up signals sent by the male species.

At times, Peter was angry at what he considered her interference; at times he was compassionate and caring; and occasionally she found him guarded and wary. The one thing she knew for certain is that he wanted her physically.

"Who is he, Minola?" Peter asked tersely.

The truth sounded strange. She didn't know how to respond, but she wanted to be honest however lame the story might sound. "I don't know who he is." Peter immediately assumed she was lying, and became withdrawn. Had he been lied to by someone? She couldn't let him think she was trying to deceive him. "Peter, I've been coming here for many months. In fact, I am here most mornings before my classes. He's been here as long, if not longer, and we have always greeted each other. I like Tom Jones' songs, and after a while he played them for me. It has always been a sweet gesture which touched me. The jukebox is great–old-fashioned, but with some wonderful songs. I finish my coffee, nod goodbye, and that is all. This is the first time I've ever seen him here in the evening."

Peter sat there with surprise, doubt, and confusion written all over his face. He no longer tried to hide his reactions from her. "Do you mean to tell me that you don't know who he is, yet he plays your favorite songs for you?"

"That is precisely what I mean. I always thought the gesture was wonderful, and to be honest, many a morning I really looked forward to that bit of impersonal romance. He began my mornings beautifully. I told you it was peculiar."

"Impersonal romance, conducted at a safe distance. Very unusual and quixotic, Miss Grey."

"What can I say, Chief Inspector? I lead a boring life."

"I rather doubt that. Are these songs personal? Do they mean something to you?" He gazed intently at her face.

"Yes, sort of..."

"Well, pray continue. I do expect a complete answer."

"I had been seeing someone. I actually thought we were in a relationship. I surprised him once in his apartment. I found him in bed with his secretary. I had never felt so betrayed in my life. I felt murderous. I like Tom Jones, hence 'Delilah'."

"Do you still feel anything for him?" Peter felt himself tense, as if his happiness depended on her answer.

"No. Whatever feelings I thought I had died that day. He tried to apologize by blaming me. He said I was unavailable and he needed a release. I felt sorry for the secretary. I have been relationship-shy ever since."

"I am sorry. The man was obviously a fool and a bastard. Unavailable, Minola?" He reached out and took her hand in his warm, firm grasp.

"Yes, Peter, unavailable. I was out of town, but I also refused to make love until I was ready. I believe he wanted sex, not love. I make a distinction between the two. He obviously did not."

A sense of joy settled in Peter's body, and he visibly relaxed. His face lit in a smile. "'Help Yourself'?"

"Ah, yes. 'Help Yourself'. How do I answer that? I like the beat." She looked at him and knew he wanted it all, so she continued. "I also feel that if love is found, it should include total commitment, physical as well as emotional. It should be given freely and completely. The song was a salve at the time, and even now it still moves me. What can I say? I am a romantic at heart.

"Now it is your turn, Peter. Is there someone in your life who left a scar? Like Alexis Yardleigh, for instance?"

"You amaze me. How did you pick up on that?"

"I saw the two of you together, remember. She is still interested in you, Chief Inspector, so what's the story?" She could not explain it, but Minola felt him withdraw from her. She assumed he still wanted Alexis.

"It's not a pretty story. We were engaged, but at the last minute, she decided that she couldn't live on a cop's salary. She needed more, so she settled for a title and a fortune," A flat statement uttered without emotion.

"Peter, I am so sorry." She tried to take her hand out of his grasp, but his grip tightened. His touch was firm. She took her other hand and caressed his cheek. "I am sorry," she whispered again. "I think she still wants you. I watched her, and I am good with faces. You can have her back, I'm sure of it," Minola said with a sinking feeling in the pit of her stomach. *I can't compete with Alexis Yardleigh.*

"That is my past, Minola. It is done." He wanted to tell her that she was his future, but God help him, he was afraid. It was too soon; she was too skittish. He now realized that it had never mattered to him how many lovers Alexis had had prior to their relationship–with Minola, however, he felt possessive and jealous. What had she done to him? The thought that there had been another man holding her, touching her, making love to her, was untenable, yet he could not stop thinking about it. He had felt her response to him, hot, passionate, and giving. The thought that she could respond to another man the same way was exquisite torture. He needed to stop thinking about it.

"Peter, are you alright? Where are you?" she asked softly. *He is thinking of her–I am a substitute.*

"I'm sorry. I'm right here, with you," he whispered.

"Peter, you can have her back," she told him again. Minola mistakenly assumed that he was reliving his past.

"No," he answered vehemently. "That is finished. Now, where were we? Good with faces?"

"What?"

"You said you were good with faces. What did you mean?"

"I have made a study of facial expressions, body language, mannerisms, so forth and so on…"

"Why?"

"Why?"

"That's what I asked you. You are quibbling, Miss Grey. Out with it."

"I never quibble, Chief Inspector. I just prefer not to answer yet."

"I see. All right, Miss Grey, we won't discuss it now. Just remember, I am a cop and I am tenacious. I mean to know."

"Yes, Chief Inspector."

Afraid she would withdraw, he asked about her classes. "Minola, are you ready to discuss your art? What precisely are you studying, is it Botticelli?"

"Oh…you remembered," she blushed.

"I remembered."

"Yes, I've studied Botticelli."

"Miss Grey, you are prevaricating."

"Yes, I know. Peter, why did you break all the rules about me?"

Peter didn't immediately respond. There wasn't much he could have said that would have made sense, not to mention sounding as bizarre to her as it did to him. He knew he needed to move slowly because of the suspicions he'd held when he couldn't reconcile her demeanor and her suspected activities at the hotel. He had followed his instincts and did nothing but wait to evaluate the situation himself.

"As you might recall, you had made an incredible first impression, I must say."

"Yes, I remember your first impression, as does the hotel staff. Thank you very much. They are still talking about it. You have given me quite a reputation, one I am still having a hard time living down. Although I must admit it has been fun, being a woman of the evening."

"The correct term, Minola, is woman of the night."

"No, Peter, woman of the evening. All my clients leave by ten. I sleep at night."

"Clients, is it?"

"Isn't that the correct term?" she asked.

Peter laughed, grateful she was able to enjoy a sense of the absurd. "I do apologize, but what was a cop to think? You certainly did nothing to dispel my notions."

Minola smiled. She remembered his arrogant approach well. "I didn't try to dissuade you because you behaved boorishly and I wasn't about to explain myself to you. I was going to let you do the legwork."

"You certainly put me in my place, and now look–you somehow became involved in this investigation. Again, I seem to behave in a totally abnormal manner. I have never before allowed a civilian, to interfere in an investigation."

"What do you mean, interfere? I am helping, and doing a great job of it, I might add. Look at the list from that office. You and your policemen can do your magic and decipher whatever it is. Robert hopefully will have all sorts of information for you on Saturday. What more can you ask?"

Peter was concerned that there could be a second murder. "I want to catch the culprit before he kills again."

Minola saw Sally and Robert walking toward them

"We stopped in the gardens, but it was chilly, so we came here for coffee. Ye gods, it's contagious, this coffee addiction." Sally sat down and rubbed her hands together to warm up.

Peter decided to establish the protocol for Saturday's dinner. "Robert, do you know anyone who could provide private information about Gernaud, and LeClerque? The senior partners at the Le Clerque firm were dear old friends of our victim. I want to know if you have ever heard any gossip about them in the financial district. I know it's short notice, but anything at this point will be helpful."

"I will check with the permanent Parisian staff, see what we can come up with," responded Robert.

Peter continued, "I would like our group to stay put at the table, or at least in the room. Should something happen, you will be protected."

"Peter," Minola sounded nervous. "What do you mean, in case something should happen? Just what do you expect to happen?"

"Call it my sixth sense, but I suspect someone is getting edgy. All of the suspects have been interviewed a second time. We have tried to make everyone feel uneasy. The Police Nationale visited Lady Yardleigh this morning. The lady wants to protect her interests, so she volunteered to talk to Edwards. She stands to inherit, assuming there is something left to inherit."

"You didn't visit Alexis Yardleigh yourself?" Minola was curious.

"No, I didn't. To avoid a potential conflict of interest, I have had very little contact with Lady Yardleigh, save for that one interview, where I had a witness. There was no other need for me to see her," he said with quiet emphasis. *She sees Alexis in my future–what the hell do I do now? I need to talk to her alone, tomorrow.*

"What you are telling us is that you have poked and prodded, and are now looking for the results."

"That is precisely what I'm telling you. People on edge tend to make mistakes. It seemed that Lord Yardleigh was very good at exchange rates. That was his business. He was a market maker, and he traded in European currency. He did quite well for himself. However, with the introduction of the Euro, he could no longer maintain a high profit margin, and the company began to slide monetarily. Yardleigh needed a large influx of cash to maintain the business. The import/export tag became very handy, since no actual product was handled except for the cash. It was easy to turn money around. This made the company solvent, but severely tied Yardleigh to the criminal elements. LeClerque provided the first and continuous influx of cash to Yardleigh. I suspect that more than one company was thus helped with cash. The stakes were high enough for more mayhem."

"This is so complicated. So what happens now?" Minola said.

"We have placed men in LeClerque's office, now we wait for the results. The local gendarmes are going through a short crash course in waiting tables. They are delighted, by the way, since the chef promised them a wonderful dinner afterward."

Minola pretended to be mildly outraged. "You mean to tell me you told Chef Etienne about this, and he said not a word to me? Left me completely out? His tip just got smaller."

"Don't take it out on the poor man, I swore him to secrecy. Restore his tip," Peter teased.

Their eyes locked–his gaze compelling. Minola became

more guarded as both friend and amateur sleuth. Minola didn't want Peter to feel pressured or uncomfortable, and knew she would have to watch herself. She was beginning to feel like a Victorian maiden, innocent and perpetually bewildered.

To break the tension, Sally announced she was going shopping Friday morning.

"Again? It looks like Peter and I are the only ones working tomorrow," Robert complained.

Peter, watching Sally and Robert, recognized the deep and abiding love between them. He desperately wanted that with Minola. *I'm in love with her. How do I get through to her?*

"No, you are the only one working tomorrow. I have a date with Minola to visit the Rodin Museum," Peter laughed. He used 'date' consciously to see how Minola would react, although her reaction was not what Peter expected.

She blushed, looked directly at Peter, and said, "It is a date, isn't it? I do remember asking you, and you said yes, so a date it is." Straightforward and refusing to play games, she generously gave him the small victory.

"Minola loves playing tour guide. She doesn't take just anyone to the Rodin Museum. It's very private and intimate, and she only shares her time there with a very few close friends." Sally glowed.

Minola turned delightfully rosy. "Sally, stop it," she begged.

Peter grinned mischievously, "Miss Grey, it would take a lot more than a date with a beautiful woman and a museum visit to frighten me."

"Thank you, kind sir. Any and all compliments are welcome. Now, it is time to head back to reality."

Sally, however, with an agenda of her own, continued talking about the magnificence and intimacy of the museum, having Minola as a guide, and her passion for Rodin's work.

Minola begged Sally to stop. Peter, on the other hand, kept watching Minola and gauging her flustered responses.

At last Robert decided to end Minola's agony. "Ladies and gentleman, since tomorrow is going to be a long day, I am going to take my wife home. We will communicate via cell phones, so Minola, make sure yours is on." He pulled Sally up, put his arm around her waist, and moved her toward the door.

"More coffee, Miss Grey?" Peter knew what her response would be, but he was trying to get her to relax. Minola started laughing, and he joined in. He got up, walked over to the old-fashioned jukebox, and selected Minola's two favorite songs.

When she heard the familiar chord of 'Help Yourself', she looked up and watched Peter walk back to her. As he reached her side, he whispered, "We shall make this more personal." His voice was like a caress.

Minola, taken aback, finally admitted to herself that she loved this man, totally and completely. She had loved him all along, but had been afraid to admit it. Peter was in her life, Alexis notwithstanding. She needed to gain some perspective and get back to a common ground, away from intimacy, or she would drown in her love for him. "Peter, earlier you talked about the conflict in this investigation.

Why did you take it on?"

For the first time, he really thought about why. "I think it was an automatic response to their call for help," he answered. "I really didn't evaluate the process. I reacted. Perhaps I should have considered the conflict that could arise out of my involvement. The relationship was over. It was over–a closed chapter in my life. Maybe guilt about the old relationship played a part. Murder certainly didn't seem to be on the horizon. I think I just fell into the investigation. I'm sorry I don't have a more profound answer."

"I certainly understand accepting something that comes along. I have done that for many a year. Have you been with anyone since Alexis? Peter, I really am not prying into your life–well, perhaps I am. I just want to understand how you relax and unwind other than going home. You see so much in your career. Who helps you to break away and regain a sense of perspective?"

"I haven't had a serious commitment since Alexis. There've been other relationships, but nothing serious," he stated, "and not many opportunities to relax. When an occasion presents itself, I simply go home, stay with my parents, and blend in with the locals. What about you? You had a disappointing relationship with a bastard. Have you recovered?"

"You certainly don't mince your words, Chief Inspector. I actually recovered very quickly. I realized almost immediately that it was comfort and convenience, not love that had perpetuated the relationship. However, it has left a rather profound mark–scarred for life, Chief Inspector."

"I rather doubt that, Miss Grey–you are too full of life.

I've chosen a profession where I see the darker side of humanity. You, however, seem to have retained your positive attitude. I was about to say innocent attitude, but given my first impression of your chosen career path, I am afraid you might retaliate. What is it, exactly, that you are doing in Paris? Are you ready to tell me about it?" His voice was warm and soothing.

"I doubt that you are afraid of many things, Chief Inspector. Now to my other selected profession. I am currently at *Les Écoles des Beaux Arts*. I love art, it is very important in my life. I do not engage, nor have I ever engaged, in the oldest profession. Do you like being a cop, Peter? Why Interpol?"

"I see. I get very vague answers, yet you want specific details from me. So be it, Miss Grey. Yes, I do like being a cop, and Interpol has well-defined roles in various sectors that make it interesting. Primarily, it allows for international cooperation since it does have a global as well as local perspective. No, I didn't read this somewhere in a recruitment poster. Since we now live in a vastly global community, I feel that international communication and understanding is the police format of the future. All right, Miss Grey, I expect an answer to my question. How have you accepted everything that came along? What did you mean?"

"I see you paid attention." she began.

"I paid attention. Pray continue."

"Chief Inspector, you are relentless. For the sake of expediency, I held a boring office job that was meaningless. It paid the bills, but offered nothing else. I was too afraid to make a change. The end of my so-called relationship inspired me to jump ship, as it were–I tendered my resignation and moved to Paris to find myself."

"And did you?"

"Find myself? In a sense, yes…I think I have faced some of my fears, although I don't think I have defined anything else. I am still a work in progress, though I do think I have a career path in mind."

"That is a very oblique answer."

"Peter, please be patient. Trust and friendship do not come easily to me," she pleaded.

"I have all the patience you need, Minola." He spoke quietly and earnestly. *That bastard must have really scarred her.* Peter did not press the issue further, he was glad that she was as forthcoming as she was.

It was late evening when they left the café. The city once again was pulsating with a beat all its own. Cobblestones echoed the life of the city. Paris was all lit up and as vital as ever. The City of Lights was living up to its romantic reputation.

They exchanged greetings with the lobby staff, then the elevator took them upstairs. They walked to Minola's door, Peter took the key from her hand, opened the door, and followed her in. Once inside, he caressed her cheek, tilted her chin, and gently touched her lips with his.

Minola's reaction was electric. She was getting used to the heat that his mouth generated. Peter deepened the kiss and explored her mouth with his tongue. By now fully aroused, he caressed her back with an urgency that betrayed his need for her. He found her intoxicating.

Minola moaned and pulled away. She looked into his eyes and saw the desire that mirrored her own. "Peter, I want you. I usually don't…I don't know how to explain." She was at a loss for words. She wanted him desperately, although Alexis Yardleigh was never far from her thoughts. *Lust, it is just lust for him. I can't do this. Once I give in, I will lose myself.*

"It's all right, my love. Why are you so afraid? I won't betray you," he whispered. Gently, he caressed her neck with his thumb and felt her shiver.

"Peter, I feel totally defenseless. Sex is not enough for me. You have a past with a woman who is now free. You wouldn't be here if it weren't for her. I'm sorry. Please be patient with me." She spoke with quiet desperation.

"I won't pressure you, just let me be with you. We can slowly get to know one another. I have a past with her, not a future." He kissed her forehead, wished her a good night, and let himself out.

In his own room, Peter sat down on the sofa and tried to rationalize his feelings for her. The effect she had on him was incredible. It was physical, emotional, everything. She had invaded his mind, body, and soul. He wanted her safe. He wanted her happy. He simply wanted her. When this investigation ended, he was going to court her, no doubt about it. If he could last that long. Courting her would be an old-fashioned approach, yet it seemed to suit her.

Peter thought of his mother. He wanted Minola to meet her, however archaic that sounded. He had never before wanted his mother to meet anyone he had a relationship with. His mother's main complaint was that he never brought anyone home to meet her. Well, she was going to meet Minola, although just how that was going to work out, he didn't know. Minola was an American temporarily living in Paris. He was an Englishman temporarily living in Paris, yet he would follow her anywhere.

Physically exhausted, he was ready for sleep, but emotionally he was wound up like a stringed instrument. Sitting on his bed, he thought about visiting the Rodin Museum. He was curious about Minola's interest in art. She appeared knowledgeable about the subject to the point of being an expert. He loved watching her face when she talked about it. Obviously it was important to her. *Clearly, I am not an idiot. I should be able to add two and two and come up with four. It has to come from her.* He clenched and unclenched his fist, forcing himself to relax.

Chapter 12

Minola awoke with a start, thinking she was late. She suddenly realized they had not set a time for their rendezvous. She quickly showered, dressed in long khaki pants and an ivory top. She put on a touch of mascara, comfortable sandals, grabbed her small purse, and she was ready. No sense in taking anything bigger, no sketching today. Peter would be with her.

As Minola opened the door, she surprised a deliveryman about to knock on it. He held a huge bouquet of flowers for her. They were stunning. She didn't bother to close the door as she deeply inhaled the fresh scent. Her head buried in the flowers, a gleam of burnished copper hair was all that was visible from the top of the bouquet.

That is how Peter found her, standing in the open door drinking in the scent of the flowers he had bought for her. He was enthralled by what he saw. He knew he would always cherish this memory.

She lifted her head, gave him a dazzling smile, and said, "I can only assume these are from you. They are exquisite. Thank you, Peter. What is the occasion?"

"No occasion. I noticed you like flowers and I wanted to thank you for a wonderful evening. We forgot to set a time for this morning, and I wanted to see you. I am glad you like the flowers."

"I love them. You not only made my morning, you've made my whole day. I hope you will like the museum. Have you had breakfast yet? More to the point, have you had coffee?"

Peter laughed out loud. "No, I have not. Where would you like to go for your morning fix?"

"Let me put these gorgeous flowers on the table. How about downstairs? They have outstanding pastries, great coffee, and thou." She looked at Peter as she voiced her feelings.

It thrilled him. "Wonderful sentiment, I could get used to this."

"Get used to what?"

"To being with you all the time."

She did not know how to respond to that. "Are you flirting with me?"

"No, just stating a fact," he replied quietly.

Flustered, she murmured. "Thank you. At least you are not bored."

"Not a chance." Peter noticed her discomfort, and realized she was not practiced in the art of flirting. Much to his delight, she wanted to make sure. She had no qualms about asking if he was flirting with her. She didn't play games.

While Peter waited at the door, Minola set the flowers down on her bedstand, pausing to enjoy their scents once more.

For Peter, the location was perfect. She would think of him as she lay in bed, at least he hoped she would.

The restaurant was already teeming with business. Once the waiter had taken their order, Minola said, "Do you think tomorrow night will really be worthwhile? There is such a buildup for it. I would hate for you to be disappointed."

"First of all, I will be with you. Therefore, I will not be disappointed. I also happen to think that, because we have made all the suspects nervous, someone will make a mistake. Minola, I need to tell you something. Please don't be angry, but since this dinner has become such an Interpol operation, I have arranged for the cost to be paid by Interpol. I just didn't know how to tell you."

"Why were you afraid to tell me? It was never a control thing. I just wanted to do something special for Robert and Sally, and Paris seemed the best setting. Sally has never been here, and it seemed like a good way to try to gather some gossip and information. They will still have their party, they will eat their favorite foods, and they will probably have a memorable time. I had the fun of planning it, and Interpol is picking up the tab. What could be better?"

"Thank you, Miss Grey." Peter was delighted with her response. He could now enjoy himself without reservation. They finished their breakfast, and started their slow hike to the museum. Soon they were on the street facing a glass panel, looking at the back of the 'Burghers of Calais.' They had arrived at their destination

It was sheer magic to catch a glimpse of the treasures offered without having entered yet. What a wonderful enticement to the beguiling museum.

They walked up to the entrance. Peter had been there

many years before; he didn't remember much, so he did not know what to expect. After paying the admission fee, he guided Minola inside. They strolled to the gardens, arms clasped.

Once inside, they were immediately presented by the colossal Gates of Hell, and the chaos that was shown in Rodin's unfinished work. The magnificent gates were originally commissioned as a museum entrance, reflecting Dante's Divine Comedy, but ultimately the Gates of Hell were the reflection of Rodin's own idea or belief of hell, torment, and the human existence, a tumultuous epic in bronze.

A little further into the garden, Minola pointed out Rodin's magnificent bronze, the 'Thinker'–the poignant face bent in contemplation, each muscle strained and visible, every sinew perfectly defined.

They walked a bit more in the peaceful, sculpture-filled gardens, Minola occasionally pointing out a special piece here and there. It was like looking for lost treasures, but once found, oh, what an incredible joy of discovery!

As they stood in front of the Burghers of Calais, she exclaimed, "Peter, look at this. You can see the rope so clearly defined; look at the pain and despair on their faces. How clearly he was able to portray the suffering–it's so visible on each face. Isn't it amazing?" Her enthusiasm knew no bounds.

"This was Rodin's heroic depiction of the siege of Calais in 1347, and their apparent willingness to sacrifice their lives for the survival of their village. It's magnificent. I love this place." She beamed.

"I can see and feel your appreciation, Minola. You absolutely amaze me." Minola's animation enraptured Peter.

They found themselves in front of the famed statue of Balzac. "Rodin absolutely loved this piece, but his critics did not. They vilified it. Today, it stands as one of his greatest triumphs–Balzac in all his arrogance and glory beyond life-size," Minola continued.

She took him inside Rodin's home, which now was a glorious museum in its own right. She shared with him Rodin's erotic side, "Do you see this piece–the Kiss? It's made of cold, hard marble, yet look at it, really look at it, Peter. Do you feel the passion, the heat, the flowing grace, the soft curves? It has been represented as a woman's submission and subordination to the greater man, but I see something else. I see the woman as a willing participant in the passion reflected, an equal partner. I don't see submission, I see equality, passion, and ardent cooperation." She stopped when she noticed Peter staring at her. "I'm sorry, I promised not to lecture."

"You take my breath away," he whispered as he pressed a kiss in her hair, and tightened his hold on her arm. Peter saw a totally different side to the woman standing next to him. All her senses were involved. He now understood this was her world, and it gave him a totally new perspective on the world of Rodin and the art world as a whole. He didn't know the depth of her commitment, but he knew this was her life. Minola understood the toil, the fierce determination, and the drive it took to produce a work of this magnitude. He suddenly realized he loved her beyond reason, she had captured his soul. He was enthralled with the alluring woman by his side.

They walked outside once again to continue their exploration. It was so peaceful. Here and there Rodin's sculptures appeared amongst the hedges and bushes. Peter was bewitched, not just with the Museum, but with Minola's earthy, gritty approach to Rodin's work. She saw everything, each curve of the hand, the stray hair, the agony reflected on some faces; the masterful carving of the ropes the Burghers were carrying, the sensuality and passion. It all came alive through her glowing explanations.

Peter had never had a museum visit quite like this. "I will never visit this particular Museum without you. I now understand what Sally meant when she said it was very intimate and personal for you."

They went back inside the house to view the clay and marble statues, so lovingly left intact, as if the pieces were still a work in progress, then returned outside to again enjoy the tranquil atmosphere of the gardens. They sat on a bench in front of the 'Thinker', copied his stance, and pondered–as many have done before and will continue to do in the future.

By late afternoon, they were thirsty and hungry, but not eager to leave quite yet.

"I could really use a cup of coffee," said Minola. "How does that café in the gardens look? Delightful, isn't it? I cannot imagine a better place to sit and relax."

"Nor can I. I have been remiss. My apologies. Coffee will be provided shortly," Peter replied. The café was brilliantly situated in the middle of the garden, surrounded by Rodin's work. They listened to birds singing and other visitors discussing their impressions of the amazing museum.

After their coffee break, they walked around the gardens one last time. Once again reaching the Gates of Hell–which stood as both entrance and exit to the museum–they paid homage one last time to the magnificent structure.

Minola couldn't resist a final comment. "Peter, notice how huge they are. You see them coming in and you see them going out, an incredible first and last impression of the museum. The Gates of Hell are massive and tortured. Just look at them, they are beyond description." She was completely bewitched. For her, The Gates were a physical, overwhelming presence. They had a profound impact on her psyche. Rodin reached her emotions as no other artist had ever done. Minola, trying to impress upon Peter her love for Rodin's work, succeeded magnificently.

"Thank you for sharing this day and the museum with me. I cannot possibly begin to tell you how much I enjoyed it. I understand your attachment; you can be my private tour guide from now on."

"I may hold you to that. I love art, and in Paris, art is everywhere. I found that to be true especially here, at the Museum. It revives the soul. It is one of the most contemplative museums I have ever been to."

"I absolutely agree with you. It is peaceful, in spite of some of the tormented pieces of art. That is quite a contradiction, but true nevertheless."

"You are a philosopher. You can look at it from the perspective of torment. Torment is certainly represented in his work, but you also see the pride, passion, love, and meditation–life in all its complexities. Ultimately, however, everything transcends and you see hope and survival. That to me is a sign of a magnificent artist."

"Who is the philosopher here?" he quipped.

"I don't want to spoil this erudite mood, but let's find a restaurant and have an early dinner. I am famished. Breakfast was a long time ago."

They found a café nearby, on the Rue des Invalides near Napoleon's tomb, artfully named The Museum Café. During the tourist season, the place usually stayed busy, although today it was quiet. They enjoyed a peaceful meal.

Their continued discussion about art and other topics, save murder, further animated Minola. This was their time together, their respite from the world. She had a calming effect on him, something he had never felt with anyone in the past.

They ordered the house specialty, a hearty casserole dish from the Normandy region: chouxcroute garnie; sauerkraut, ham, sausage, and potatoes. Also included were salad, cheese tray, and of course more coffee.

The walk back to the hotel allowed Peter the luxury of contemplation, his mind full of Minola Grey. His arm encircled her waist. His hold tightened as he felt her lean into him, they walked in agreeable silence.

They found Sally waiting for them in the lobby. "I just had dinner with James and Samantha. Robert is working late and will pick me up here. So what are we going to do? Something relaxing, I hope. I am exhausted."

Minola, never one to let an opportunity for her favorite brew slide by, suggested, "Let's have coffee."

"We just had coffee with dinner," Peter replied.

"Precisely, *with* dinner. This is *after* dinner," Minola countered with a grin. She decided tonight would be the perfect time to present the anniversary portrait. Tomorrow was going to be hectic; besides, this was personal and tonight was theirs alone.

"Sally, can you and Robert stop by my room tonight before you go home? Peter, please join us." Minola did not want Peter to feel left out. She felt apprehensive, but he might as well learn all about her so-called visitors.

"Is something the matter, Minola? You seem uneasy all of a sudden," Peter voiced his concern.

"No, no, everything is fine." Minola got up and walked to the front desk. She asked them to get the painting out of storage and bring it to her room. She returned, smiling, and led them to the little café.

Robert arrived, and knew exactly where to find them. Greeting everyone, he kissed Sally and joined them for coffee. "So, is everyone ready for the big day tomorrow? I just happen to have some information for you." He handed Peter a file. "This will give you some sense of where the money was coming from. Just don't ask how I got it."

Robert continued, "More work for you tonight–a bit of information about the LeClerque accounting firm. Take a look at the report; we can talk tomorrow after the dinner. So, wife of mine, are you ready to go home?"

"Robert, Minola asked us to stop by her room tonight, but she won't tell me why." Robert looked at Minola, instantly understanding the reason for the request.

Before going upstairs, Minola stopped to order dessert and a bottle of champagne. In her room, the covered painting had been placed in the center of the room. Sally was dying of curiosity. "So, what is your newest project, and how come I haven't seen it? Is this when Peter finds out about your activities when not sleuthing?"

"What activities?" Peter demanded.

Just as Minola was about to answer, the doorbell rang, and room service made the champagne and dessert delivery. Sally looked at the champagne and could not wait. "What is going on? Minola, tell me before I burst out with something you will probably regret."

"We are going to toast your anniversary tonight, since tomorrow will be too busy. I have your anniversary gift here. So, let's pour the champagne and drink to a wonderful couple and dearest friends."

Peter made himself useful by popping the cork.

Sally told him to pour just a tad for Minola, since she didn't like champagne. Minola happily replied, "It is scary to have friends who know you so well."

They toasted the anniversary, then Minola walked over to the portrait, removed the cover, and presented it to Sally and Robert.

Sally started crying and hugged the stunned Robert.

Peter was completely taken aback. He still had no idea Minola was the artist, but he loved the painting. It depicted the couple perfectly. She had found something magnificent.

It portrayed a partnership in every sense of the word— soft, passionate, and determined. They were almost facing each other, but looking beyond to their future. Robert's arm gently encircled Sally's waist; a wisp of her hair touched his cheek.

Once Sally stopped crying, she turned to Minola, gave her a big hug, and thanked her profusely. "I love it…how…when… I am speechless!"

"I have to paint your portrait to get you to be speechless, hmm? I guess that means you like it."

"Like it? You have no idea. It's brilliant. I am at a loss, I-It's incredible. Seriously, when did you have the time to do this? I know how long it takes you to finish a project like this."

"Sally, it was a labor of love. Your wonderful husband asked me to do this as soon as he arrived in Paris. Robert, you have not said a word. I hope it meets with your approval?"

Peter in the meantime stared at Minola, total comprehension dawning in his eyes. He felt like an idiot. All the clues had been there. He was supposed to be a detective, but only now did it all make sense to him. He thought back to his original impression of her, and smiled.

Minola looked at him and returned the grin. "So, Peter," Minola teased, "is this a better profession than the one you had envisioned for me earlier? Do you like it? Robert seems to have lost his capacity for speech."

Peter looked at the wall and the prints he had admired earlier. "The portrait is stunning. I should love to see your other efforts." Minola followed his gaze and nodded in agreement.

"My other efforts, as you put it, are in the other room, the one I use as a studio."

"Now I understand the need for the extra room. Your work is outstanding. I think Robert and Sally are going to be unavailable for a few minutes." They turned and looked at the couple sitting on the couch, hugging and contemplating their painting.

"They seem to be very taken with your gift, and I can understand why. I do beg your pardon for my original observation."

"Oh, so you call it an observation. An interesting choice of words."

"I will never live this down, will I?" asked Peter, sheepishly grinning.

"Not any time soon, Chief Inspector." She led him to the other room. Minola's big easel sat by the window, at an angle to catch the best light. She had a comfortable chair, and a couch next to a small table holding a vase of flowers. The bed had been removed, and the rest of the space was occupied by canvases, easels, and all sizes of sketchpads. Along one wall was a table filled with various paints, palettes, and more paper. It was a working room.

Peter looked around, noticed all the details, and was amazed at the woman standing next to him. How could he ever have thought she could be capable of any devious behavior? Her talent was undeniable. What he wanted to do at this moment was to take her in his arms and love her, but they were not alone. Instead, he walked around the room yet again and looked at everything visible. He caught a glimpse of a well-used sketchpad, but did not ask to see it. He felt that might be an infringement on her privacy.

Minola watched him look at the exposed pieces and noticed his glance at the sketchpad, but did not offer it to him. His face covered most of the pages–not something she wanted to explain. She did, however, offer him the colored charcoal drawing that reflected the menu scenes.

"What do you mean, 'You can have this canvas'?"

"Let's see. Which part of 'If you like it you can have it' are you having trouble with?" Minola inquired.

"I think it is beautiful. It seems to have a story behind it. Why the multiple scenes? How can you part with it?"

"Well, actually, this will be a souvenir for you of Saturday night. I decided to draw menu cards/seating cards, but I wanted each one to be unique. I was not sure what I wanted, so I drew on one canvas, separated the scenes, and this is the result. The place cards are on the table. Peter, most times I sell my art. That is my business. You know-the many visitors? There are a few pieces I cannot part with, and those will never be offered for sale."

"Yes, I know, the many visitors. My abject apologies, Miss Grey." Peter continued to digest the whole concept of Minola the artist, the dinner, and the trouble Minola took to make it so special. She was one hell of a friend. He didn't just want that drawing, he craved it. It was like having a part of her with him–of course he wanted it. He knew he couldn't offer her money. What could he do to show his appreciation? He would have to find something truly unique, something that reflected her taste and spirit.

He walked over to the table to look at the neat pile with the various scenes reflected in miniature, beautifully done. There was one with his name on it.

She scrutinized his every movement, and waited patiently for him to finish. Peter turned around, walked over to her, caressed her cheek, and whispered, "You have invaded my very soul."

Minola touched her forehead to his and took his hands in hers.

Precisely at that moment, Sally walked in.

Peter and Minola quickly moved apart, but not before Sally noticed the near embrace. "Sorry, I did not mean to interrupt. I just had to thank you again, for the incredible gift."

"I am sorry I didn't have time to get it framed. I will arrange to have it done soon."

Peter interrupted. "Actually, I haven't had a chance to buy you a gift, and I really did want to celebrate your anniversary. Would you please allow me to have it framed for you?"

"It is so generous of you, but..." Sally did not want to insult him, but knew it would be very expensive. She did not want Peter to have to get such an extravagant gift on a cop's salary. Nor, for that matter, did she want Minola to incur such an additional expense.

Minola glanced at Peter and realized he understood Sally's hesitation. He was grateful that she cared enough to take his finances under consideration.

"Sally, I really would like to frame the portrait for you. I will ask Minola to recommend someone she uses. Please allow us to pick out the frame." Peter wanted to take even a miniscule part in this gift. In an odd way, it made him somehow feel closer to Minola, although he couldn't quite explain it to himself.

Sally looked at Minola, who nodded. "Thank you. Of course I trust you both. I just cannot bear to be parted from the painting for any length of time. Robert is still sitting on the couch staring at it."

She walked over and hugged Minola yet again, then turned and embraced Peter as well. "I'm absolutely astounded at the magnitude of this fantastic present."

"Good. I'm glad you like it, since you cannot return it anywhere." Minola reminded Sally about her predisposition to return most gifts she received.

"Return it? You wish…"

Peter listened to the exchange. He looked at Minola's radiant face and realized he loved her beyond reason. Completely and totally. The reality of the depth of his love overwhelmed him. For a jaded cop, this came as quite a revelation. *When is she going to realize what she means to me?*

Sally turned, returning to the other room. Minola and Peter wordlessly followed.

Robert rose from the sofa, enveloped Minola in his arms, and lovingly kissed her cheek. His eyes were moist, and she acknowledged the emotion reflected in his face.

Sally remembering that Robert had asked Minola to do the portrait, walked over to her husband to hug him, and said, "Husband, you have done very well. This anniversary will be impossible to top." Noticing how tired Minola looked, Sally added, "Robert, I think it is time to go home. I hate to part with this painting, but tomorrow is going to be a long day." They called downstairs to request a taxi. After more hugs, they took their leave.

Alone with Minola, at last, Peter walked over and took Minola in his arms and kissed her. Without coyness, she returned his kiss with ardor. He kissed her again as he muttered, "Your work is magnificent, and your generosity overwhelming." His lips seared a path from her mouth, down her neck, and back to her lips. He pressed her closer and deepened the kiss. Her mouth opened to him, and he felt her moan as his tongue invaded her mouth. The kiss was an insistent force, one that both demanded and gave total possession.

"I want you," he groaned. "God, I want you." He shuddered as he kissed her again and molded her body to his. She fit so perfectly.

When he finally released her, she was limp from desire. No man had ever affected her in this way. *But he said nothing about love, nothing.*

For Peter, his arousal was complete and damned uncomfortable. Nothing new there…it'll be another cold shower, he thought grimly. If he stayed, they would make love and he knew she was not ready, although he sure as hell was. It was too early; one look at her face was enough. Her hesitancy, and the fear in her eyes was haunting. He had to leave.

"I know it is time to say good night. Sleep well, my love." He bent down to give her another hungry kiss, and crushed her to him. She was worth every ounce of patience he had in him, and more. It was so damn hard to leave her.

Ready to go, he gave her another sweet kiss. Minola wrapped her arms around his neck and deepened the kiss. She couldn't let him go. She caressed his back and pressed herself closer. She could feel his erection through her clothes, further igniting her response. She showered kisses around his lips and his jaw, then kissed him again, savoring his taste on her mouth.

He explored her mouth ruthlessly, then, moving lower, kissed her breasts through her blouse. He cupped a breast in his hand, it fit perfectly. Vaguely aware of her moan, he moved back to her mouth, leaving a trail of hot kisses on her neck and behind her earlobes.

For Peter, this was sheer torture. "What are you doing to me?" he whispered hoarsely against her mouth. He tore himself away from her embrace and whispered, "I need to leave. I desperately want to love you. Are you ready for that next step?" With trembling hands he touched her face–he wanted to see her eyes. There was need and desire there, but most of all he saw her fear. "It's all right, my love." He held her tightly and waited for passion to subside.

"Peter, I am so sorry. I want you too. I–" She almost told him she loved him, but she couldn't. She couldn't bear to have him feel obligated, and there was always Alexis, damn it.

"*Shh*...I do understand. Good night," he whispered hoarsely. His breath was hot against her face. "Sleep well, love." He remembered to take her gift, and quietly left. Minola sat down on the bed before her knees buckled.

Peter did the same thing when he entered his room–sat on the bed and thought of Minola and the amazing evening he had just had. After taking another look at the painting given him, he called his mother. Told her she was going to meet the most astounding woman he had ever known, wished her good night, and ended the call. No doubt about it, he was behaving erratically and that was unlike him.

Chapter 13

Saturday morning Minola woke up blissfully happy. It was going to be a great day. Sally and Robert loved the painting; she had managed to convince an Interpol man that her many visitors were legal, leaving him speechless; and tonight they were going to try to corner a murderer.

She couldn't stop thinking about last night. She was thrilled she no longer had any secrets from him, except that she was madly in love with him.

She quickly showered and dressed in dark blue Capri pants and a pink T-shirt. With her hair pulled back in a bun and a touch of mascara, she was good to go. She beamed at her image in the mirror.

Her lack of coffee brought her back to earth. She went in search of sustenance, taking the menu cards with her since they would be needed. She grabbed a newspaper from the little table in the lobby, and was all set to enjoy coffee and the news on a quiet Saturday morning. It was wonderful to be alive, in love, and in Paris.

While Minola was sipping her coffee, Peter was waking up. He studied Minola's canvas, where he had placed it on the desk, facing the bed. He needed to get her advice about framing it. He wanted to have it done at the same time as

Sally and Robert's painting. He still was not sure about what to get Minola–perhaps a piece of jewelry or a vintage Art Deco piece? Whatever it was going to be, it would have to be special. He finished getting ready, eagerly anticipating seeing her. He knew where he would find her, she was totally predictable in that respect.

He went out the door and ran into Mr. Edwards, who greeted him effusively and hinted that he had yet to meet with Miss Grey.

Peter responded, "I'm having breakfast with Miss Grey. I will convey your message. I am sure she is looking forward to it. Miss Grey is hosting the party for Robert and Sally Jones. Among the invited are Giselle Armand, and Mr. LeClerque. So most likely your meeting with her will occur after the dinner."

Peter noted Edwards expressed surprise that board members and top management from LeClerque would be attending the dinner. Peter explained they were people who traveled in Robert's business circle. "It is an anniversary celebration."

"Are you attending, Chief Inspector?"

Smiling, Peter told him, "I'm Miss Grey's guest for the evening."

He had baited the fish well. "Good day, Mr. Edwards," he said, and proceeded to the elevator.

From the entry, he saw Minola at the table sipping her nectar and reading the paper. Peter quietly walked up to her and whispered, "Good morning. Sleep well?" He couldn't take his eyes off her face. Surely, she must know what she meant to him.

"Good morning." She looked up with a blinding smile, and said, "It took a bit…never better…it was a wonderful evening. Thank you, for making it so perfect."

"How did I manage to do that? I seem to remember you making it perfect." Peter was going to say something more, but he saw Sally approaching, Robert trailing behind her with suitcases. *She does have the most inopportune timing.*

"Good morning," Sally glowed.

"Are you two moving somewhere?" Minola looked at the two big suitcases Robert was dragging.

"No," Robert responded. "Although it may look like it. This one holds my tuxedo and the other, Sally's clothes for the evening. She couldn't decide what she was going to wear, even with all the shopping you two managed to do. She also thought it will be more fun if we booked a room here for two nights, on your side, one floor below."

"Now that will be fun." Minola looked forward to the camaraderie. Peter, however, wasn't so sure. As much as he enjoyed their company, he wanted time alone with Minola tonight.

"Robert can't stay too long, he has an early Saturday morning meeting. So let's cover whatever it is we need to do." Sally wanted Robert to leave so she could spend some time with James and Samantha.

"I might as well start," Peter began. "On my way downstairs, I ran into Mr. Edwards and told him about the dinner. By the way, Minola, he mentioned you had not seen him yet. You might want to schedule something after dinner tonight. I'm sure he knows you met with Giselle Armand."

Looking at Minola, Peter asked with a wide grin, "Have

you started the portrait yet? It does seem odd."

Minola was fully aware of what Peter was thinking, but she wanted him to spell it out. "What seems odd, Peter?"

"The fact that you really are an artist, a remarkable one at that. There, I have said it."

"Thank you, Peter. Yes, I have started. Enough to let Mr. Edwards know it is a real effort. His suspicions should be groundless. What's next on the agenda?"

"I have with me the seating arrangements. We have three tables, and we will seat eight people at each table. One will host the three key people from LeClerque and four members from the Yardleigh board; we will put Giselle Armand at that table. The second table will seat three LeClerque accountants, people who actually do the ledgers, plus two additional board members who are not so active in the business. We will fill in the other three seats with names from Robert's division. I believe they all know each other—it is a rather small community. Then, of course, there is our table."

Sally was curious how the police were going to participate. "Peter, just exactly what will the police do?"

"Most of the wait staff will be from the Police Nationale, with a few from Interpol. They'll pay attention to the conversations. After dinner we will dissect everything."

Minola listened as if in a dream. This had to be the most bizarre murder investigation in the annals of Interpol. She felt she might as well bring her bit of news into the final arrangements. "I have brought down the name cards. They are all labeled, and I have asked that my easel be brought down. I have a rather large card, which everyone will be asked to sign. I basically drew the restaurant, and jotted down the date and the food selection. It looks like a very large restaurant menu. I thought that would be fun. We may as well make this dinner look as real as possible."

Peter, in a serious tone, said, "I ask that you please stay together around our table. We have shaken the tree; let's see what falls." Peter looked around to see if anyone had any questions. "I think that covers it."

Sally, in a hurry to spend time with her in-laws, succeeded in pushing Robert out the door. She turned back to Minola and Peter. "I am going up to get James and Samantha. We are going sightseeing." She got up, said goodbye, and left.

Minola and Peter lingered over coffee.

"Peter, what are your plans for the day?"

"What I want to do is spend time alone with you, but I have to visit with Lanier. What about you?"

"I'm going to make sure the café is all set, and then I'm going to relax, read, and paint. I have a show that I need to get ready for."

"A show, Miss Grey?"

"Yes, Chief Inspector. I will extend an invitation."

"I would greatly appreciate it. How are you preparing for it? Do you have specific paintings you need to do?"

"No, no theme, just whatever I finish. I had an idea and the gallery owner actually went for it. We are going to present my work, but we will also exhibit the works of some promising students from the school. Plus, I wanted to do a lecture series on current artists. The first night we will have cheese, wine, art, and music. I thought that might make it a bit more special."

"Sounds like a delightful evening, but then any time with you is delightful. Will there be dancing? We haven't danced together yet."

"Maybe we'll dance."

"Good." With a sigh, he got up. "I have to go if I don't want to be late for my meeting." He brushed his lips against her cheek and whispered, "I mean to have you, my love. We will make love soon." He zeroed in on her lips; the kiss was as quick as it was branding. She was his.

Peter needed the walk to clear his head. He was full of Minola. His thoughts on Minola, he suddenly noticed footsteps behind him. Was paranoia setting in or was he being followed? He passed a little jewelry shop, and decided to stop.

He wanted to buy her a vintage Art Deco something. She loved that period in art, as did he. He found nothing in the little shop. He did, however, find his intuition was on target–Mr. Edwards was loitering in the vicinity. Peter walked out and headed for Edwards. "Good morning. Are you shopping as well, Mr. Edwards?" Peter asked politely.

"No, just taking a walk."

"I see, quite. You seem apprehensive. Is there anything you wish to tell me, Mr. Edwards? Now is as good a time as any. If you know something, or suspect someone, I suggest you talk to the Police Nationale, if not to me."

"No, I am just going to the office. We still have some accounting to finish up. Until this murder is solved, it is difficult to run the business properly."

"How so, Mr. Edwards? Isn't the office in the opposite

direction? You were following me, were you not?" Peter, abruptly tired of the conversational fencing, nonetheless needed to know why Edwards was there. It seemed a great length to go to for idle curiosity.

"Yes. Yes, I was. I wanted to know how soon all this is going to end." Edwards seemed troubled and on edge.

"It will end when we catch the murderer. Now, what is happening to the business? Why are you so concerned about the timely apprehension of the murderer?" Peter noticed Edwards' face had turned pale grey. He looked frightened. "Mr. Edwards, I can help if you will let me."

Edwards seemed to mentally shake himself, donned a look of defiance. "The transition is more difficult. Yardleigh was a great speculator in currency. Now it is more challenging."

"Mr. Edwards, please don't take me for a fool. Speculation pretty much ended with the introduction of the Euro currency, and that is when your problems began. Here is my card. Please call me any time if you want to talk to me. Think it through, Mr. Edwards, please." Edwards took the card and put it in his wallet as he turned away. Peter waited a few seconds, then continued to his destination.

He wanted to finish early at the police station, and then pick up a gift for Minola. He wanted his afternoon free to sort everything out. Papers had been piling up as always. Too bad Yardleigh's guests didn't have to check in at the hotel desk, he thought. There would have been a record; instead, the only constant seemed to be Edwards and the hotel staff.

His arrival at the police station was greeted with

anticipation. "Good morning, gentlemen." They didn't give him a chance to settle in before the questions started, "Chief Inspector, what are we to wear?"

They never worried about clothes. This undercover job had really gotten them involved—or was it the gourmet meal that had been promised? Peter was not sure.

"Glad you brought that up. It will be white shirts and black pants for tonight. The hotel has the uniforms all ready for you. I took the liberty of estimating your sizes, and hopefully everyone owns a pair of black shoes. Please arrive an hour early. The hotel staff will give you last-minute instructions. The chef, as promised, will have an outstanding meal for everyone after the formal dinner. It will, however, have to be eaten in the kitchen, and will be accompanied by a meeting. We do not want to arouse any suspicion whatsoever. Sergeants Aubergne and Jouard did an excellent job of cleaning the LeClerque offices. It added nicely to my already high pile of reports. Well done, Gentlemen, thank you."

"Sir, we were happy to add to your pile." Sergeant Aubergne replied with a chuckle.

"Now to our current assignment. We are looking for any information, be it gossip, financial discussions, anything at all, no matter how trivial it may seem."

"Where will you be, sir?" asked Sergeant Jouard, grinning. Peter responded in the same vein. "I'm a guest—Miss Grey's guest to be exact, sitting with the hostess and her friends. The pertinent conversations will be at the other two tables, our table will be serviced by the regular staff."

"Are we to take notes? That would be rather obvious,"

Sergeant Aubergne asked.

Those two make a good team, Peter thought. "No, Sergeant, not precisely. You will have a small order pad with you for drinks, coffee, etc. Use it to jot anything down, but only when you are taking orders. Otherwise, you will have to rely on your memory, so stay sharp."

Another officer asked, "Are we to concentrate on a specific person at our table?"

"Yes, there will be three of you at each table, two waiters and the bus boy. Each waiter will take four people, and will pay attention specifically to that group. The bus boy will try to pay attention to body language, and again the table conversation as a whole, a backup, if you will.

"Pay particular attention to Giselle Armand. She was fond of the victim, and she is an accountant who, until last year, worked on their books. After Yardleigh's death, Edwards asked for her help again.

"Gentlemen, be careful. I don't need to remind you that this person has already killed once. I don't believe you are in eminent danger; however, we cannot discount a trapped man."

Another officer queried, "Chief Inspector, do you really think this will work? Could it be this easy?"

"I do not think this is easy at all. Remember, people are on edge, we have made sure of that. Also bear in mind that alcohol will be served. We hope to loosen a few tongues.

"Just as a reminder, we do not know each other. All right, gentlemen, any other questions?" He wanted everyone comfortable with the task at hand. No one said anything. Peter finished, "If not, I will see you at the hotel. *Bonne*

Chance et merci." He thanked Lanier and his men, and left the station.

Cartier was the jeweler of choice. Once inside, Peter got the proverbial once-over twice…this was Cartier, after all, and a full scan was expected from a sales clerk. He did not find exactly what he went in to find, but a blazing Australian Fire Opal pendant caught his eye. The stone blazed every color in a palette, a square-cut riot of color nestled in a gold frame. Perfect. He bought it instantly, much to the surprise of the saleswoman.

Now he could go back to the hotel and go over more reports. The pendent seemed to burn a hole in his pocket as he anticipated Minola's reaction when she saw it. He looked at his watch, and quickened his pace. He hadn't realized how late it was, already two o'clock.

As he walked into the lobby, headed for coffee, he saw Minola sitting there, talking to a stranger. She looked up, a wide smile lighting her face in welcome.

"Peter, I would like you to meet a friend of Robert's, Steven O'Connell, who will be at tonight's dinner. He delivered some papers for you. Robert wanted you to have them right away."

As Peter sat down, he could see Steven was interested in Minola. Steven and Minola had met before, and the stranger watched every move Minola made. Peter accepted the envelope and thanked him for the delivery.

Steven indicated he had a meeting scheduled close by, so it was not an effort, but he had to leave to make his meeting. He got up and shook Peter's hand, gave Minola a warm hug, and left.

Minola, glad to see Peter, gave him another heart-melting smile. She ordered coffee and something to eat for him, saying, "I'll bet you haven't eaten since breakfast. How did the meeting go?"

"You are right, I haven't. The meeting went well. The men are looking forward to the assignment or, more likely, to the meal. How well do you know this Steven O'Connell?" he demanded grimly.

Surprised at the tone of his voice, she answered, "I met him several times back home. He and Robert have known each other a long time. He is an acquaintance."

"An acquaintance who seems very interested in you," Peter continued in the same vein.

"You just met the man. How can you say that?"

"I saw him looking at you."

"I don't know what to say, except you are imagining things. We've seen each other socially, and attended some of the same functions, that's all. Just in case you did not know, I haven't dated much. For the most part, it seemed like a waste of time."

"Why a waste of time?" He was sure he had not imagined things. He knew that look. He looked the same every time he was with her. Peter gritted his teeth, so jealous he wasn't even sure what he was eating.

"I really don't know. There wasn't any depth to the relationships. I do like my own company, so I don't feel it necessary to be continuously surrounded by people. I don't believe in casual sex. I am not interested in sports to any great extent, nor are many men fond of museums, theater, and the like. I never have felt the need to have a man in my life just to have a man in my life, so there didn't seem to be any point in wasting time, theirs or mine. The one time I really ventured out was a total disaster."

"That seems very straightforward. How did you feel about our date?" Peter spoke in earnest. He needed to know how she had felt about their time together.

"Peter, I…" Minola didn't get to finish, as Sally seemed to appear out of nowhere with James and Samantha lagging behind her. Peter knew he was *seriously* going to have to have a talk with Sally. Her timing was appalling.

"I thought I would find you here." Sally, very excited, sat down, inviting James and Samantha to do the same. She proceeded to tell them all about her day playing tour guide in Paris. They had done some serious shopping, and were exhausted. Peter listened for a while, then excused himself, saying he had the new reports to go over.

His glance lingered briefly on Minola before he walked out. Minola looked at Peter's grim face, and knew she needed to answer his question privately, as soon as was possible. After a few minutes, Minola made her excuses and went in search of Peter. She knocked on his door.

He answered, surprised to see her, and asked her to come in. No tie, sleeves rolled up, he was hard at work. The desk light was on, and papers were strewn all over. It looked like he was comparing ledgers with the reports that Steven had delivered. Behind all the papers was her drawing, facing his bed. He asked if everything was all right.

"Peter, this might be presumptuous of me, but I wanted to let you know that I had a terrific time on our date. I was talking about my experiences in general. It had absolutely nothing to do with any of the time we have spent together."

They were standing very close. Peter reluctantly moved away, went over to his coat pocket, and extricated the small, beautifully wrapped box. He gave it to her, and asked her to open it.

"Peter, I can't." She recognized the Cartier wrapping paper.

"Yes, you can. Please open the box," he exclaimed.

Minola opened the box and gasped. She looked up at him. "Peter, I can't accept such an expensive gift."

"At the risk of repeating myself, yes, you can, and you will. I wanted to get you something that had to do with art, and you seem to have all the supplies you need. Besides, I wanted to get you something that will last and will always remind you of me. Pretty selfish, I admit, but there it is. This stone has a beautiful range of colors–when I saw it, I knew it was perfect for you."

Minola kept staring at Peter as he talked. He was a cop, living on a cop's salary, yet how could she refuse? She reached up, drew his head to her, and gave him a long, deep, lingering kiss, which he passionately returned.

"Peter, this is too extravagant. I don't need…"

"Don't even think of refusing." He still held her, unwilling ton let go.

"Peter, I don't want to be rude. You paid a Cartier price for this. I can't accept that. You are a policeman. I don't need…" She was amazed at the thought that accompanied this gift, but she couldn't accept it.

"Damn it, Minola. If I couldn't afford it, I wouldn't have

bought it," he barked.

"Why, Peter?"

"Why what?" he demanded.

"Why did you buy it?" she asked gently.

"I bought it because it reminded me of you. I bought it because I wanted you to wear something that I gave you. I bought it because, every time you wear it, there will be a part of me on your body."

Her eyes were damp with unshed tears. "Peter, I am sorry. I didn't want you to feel you had to buy me something. The quid pro quo routine…I don't believe in it."

"Neither do I, and I am done with this conversation. You will keep the necklace." He kissed her, plundering and bruising her lips in anger and pain.

She felt both, and responded with tenderness. It was his undoing. In response, he softened the kiss. He cupped her face in his hands and seduced her with passionate kisses that lingered on her mouth. He could taste her sweetness through her swollen, red lips. "I'm sorry I hurt you. Forgive me," he whispered as he ran his finger over her mouth.

"You have nothing to apologize for, except maybe for turning my knees to jelly." Her hands weren't quite…steady and she trembled. The power he had over her terrified her. "Peter, thank you for the pendant," she said.

"I turn your knees to jelly? I won't discuss what you do to me, and that, Miss Grey, is a very good beginning. We are making progress." He tried to lighten the tension between them. "Thank you for accepting it." He relaxed against her, and this time he initiated the embrace. Feeling her response, he deepened the kiss.

His senses reeled as she opened herself to his embrace. He felt her arousal. When Peter finally released her, he shook. *I need to love her. I need to be inside her. Bloody hell, what is happening to me?* His emotional and physical need for her was devastating.

"Can you help me to put the pendant on?" Minola needed a distraction, but soon realized it was the wrong thing to ask. She felt his fingers on her neck and shivered at his touch.

He brushed her hair aside, closed the clasp, and left a trail of feather kisses on the back of her neck. He turned her around, took her in his arms, and held her.

"I should get going. I still need to change." She reached up to caress his cheek. He turned his head, dropping light erotic kisses over her wrist.

Suddenly, there was a knock on the door and Sally walked in. Suitcase in hand, she asked for Minola. She had knocked on Minola's door, when there was no answer, she decided to try Peter. She needed advice on what to wear. She looked at Minola, noticed the opal pendant, and whistled. "Peter, you have excellent taste in jewelry, and obviously know Minola well. It's gorgeous."

As Minola shooed Sally out the door, Peter whispered that he would pick her up at seven. He pressed her lips to his, caressing her mouth. She felt his lips touch hers like a whisper. She shivered.

Once in her room, Minola started to dress for dinner. Sally, wanting details, followed her into the bedroom. "Minola, he is the one. He adores you."

"Yes, he is the one," replied Minola. "However, you are

forgetting the gorgeous Alexis. He has a long history with her, and she is both stunning and available."

"Don't be silly, it's you he wants," Sally said firmly, excited, because one look at Minola's radiant face told her all she needed to know.

The process of getting ready was always slow for Sally...she could not decide what to wear, the peach dress purchased earlier notwithstanding. That is where her friend came in handy. They went through the suitcase, and finally found all the accessories, but which dress still remained a question mark. It had to coordinate with the items already selected. This backwards process worked for Sally, and only Sally.

Minola knew exactly what she was going to wear. She chose a long, flowing, black chiffon dress especially made for her by a local seamstress, based on Minola's design. It had a low-cut front, see-through long sleeves and back, and a slit in the front that reached to just above the knee. Peter's opal would be a striking contrast to the stark dress. Minola was nearly ready.

Finally, her dress selected, with suitcase in tow, Sally returned to her room to wait for Robert.

Left alone, Minola decided on minimal make-up. With a few minutes to spare she picked up the pad full of drawings of Peter, and looked through it, trying to decide which sketch to turn into a full portrait. Hearing a knock, she left the pad on the table, and went to answer the door. Peter, looking very elegant in a tux, greeted her. *How am I going to walk away from him when Alexis takes him back?*

Is one night better with him than nothing at all? I know he wants me.

Minola took Peter's breath away. Her dress was distinctive, and it fit her perfectly. He noticed her only piece of jewelry was the opal around her neck.

She asked him to come in, and told him he looked marvelous. Peter returned the compliment. He took her in his arms, kissed her. "Are you ready for another adventure?"

"Tonight, I am ready for anything that comes my way," she replied, thinking about one night with him.

Peter gave her a long steady look and asked, "Are you ready to accept me in your life?" Afraid she was going to say no, he quickly asked her to think about it.

She didn't hesitate. "Peter, in case you have not noticed, you already are in my life. I would not have accepted your remarkable gift otherwise." The embrace following that declaration left them both winded. The kiss was an exploration of their senses. He followed the outline of her mouth with his tongue, deepened the kiss, and felt her melt against him. He lifted his head, kissed the tip of her nose, and held her close. Kisses, however intense, were no longer enough–he wanted more. Needing to stop and concentrate on something other than the woman he held in his arms before he lost what little control he still possessed, he glanced at the table and noticed his likeness on her sketch pad.

"May I look at these?" he asked.

"I know they are sketches of you, and you have every right to see them, but right now I am not ready. I will be more than willing to share them with you, but not yet. I can't explain it further." She felt the drawings revealed her feelings for Peter. She had sketched him with a great deal of intimacy she did not want to justify, afraid he would see through it. Above all, she did not want him to feel obligated. She loved him, but was not sure he returned the sentiment. She knew he wanted her, but love? She needed and wanted more. *Why was I so careless?*

"Minola, we are not drifting into some sort of an arrangement. This is real, very real, at least for me. We need to talk after this mess is finished. In the meantime, I will respect your wishes." He looked again at the exposed drawing, at the passion, and recognized his own feelings displayed on the sketch. "I've seen enough of your work to know that you honestly express what you see. My emotions are reflected in those sketches, not yours."

Stunned that he so quickly understood her reasons and fears, and grateful he did not try to influence her in any way, she thanked him, closed the pad, and walked back to him. She raised her hands, caressed his cheek, and gently kissed him.

"Peter, I apologize for having made a mess of this evening, I promise we will talk about the drawings soon. They are just brief sketches I've done of you."

"You haven't made a mess of anything. I am still your date for the evening, and I have no intention of going anywhere. I am afraid you are stuck with me. I'll wait until you are ready." He held her tightly, afraid she would somehow slip away from him.

A knock on the door revealed an animated Sally and Robert, ready for their venture in subterfuge. Peter and Minola regained their composure, and the foursome went downstairs together, anticipating a break in the investigation and eager to enjoy the anniversary dinner.

Chapter 14

The alcove where the dinner was being held was ready, the setting perfection in its simplicity. The lights were dimmed, and the glow of candles cast wonderful shadows on the tables and walls of the intimate room. The menu cards were neatly held in place on tiny easels. It was a romantic, elegant presentation. The restaurant staff had done an outstanding job. The flower arrangements were colorful, perfect bouquets reflecting the joyous occasion being celebrated tonight. Even though there was an ulterior motive, this was still Sally and Robert's anniversary party.

The huge card Minola had done added to the ambiance, since it was displayed on one of Minola's full easels as a work of art. It gave an eclectic feel to the decor.

In the lobby, the guests milled around, drinking cocktails and eating the appetizers being passed around by the police 'waiters'. Some guests greeted each other as old friends, while others introduced themselves without waiting for Robert and Sally to do so.

The most popular spot appeared to be the little bar area set up in the lobby right outside the restaurant–secluded, charming, and very unobtrusive.

It was a perfect observation area, Minola decided. She could see everyone who entered in their Parisian finery.

Casting an oblique glance, she noticed Mr. LeClerque was a frequent visitor to the bar. He was flawlessly dressed, right down to the immense tie tack that caught Minola's eye. It was an unusual piece that would fit right in with Erte's style. Colorful precious and semiprecious stones arranged to look like the Winged Victory, Art Deco style.

The police, ever vigilant, served the appetizers. Minola hoped tonight would be the turning point in the investigation. Peter, doing his bit as he casually observed interactions between the guests, so far couldn't find anything out of the ordinary.

Minola thoroughly disliked 'cocktail intermissions', as she termed them. She functioned much better in smaller circles. Peter's arm around her waist offered the support she needed, as if he sensed her discomfort.

So far, everything was going well. It appeared to be a very amiable gathering. While a few trips were made to the restrooms, guests generally stayed within the serving area. No one behaved atypically. Peter thought he had seen Edwards walking out of the main restaurant, but he seemed to have disappeared almost immediately. Their area was secluded and screened in the corner, while the rest of the restaurant was open for business as usual.

Once everyone was seated, Sally introduced James and Samantha as they walked into the room. This little surprise made it much more real, adding to the celebration. A stunned Robert stood up, gave Sally a kiss, and walked over to his brother and sister-in-law to welcome them to Paris.

Minola toasted the couple and asked everyone to sign the anniversary card. Since it was such an unusual card, she was asked where she got it. When she told them, everyone looked down at their menu cards and made the connection. Minola let everyone know the cards were theirs to keep, if they wished to do so.

The menus were read and carefully set aside as conversations flowed; the servers started their work in earnest. Peter watched the men operate. They were doing an excellent job—one could not tell them from the regular staff.

James and Samantha, not yet aware of the more ominous reason for this dinner, talked about their day touring Paris.

Sally, sitting next to Minola, flashed her right hand. A new and quite sizable diamond adorned her finger, Robert's gift to his wife. Minola turned and hugged her best friend. "Sally, it is absolutely stunning. Robert did really well." They hugged again. Sitting on the other side of Minola, Peter wondered at this great friendship between the two women.

Sally again told Peter that Minola's pendant was incredible, and it looked beautiful on her.

Peter's gaze lingered on Minola. He wholeheartedly agreed. Although for Peter this was a working dinner, he had time to observe Minola, acutely aware of her every move and the quiet, elegant way she handled the guests. He sensed she was uncomfortable in large crowds, yet she was able to overcome her shyness and make everyone feel welcome and part of this celebration.

The general chatter at their table continued. James and Samantha were overjoyed to be in Paris. Sally had taken very good care of them while hiding them from Robert.

James was ecstatic about the incredible variety of French architecture, especially the juxtaposition of the great Renaissance Louvre structure and I.M. Pei's Pyramid, the main entrance to the renowned museum. "I can't identify the style of the Pompidou Center. Ultramodern, future modern, I don't know. It is what it is, well worth a visit, though."

They discussed the must-see Eiffel Tower, as well as the bookstalls along the Seine, truly a Parisian institution. The quais are lined with all sorts of books from antique comic books to current literature to old manuscripts.

Minola, with a faraway look in her eyes, stated, "The stalls evoke a romantic familiarity along the Seine in the evening hours. Yet, a stroll along the quais in the early morning presents a desolate view of closed and locked stalls. Paris has yet to awaken, but that never stops romantic couples from strolling along the Seine, before turbulent sightseers fill the area, that is. It is perfect there, morning, noon, and night," Minola quietly concluded.

Peter leaned over to whisper, "Miss Grey, would you join me tomorrow morning for breakfast and a leisurely stroll down the quais?"

"Chief Inspector, I would be delighted," she replied. Minola thought back to the Seine. The emergence of tourists signaled a new day for the stalls. One by one they would open and the articles of choice would be set out, hung up, and arranged any which way, ready for business. This awakening occurred at various times in the morning and lasted till late evening. There were no specific hours, one by one they would open, and one by one they would close. She was glad that James got to see this Parisian institution both in the morning and at night, and delighted she would get an opportunity to do the same with Peter.

While James raved about buildings, books, and stalls, the women made a pact to go out on the town tomorrow. Later, everyone would meet for dinner. Peter was, of course, included in all these decisions.

The staff efficiently worked the tables, the men taking down various written orders. After the main entrée, there was a break between dessert and the obligatory but delectable cheese selection. Aperitifs were served in the bar area. Again, the guests milled around, going to the restrooms, to the bar, or back to their tables. Chef Etienne, in his splendid high toque, greeted everyone as he asked if the meal was cooked to their satisfaction. He actually received an ovation, and took several bows. Etienne was a ham at heart.

Giselle Armand ventured over to Minola to thank her for a most remarkable invitation; Minola, in turn, introduced her to everyone at their table. Giselle offered Sally a package rolled up in plain brown paper. Sally untied the ribbon, revealing a view of Notre Dame from the little café where they had first met. Stunned, Sally hugged the colorful woman. Robert shook her hand and thanked her for the thoughtful gift. Giselle complimented Minola on her efforts, saying it was most unusual, and asked if Peter was her young man.

Peter, amused, looked at Minola, and waited for her reply.

Blushing, she faced him squarely and asked, "Are you my young man?"

Unequivocally he stated, "Yes, I am yours completely, body and soul."

Sally let out a jubilant "Yes."

Peter laughed out loud.

Minola whispered in his ear; "Let's discuss this body and soul part."

Peter chuckled and muttered, "Anytime. I am all yours, my love."

Giselle returned to her table as the other guests were being ushered back for dessert, cheese, and coffee. Everyone eagerly complied with this request, it seemed as if no one wanted to miss anything. From that perspective, the evening was a monumental success, although whether anyone had said anything of interest to the murder investigation had yet to be determined.

Minola went to the bar, where she ordered Chambord, her favorite liqueur. As she watched a couple enter the lobby, she felt a big gust of wind hit her face. The weather had turned.

Mr. LeClerque, looking grim, had returned to the bar. The blustery wind was so strong that it blew his tie right up into his face. Jerkily, with shaking hands, he quickly put his hand over the tie and pulled it back into place. *He is watching me. What on earth for?* As she walked back to her group, she acknowledged his glare with a tentative smile.

The kitchen was a hub of activity, and not just with food preparation. Sergeant Welsey sat at a table collecting assorted bits of information. He sorted the pieces of paper sporadically presented to him; each slip marked and identified. Periodically, he checked the lobby to look for anything out of the ordinary, anyone out of place.

During one particular turn, he walked into the men's room and found a body. Edwards was beyond help. Another damn body and nothing else. The proximity of the body to the urinal indicated that the urinal had been used as a murder weapon.

The sergeant closed the door behind him and summoned another cop to stand watch. "Absolutely no one may enter the lavatory. I am going to get help."

The officer tacked a sign on the door indicating the bathroom was out of order, and the door was locked. The sergeant pocketed the key, and went in search of Peter.

Forensics and the crime lab group were called as the sergeant reached Peter and urgently whispered in his ear. Peter excused himself from the table and went over to the main restaurant, talked to the maitre'd, and asked that no one leave, there had been an accident.

Peter returned to his table and calmly said, "Edwards is dead. Please do not leave the table. The police will be here soon. I will make a general announcement. I was afraid of this, the bloody fool. What a useless loss of life."

"Peter, I assume it was not an accident. Was it because of this dinner?" Minola was visibly distressed at this turn of events.

"No, love, it was not. He had a chance to talk to me. Instead, he played his own game and lost." Peter looked at James and Samantha, saw the confusion on their faces, and turned to Robert and Sally. "I think you should tell them what is going on. If anyone needs to go to the bathroom, go to your rooms, don't go alone, and let the police know before you leave."

Sergeant Welsey by his side, Peter stood up and asked for everyone's attention. "Ladies and gentlemen, I am Miss Grey's guest, but I am also a police officer with Interpol. There was an accident in the men's bathroom. I'm going to ask you all to remain seated. Don't leave this room until the police are finished with their questions."

The room stilled completely for a brief moment. Then, almost simultaneously, a clatter of voices drowned out everything else, all requesting information.

Peter was as honest as he could afford to be. "At this stage, we simply don't have many details. A hotel guest had an accident. Please be patient. I'll ask the staff to bring in more coffee, and anything else you may require. We will work as quickly as possible." He turned to face Minola, and embraced her. "Stay with the group, please. It will be safer." He caressed her cheek, and quickly walked out into the lobby.

The sergeant had never witnessed such a public display of affection from Peter. He had known him a long time, had seen him with women, and realized this one was different. He eyed Minola, who returned his gaze openly and candidly. The sergeant, sized her up, seemed satisfied. He briefly nodded, turned, and followed Peter.

Minola looked around the tables. Giselle was visibly upset. There was an air of excitement in the room, but everyone behaved above suspicion. At her own table, Robert and Sally were taking turns explaining everything to James and Samantha. Minola knew they were in for another interrogation, and she was sure this time the murderer was one of their guests.

The kitchen became the point of operation. Peter asked the police servers to stay in character for a little bit longer, and to go ahead and serve coffee, dessert, and fruit, whatever was available to keep the guests quiet and content for as long as possible. He wanted them to continue to eavesdrop on all the conversations.

Etienne had been asked to feed the working policemen in shifts. Peter wanted them fed, but alert, so he asked the regular staff to have coffee available. It was going to be a long night. The staff willingly complied. During the training period they'd gotten to know the officers, and were eager to make things as easy for them as possible.

Peter and Sergeant Welsey returned to the men's room so Peter could view the crime scene. The skin on Edwards's neck had not been broken; it looked like his head had been bashed against the urinal.

If there had been a struggle, it was minimal. "Sergeant, look at Edwards' knuckles, they are red, but not bloodied. He must have been shoved hard enough against the urinal to cause whiplash, and his neck probably snapped." Peter looked more closely at the body under the urinal, and a blaze of tiny colorful specks caught his eye. "What the hell are those? Sergeant, make sure these are tagged. They are small and might be missed. No ring on fingers, no cuff links, no damaged jewelry anywhere."

"Yes, sir."

"This killing doesn't look planned. More of a crime of opportunity." Peter felt they had finally gotten a break.

Unfortunately, it cost another life. With this murder, they had a tidy list of suspects to work with. He ruled nothing out, as it was too early to make snap decisions. They left the room, relocked the door, and Peter returned to his table while the Sergeant waited in the lobby for the arrival of the police.

Minola asked if there was anything new. He gripped her hand for comfort and answered, "No, other than one of our guests is a murderer. While we wait for the police, our crew is staying undercover for a bit longer."

"Peter, are you sure it's one of our guests?" Robert wanted confirmation.

"I'm afraid so. We observed all arrivals, their destinations, and departures."

"Are you sure it wasn't an accident?"

"No, love. I'm sorry, but it was not. One hit on the head maybe, but not two. I suspect his death was caused by the second blow—there are signs on his hands of a scuffle. He most likely was meeting someone. It had to be one of our guests." He didn't release his hold on her hand.

"How does a person who just committed a murder act normally, as if nothing had happened? I was watching everyone. It all looked ordinary, no one behaved erratically."

"I wish I could answer that. This was a crime of opportunity, and most likely survival. I am not a criminalist or a profiler, but from experience I think it was committed by an individual who feels superior to all others, whose existence is more important in relation to others." Peter saw the despair in her eyes. He could offer nothing but a touch.

An eerie silence pervaded the room as Lanier walked over to Peter and asked to speak with him outside.

The forensic and crime teams had arrived. Peter gave them the washroom key. The medical examiner inspected the body, and knew better than to ask if anything had been moved. Peter's original assessment had been correct. Besides minor bruises, two blows had been delivered to the head. One knocked him out, the second one finished him off.

After the scene had been taped and photographed from every angle, the body was removed to the morgue. Every piece of scrap was bagged and labeled for microscopic evaluation, along with the clothes the victim wore. The drain in the toilet was secured and examined. The sparkling specks were carefully collected.

The questions began in earnest. Every guest was asked to account for his or her time, including bathroom breaks, visits to the lobby, time of arrival, and any possible connection to Edwards, real or imagined. This was the tedious part of the routine, but one that had to be followed with meticulous attention to detail.

A man, wearing a brown suit obviously too big for his body, shuffled into the room and lazily surveyed the group. He looked as if his sleep had been interrupted, but his appearance was deceptive. He was a shrewd, wily cop, easily underestimated.

He sauntered to the table where Giselle Armand sat and introduced himself. "*Bon soir*, Madame, Messieurs. *Je m'appelle Gautier*." He changed to English. "I am with the Police Nationale." He did not indicate his rank. He was a

Captain, but preferred to remain somewhat anonymous. This was one of his many quirks. He was simply known as Gautier.

He flashed a badge, put it back in his pocket, then took out an old, worn, rumpled pad of paper. "You have been told of an unfortunate accident that occurred here earlier this evening. It is my sad duty to question everyone's whereabouts." He heard a sharp intake of breath, but didn't know where it came from. Since Giselle Armand looked the most distressed, he started with her. If she was surprised he knew her name, she didn't let on. "Madame Armand, can you tell me exactly when and how often you went to the lobby during this event?"

"Certainly…er…Monsieur Gautier. I went to the bar earlier, before we sat down, and again during the break. I also went to the ladies' bathroom sometime before the main course was served."

"Did you notice anything unusual?" he asked quietly.

"No, I didn't. I saw a friend I know coming out of the restaurant and I said 'good evening' to him, but I didn't see anything else, nor did I recognize anyone else. What kind of accident? It must have been serious." Giselle was obviously shaken.

"Who was your friend?"

"Mr. Edwards."

"How did you meet him?"

"He was an assistant to Lord Yardleigh. Lord Yardleigh and I were friends. What type of accident? What happened?" She asked again.

Gautier did not respond, but continued the tiresome by-the-book questions.

The little dining room was a den of activity. One officer was assigned to each table, and the questions were relentless. Even though Peter already had the information, duplication was needed to establish the official investigation.

Peter's table wasn't safe from the police; however, it had a gentler tone. Sergeant Welsey, who had finished his duties in the kitchen, took his turn in the dining room at Minola's table. He needed to ask something, so he chose the most common question of all. "Miss Grey, did you notice anything out of the ordinary this evening, anyone behaving differently since their arrival?"

"No, sergeant. That's just it. Everything and everyone seemed normal. We walked around and tried to meet as many guests as possible, but I wouldn't be able to notice a different behavior pattern since I don't know these people. I can't even tell you how alcohol affects them."

Robert told Sergeant Welsey to question the bartender. "He would be able to observe a change in behavior. Bartenders are really very discerning."

"Very good, Mr. Jones. We have already spoken to the bartender, and he mentioned a few guests were drinking rather heavily."

Sally, not about to be left out, asked a question. "Sergeant, did anyone appear disheveled, or unkempt? Did the bartender notice anything like that?"

"No, Mrs. Jones, he did not. But I thought I was supposed be asking the questions?"

Peter approached and asked how things were going.

The Sergeant, tongue in cheek, explained that he had answered all their questions to the best of his ability. Peter smiled and asked the group to give the Sergeant a break, then he filled them in on the latest developments.

"We have all the information we need for right now, and everyone will be released soon along with a warning not to leave town. Someone is running scared. Edwards was seriously involved; my guess is he panicked and became vulnerable, or else he wanted a bigger piece of the pie and became a liability. Either way, he became expendable."

Peter's focus shifted to Minola. Her face seemed pale and drawn. He wanted to insulate her from this business, but he could not. Nor, he suspected, would she want him to. This was his world. She knew that, and hopefully she accepted it. Peter gently touched her shoulder, just to let her know he was there. He looked around the room and casually glanced at every guest, but nothing tangible stood out.

The hotel was buzzing with the latest disaster; word had got out that it was murder. The lobby, usually a quiet and contemplative area, was enveloped in whispers.

The guests at the restaurant behaved with decorum. No one objected to giving up their name, address, or phone number. Most had indicated the exceptional food as reason for the visit. Were it not for the murder, this would have been a wonderful accolade for Etienne.

Chapter 15

After being released by the police, Sally and her retinue went up to her room. Minola agreed to join them later, but first she needed to catch her breath in her own surroundings. Somehow, she felt responsible–if she had not insisted on this dinner, Edwards would still be alive.

Peter recognized her despair and wanted to tell her again it wasn't her fault. He asked for her room key from the front desk, told the Sergeant where he could be found if needed, and went upstairs.

Standing by the window, he could tell she'd been crying when she turned to face him.

"Minola, I don't want you here alone. It was *not* your fault. Please, love, go see Sally." He took her in his arms and held her; after a few minutes, he walked her out to join the others.

Upon arrival, he was assaulted by a barrage of questions.

"Peter, how could this have happened? There were police everywhere." Robert was the first to voice his question.

"This appears to have been a crime of opportunity. We really don't know anything yet. We have narrowed down the time of death. I saw him before everyone sat down to eat."

Peter listened to the continuing discussion while James and Samantha observed in silence, shocked at the depth of the tragedy in which family and friends were involved however peripherally.

Robert insisted the answers were in the books, and that they were cooked.

"So you keep telling me. I got firsts in math, and I am confused." Peter said irritably. "We haven't really had much time to investigate this scheme; Yardleigh was eliminated fairly soon after contacting us."

"Okay, I'll try to explain in sentences of one syllable or less," Robert smiled. "The currency exchange markets operate like a barter system. They might as well be trading colored chips."

"All right, I follow you so far. There does not have to be an exchange of goods, just pure currency. I do understand the basics of money laundering. It is our bread and butter. This isn't the sort of business you do with people you don't trust or don't think you can control."

"That is certain. Anyway, suppose Yardleigh is contacted by someone he knows has money to launder. Why or how it became dirty doesn't really matter, it might be profits from drugs, gambling, fencing operations, prostitution, whatever. You are a cop, so you know the endless possibilities. They pass the cash to Yardleigh who exchanges the cash, dirty money for clean money at a deep discount. With fluctuating exchange rates, you don't get back the same number of dollars you started with; sometimes you get more, sometimes you get less. What gave this away is Yardleigh's investors didn't seem to mind losing 20 or 30 percent. He kept getting money from them and returning money to them, always within a short period of time, and always a quarter less than what they gave him. Most legitimate investors frown on heavy losses."

"Yardleigh just kept records of all these transactions so you could follow them. We didn't find anything, and we had experts go through the books," Peter scowled.

"Well, not exactly. I might not have caught on if he hadn't used four sets of homophonic names as codes for companies, and the money almost always went through another firm first: LeClerque. Remember the codes Minola saw in the little black book she found in his office?"

"What homophonic names? I think I am getting a migraine."

"You know, words with a common syllable; for example, Samsung, Samsonite, etc. I have everything documented for you. It makes sense. When you look at the sums involved, you have motive enough for several murders."

"Robert, how could an accounting firm allow such practices? You have just pointed a finger directly at the LeClerque firm. How do we prove it?" Sally asked, looking confused.

Robert replied, "That my dear, will be a bit more difficult and is best left to the able hands of the police. Most likely, papers have been destroyed. Besides, the man sitting next to Giselle Armand at dinner did not strike me as the careless type. His tracks must be well covered. Peter, just a thought…Giselle Armand is an accountant. Why not talk to her again, alone? Something may surface."

He nodded in agreement. "Everyone will be interviewed at least once more. I've a strange feeling I have missed something this evening, but I can't quite put my finger on it."

No one wanted to break up the discussion until Peter said, "I believe we are all staying here in the hotel. The best thing to do under the circumstances is to go to our respective rooms. Get some sleep. It has been a difficult evening. I need to go back downstairs." He looked around to see tired faces nodding in agreement.

Sally made sure they could all meet tomorrow morning for breakfast downstairs, an attempt to keep some semblance of normalcy.

Looking at Minola, Peter fully realized the toll the evening had taken. Her job was painting–making beautiful pictures, vital, alive faces on canvas–not murders. How could she ever understand his world?

Scrutinizing her profile, he had his doubts as he walked with her back to her room. "Get some sleep, love, it does get better." He stood very close to her. Without too much effort he knew he could reach out and love her, but decided against it. She was too vulnerable.

"It was my fault. I never should have planned the dinner. What hubris to think I could get involved and help. I know nothing about solving crime. Reading mystery novels, for God's sake, is the extent of my knowledge. I am just as culpable as the murderer; a man was killed because I interfered."

He tasted her bitterness, and had to try to remove it, explaining, "No, Minola, you are not at fault. You had nothing to do with Edwards' death. If he had not died here, today, he would have been killed somewhere else. Please believe me, he became a liability to himself."

"Would you do me a favor? Could you spend the night on the couch here? I don't want to be alone. If you have a bad back or anything, I can sleep on the couch and you can have the bed."

She looked at him so earnestly that he chuckled–the first and only sound of laughter from him since the murder.

He replied, as earnestly as she had asked, "No, I don't have a bad back or anything. It will be my pleasure to sleep on the sofa. I will call housekeeping and order extra bedding. That will certainly set tongues wagging quickly. Minola, I do need to go downstairs and meet with the men. Call Sally and ask her to keep you company till I get back. I won't be gone long, I promise. Thank you." He turned to leave.

Minola stopped him by putting her hand on his arm. "Why 'thank you'? I am the one who asked you to stay."

He briefly touched her hand and replied, "For trusting me. Call Sally, I'll wait till she gets here."

As Minola reached for the phone, there was a knock on the door. She opened the door to Alexis Yardleigh, shocking Minola to silence.

Peter stood, dumbfounded. Alexis entered without invitation. She smiled when she reached Peter and kissed him possessively, running her tongue over his closed lips. "Hmm…He is good in bed, isn't he?" she smiled provocatively.

At first, Peter was too stunned to react. He did not reach

out to her nor touch her, but neither did he move away from her. When he saw Minola's face drain of color, he pushed Alexis away from him, took her arm, and forcibly dragged her out into the hall.

"What the hell are you doing?" he demanded, as he grabbed the door and slammed it shut behind him, his knuckles white.

"Peter, how are you? They told me you were upstairs visiting Miss Grey. I can see that you are."

He reached for his phone and dialed Sergeant Welsey, asking him to come upstairs.

"What the hell are you doing here?"

"The police called and told me of Edwards' death, so I decided to come and see you. I need you. We were..."

Peter, livid, cut her off. Alexis' possessive greeting had done little to settle Minola's fears of betrayal—one look at her anguished face told him as much. *Damn it to hell. Damn, damn, damn. She thinks I deceived her too. How the hell am I going to explain this?*

Both his hands now clenched, his eyes icy in anger, Peter said. "Damn you, we have no future. We have nothing."

Peripherally, Peter heard the elevator doors open. In a cold flat monotone, Peter added, "Have you finished? I certainly have. There is nothing to be gained here, Alexis. If you have any information, go downstairs, find a cop, and tell him what you have. You and I are finished here. Do not *ever* attempt another stunt like this." Peter looked up, saw the Sergeant, and asked him to escort Alexis Yardleigh downstairs.

Minola misunderstood everything. *I can never compete against that woman.* She stood in the middle of the room, facing the closed door. As if in a trance, she vaguely heard it open. Peter came back in alone. Still in a daze, she reached out and touched his arm to offer her support.

He recoiled as if something had hit him. Still furious at Alexis, Minola's touch was like an electric current going through him. It was so unexpected. Minola snatched back her hand. "I'm sorry," she whispered.

Peter, recalled from his furious thought, realized what he had done, but it was too late. Minola had completely closed in on herself. "Minola, forgive me. I should have told you I didn't expect you to reach out to me just now," his anger still evident. "Please understand I…." He reached out to her, just as there was another knock. "Bloody hell," he ground out.

Sally stood at the door. Buoyant as ever and no longer tired, she wondered if Minola wanted some company and a cup of coffee.

Peter needed to be downstairs. He didn't want to leave Minola right now, but he had no choice. He turned to her and murmured, "Minola, please, we need to talk. I will be back later, and I have every intention of sleeping on that couch tonight."

"Peter, you don't have to say anything to me. I really do understand. She is a beautiful woman, and she is free."

He realized what she was trying to tell him, but she was so bloody wrong. If he told her now that she meant the world to him, she wouldn't believe him.

"I will be back as soon as we are finished." Turning

toward Sally, he added, "Stay with her till I get back, please." He turned and walked out of the room.

Dejected, Minola sat on her bed. Desolate, guilty over the death of Edwards, and reeling from her sudden loss of Peter, she felt empty.

Whenever Minola became stressed or depressed, she painted, she drew, and she hid in her art. *I'm going to paint a formal portrait of Peter. It will be my memory, my own gate of hell.* Sally knew something was wrong, but understood her friend well enough to wait.

Minola rose, got a sketchpad, and began to draw Peter and the dinner guests. Sally watched as the tables and various guests appeared on the paper. Minola frowned and seemed puzzled, momentarily.

Sally quietly told Minola Robert was staying in Paris for an indefinite time. "I am staying with him. I guess that means I am staying with you too."

Upon hearing the news, Minola cheered up a little. She would at least have her friend for comfort.

Sally got up off the couch, went to the phone, and ordered coffee. Minola intently continued drawing. By the time room service arrived, she was finished. Looking at the sketches, she asked, "Do you see anything wrong here? Something is missing."

Sipping her coffee, Sally considered the drawing, but couldn't find anything out of the ordinary. "What do you mean, something is missing? You have everyone drawn to perfection. What are you looking for?"

"I don't know, I just remember staring at Giselle's table after the last break. Something was not right. I thought if I drew it, it would come back to me."

"I think you should talk to Peter. Maybe you noticed something or someone. Think. What was it? Did someone leave the table? Anything at all unusual, torn shirt, anything?"

"I am thinking. I just can't put my finger on it." She set the pad down and reached for the brew. "That coffee looks wonderful. I need to get away from this. Let's talk about your stay in Paris."

"Show me what you are working on. That always brings you out of a funk."

"I have a couple completed pieces for the upcoming show, and a few unfinished pieces. I am really nervous. I've never exhibited on this scale before, and in Paris."

A knock on the door announced Housekeeping. Minola took the bedding, thanked the woman, and set it on the couch. Sally took one look, laughed, and said, "Peter spending the night on the couch?"

Minola hardly gave Sally a chance to finish her sentence before she fired back. "Yes, I asked him to stay, and he graciously consented."

"Minola, I get the feeling he would graciously consent to anything you ask of him."

"I don't think so. We're just friends," she said sadly.

"I've seen him looking at you, and I don't see 'just friends'. I've seen you looking at him, and I see so much more. Remember me? I'm your best friend, and I know you. So, what happened tonight?"

"He was, and probably still wants to be, involved with Alexis Yardleigh. Remember her, the stunning woman in the café? I don't want to talk about it right now. Do me a favor. Give me your impressions of the dinner. Let's make a list and see if anything jogs our memories, from beginning to end."

"We can do that. Get a pad of paper and let's get to work. This is a good idea, but first you need to tell me more about the gorgeous widow Yardleigh. Why are you worried about her?"

"Not much more to tell. They were engaged to be married. She threw him over for the rich Lord Yardleigh, and now she wants him back. She was here. He wants her back, end of story. I really don't want to talk about it."

"Minola, you are wrong. She may want him back, but he has eyes only for you. He cares about you."

"I don't think Peter wants to hurt my feelings, but I want it all or nothing. No compromise. So, what do you remember about the dinner? Write it all down. I'll sketch while you write every thing you can think of, Sally, no matter how trivial it may seem at the moment."

The only thing to come out of this collaboration was further exhaustion and a few sketches done by Minola. The missing link seemed to be as elusive as before.

Chapter 16

Peter walked into the dining alcove looking for his men, and found Sergeant Welsey, who informed him the men were in the kitchen waiting for him. The kitchen's sleek stainless steel table was made up to look like the traditional chef's dining table. It was in vivid contrast to the rest of the working kitchen. While waiting for Peter, the policemen were obviously enjoying the meal; one Etienne rarely served himself. In this instance, he had made an exception and thoroughly enjoyed it. He had prepared the traditional steak and potatoes, but with a flourish–a Bordelaise sauce accompanied the flattened filet. Roasted new potatoes covered in butter and dill, and asparagus with a hint of lime accompanied the entree. For dessert, Etienne had prepared his signature crème brulee. The meal ended with an exquisite selection of cheeses. Etienne received raves for the meal.

Sated, the men were ready to return to their investigation, while coffee flowed to keep everyone awake and alert. The Sergeant brought with him several reports, among them copies of the code Minola had found in Yardleigh's office. Someone at Interpol had guessed that, along with everything else, it indicated a pick up-point, apparently, the painting's placement on the wall signaled the location as being east, west, etc.

The specific locations, however, were still unknown. They did not know if the location signaled a pick up or drop, or whether drugs or money were involved. The black book and the painting somehow provided the signal for activity, but, they had not yet broken the code

On his way back to Minola's, Peter stopped in his room to pick up some essentials. He had kept her key, but softly knocked and let himself in. Noticing the door to her studio was open; he crossed the threshold to the small room and watched.

Sitting on the windowsill, a big easel nearby, she was drawing, earphones plugged in her ears, pad on her lap. She was adding a section to a landscape she planned to use in the show, but drawing it first on the sketchpad. He would have to ask her why she did that, assuming she would ever openly discuss anything with him again. He could see she loved listening to music while she painted–disc covers lay all over the table.

It is amazing the little things he noticed about her. He stood and watched for a quite a while.

Suddenly Minola removed her earphones and turned to face him. "I didn't hear you come in. You should have let me know you were back. How did things go?"

"I enjoy watching you work. Things went reasonably well. The gist of the conversations ran the gamut from Giselle expounding on your artistic talents to Le Clerque complaining about the state of the economy. One very interesting thing came out of the dinner. It appears that Le

Clerque wants to pull out of the Yardleigh business altogether, and soon. Giselle did not say much, but it seems money has been disappearing. It's just gossip, nothing specific. Maybe Le Clerque wants to cover his tracks by disassociation. The finger of suspicion for the missing funds pointed to Edwards."

"So, it was not a total waste of time," replied Minola.

"No, it was not. I really do not want to discuss business at the moment. I think we need to clear things up between us."

"There is nothing to clear up. Alexis is free and she clearly wants you back. She is a beautiful woman."

"Let me ask you a question. Do you think I deserve to be chucked again when another wealthy man comes along? Does it not matter what I want?"

"That is a ridiculous question, and you know it. It is not what you deserve, it is what you feel for her and what you want from the relationship. I certainly will not stay around and be second best, so you won't get chucked again, as you put it. If you don't mind, I really am tired, and I would like to be alone tonight." Minola groaned at the expression. "That is so Garbo." She put the back of her hand on her forehead to emphasize her point.

Peter chuckled, but quickly became serious. Alexis would have to wait. "The one thing to come out of the dinner that I didn't mention before was that the Sergeant noticed Mr. LeClerque staring at you after the second break. You and LeClerque obviously noticed something. Do you have any idea what happened?"

"Funny that you should mention that. There is

something, but I just can't put my finger on it. Sally and I tried to work it out earlier. I did some sketches–sometimes that works for me–but I needed to get away from it for a while."

"I think you did notice something. Until this case is solved, you will be protected either by me or my Sergeant. I certainly will not ask him to sleep on the couch–that is my prerogative. Besides, we have issues to resolve."

"Peter, what is it you want from me? I touched your arm to offer comfort earlier this evening, and I thought you were going to jump through the roof. I certainly don't need, nor do I want, it spelled out for me any further. Please, please, leave me be. If you want to sleep on the couch, then by all means do so. I am not rehashing the meeting with Alexis Yardleigh to ease your discomfort, and I don't want you to feel sorry for me." She would not settle for, nor accept Peter's pity for her…that was something she could not bear. She could not live in that kind of a relationship– not with Peter, not with anyone.

Peter, on the other hand, did not know what to do. He understood why she fought him, and that she wouldn't believe anything he could possibly tell her tonight. She was too wound up. He simply had to prove to her that there was no one but her for him. Since meeting Minola, he knew what he had felt for Alexis was not real, had never been real, and could never compare with his feelings for Minola. *How do I convince her?*

"Minola, we are both very tired, but this definitely is not over. How on earth can you think I feel sorry for you? Your touch was unexpected and disturbing, but not in the sense that you interpreted it. I thought I had lost you, and your generosity caught me off guard. You are a beautiful, accomplished woman. There is no future with Alexis. I don't *want* Alexis, and I am not going anywhere. I am…"

At the sudden knock at the door, Peter swore. "Who the hell is that? It is one o'clock in the morning." He slowly opened the door.

Ian Stoddard, the reporter who authorized the portrait of Yardleigh for the *Daily Sentinel* entered and enveloped Minola in a great huge hug. He added a generous kiss, which she promptly returned with delight.

"Ian, what on earth are you doing here?"

"I came to check on my investment. I had been reading…reading, mind you, not writing about the Yardleigh investigation. So here I am. After all, I am a reporter, you may have forgotten that fact. I ran into Robert downstairs getting something for Sally at the front desk. He told me which room was yours, and that there was another murder. In reality, I am here on an altogether different story and thought I would stop by and see an old friend. I am worried about you."

Peter, who appeared to be casually leaning against the armoire, watched this exchange in utter silence, his hands clenched at his side.

Ian finally looked around, noticed Peter, and promptly asked who the stranger was.

Minola apologized and introduced them. "Ian, this is Chief Inspector Peter Riley, Interpol. Peter, Ian Stoddard, reporter par excellence from the *Sentinel*."

Ian flared, "Minola, what the hell is going on? How are

you involved? Are you in any danger?"

"Oh, so now you are worried about me. What did you think I was going to do when I called and asked you for permission to paint the portrait? I used your paper as an excuse."

"I always worry about you. To be honest, I did not think." Turning to Peter, he said. "So, Chief Inspector, is she safe, and well protected? With two murders, maybe I should stay around for a while."

Peter did not say a word, just observed and waited for Minola to answer. His stony silence spoke volumes.

"Ian, I am fine. Are you staying here at the hotel? We have a breakfast scheduled tomorrow morning. Meet us downstairs, say, ten thirty? It is late and I am tired."

Ian took the hint. On his way out he asked if Peter was leaving as well. This time, Peter responded by saying he had a few things to discuss with Miss Grey, and Ian left.

"You seem to have friends all over the place, including Fleet Street. Just how close a friend is he?" Peter questioned.

"Peter, you knew about him—remember the portrait? And if you are asking me whether I have discussed this case with him, you can see I have not. He has not written one iota about the murder. He is, however, a good friend. Now, I am tired and I assume, since you locked the door, that you are determined to spend the night. I really will be fine."

"Nevertheless, I am staying. The couch is long enough and actually quite comfortable, and I brought my things with me. Minola, please don't take this lightly. I do believe you are in some sort of danger. I just don't know the extent of that danger."

"I believe you. It has been a long day. Do you want bathroom privileges first?"

"No, please go ahead. Would you mind if I looked at your work in the studio?"

"No, you can look at anything that you want. My art is an open sketch pad." She rolled her eyes, her mouth curved in a tentative smile. "God, I must be tired. I won't take long."

Peter walked into the studio, and looked around. He noticed her current landscape reflected an early spring pasture in beautiful pastel colors, with a lovely barn mirrored in the stream. It was a peaceful painting in direct conflict to her emotional day. On the table, he found the sketches she had done with Sally. He took a closer look at them.

It was clearly visible that LeClerque was staring at her. She had captured his face vividly, and his penetrating gaze looked haunted, frightened, and cold. Peter's concern for Minola grew. Something had happened. He kept looking at the sketches. An idea began to take form. Maybe Minola could sketch the tables before the second break, prior to the murder, to see if there were any discernible differences. He would ask her tomorrow.

He looked at the other sketch pads laid out on the table, and finally found what he was looking for. He felt guilty, but she did give him a clear field, and shamelessly he took advantage of it. He opened the pad and found his own likeness. This one must have been done when they first met. He saw his disheveled hair and piercing, mocking eyes, done when he suspected her of being what? He couldn't even think of the word and apply it to her now. Somehow, she had exactly captured the contradiction in his eyes.

He glanced through the rest of the pad. He saw a sketch of his exhausted face. She had drawn him perfectly. Before him lay an amazing history of his life since they had met, and of his growing love for her. He was stunned at the accuracy of the depictions.

Minola found Peter in the studio. She stood in the doorway, watching him. He was looking at the pad she had earlier refused to let him see.

"Judging by your face, you like what you see. That is my gift to you, Peter, something to remember me by," she said quietly.

"Remember you by? What are you talking about? You cannot possibly convict me without a fair hearing. Minola, I beg of you. Please, let us not make any decisions till this is over."

"Will it be over? How is he going to get caught? I assume it is a 'him'. There is something I am missing, and I have tried so hard to remember."

"You are exhausted. Tomorrow, we will go over everything–the sketches, everything, but tonight you need to rest."

He got up and went into the bathroom, showered, and changed back to clean day clothes. He did not want Minola to be more apprehensive about the situation, and it would not be the first time he had slept in his shirt and pants. At least these were clean.

Minola had made up the couch as comfortably as she

could, with an extra blanket so he wouldn't be cold.

When he came out and saw the couch all ready, he thanked her and whispered, "Sleep well, love."

"You are welcome. Goodnight Peter, and thank you." She looked him over, noticed the clothes he wore, and decided not to say a word. He did not even feel comfortable enough around her to wear pajamas. She hoped Alexis loved him enough this time around. She turned the lights off, and both fell into uneasy sleep

In the early dawn, he heard her crying. He could not decide what to do. He knew what he wanted to do, but was afraid it would frighten her. He finally made up his mind, grabbed his blanket, and went over to the bed. He lay down on top of her covers and held her till she fell asleep again, neither one saying a word. When he knew she was sound asleep again, he kissed her hair and returned to the sofa.

Chapter 17

Peter awakened first. He took care of his toilette, then strolled to the window to gaze at the city at dawn through an early morning haze. Paris was coming to life. Soon, he would hear the Notre Dame bells peal, signaling the Sunday services. He did not want to wake Minola up. She needed the sleep. He thought he knew what had caused her tears last night. Damn Alexis.

One thing for sure, she was not leaving him. He was convinced she loved him, and he was equally sure that she doubted his love for her.

Minola, sat up in bed, and watched Peter standing at the window, his back to her. She was confused. She remembered his kindness last night. Did she get it all wrong? Did Peter really love her? How could he, with the beautiful, perfect Alexis wanting him back? She remembered how Alexis had claimed him. She refused to inflict more pain by putting any pressure on him.

He did not know she was awake until he heard the water running in the bathroom sink. Minola emerged moments later and went straight to his opened arms. He could think about nothing but the woman in his arms.

"Thank you, Peter, for last night. You are a very generous friend."

"I'm more than that, my love. You don't believe it yet, but you will. I am a patient man."

Minola refused to listen and changed the subject. "What time is it? We have a breakfast to go to." She looked at the table clock and noticed that it was not quite seven. "I didn't realize it was so early. Do you feel like going out for a walk to the café near Notre Dame before our group breakfast?"

Minola was always ready for an early morning walk. The full force of the traffic has not yet picked up speed; there is a hush before the monumental crescendo that will wake the city. Paris took on an aura all it's own as it got ready for another bustling day. Even on a Sunday, the cafés will soon come to life and the pace quickened almost instantly.

"The cafés should open soon. Maybe we can get a start on coffee consumption." Laughing delightedly, still in his arms she locked herself into the embrace. *I feel so safe and secure.*

He bent down to give her a slow drugging kiss, the most sensual kiss imaginable. He caressed her face, and felt teardrops on her cheeks. He wiped them away and continued to hold her, feeling elated that she did not refuse the kiss, but had returned it. The walk would lighten their spirits, and maybe even put things in perspective for them both.

He knew what needed to be done. He had to close this case and sever all ties with Alexis. As he started toward the bathroom to change into clean clothes, the phone rang. Sergeant Wesley said Peter was needed downstairs. He dressed quickly, picked up his cell phone, and went to meet the Sergeant.

Minola stood a bit longer looking out into the city. She heard a knock on the door, remembered Peter's advice, and checked to see who was there. Sally stood at the door.

Still in her pajamas, she had come to visit and pump Minola for information. There was no discrimination, gossip was gossip. She did, however, have the presence of mind to call and order coffee prior to her arrival.

Minola was glad to see her, especially after being told coffee was on the way. A knock on the door was the answer to her prayers…coffee! She remembered Peter's warning, checked the peephole, and saw it was Roland, the young porter. She briefly wondered why he was delivering coffee, than she remembered that it was Sunday. He was probably pinch-hitting to earn extra funds. He was, after all a student. She opened the door.

First, she saw his brightly polished shoes, then the coffee tray in his left hand, and a gun in his right. It was long, probably with a silencer on it; at least she assumed it was a silencer.

A piercing scream from Sally alerted Minola to her danger. She swerved behind the door as she heard a subdued pop. The bullet hit her in the left shoulder. Surprised at how much pain such a small, quiet instrument could inflict, she managed to slam shut the door, but just before Roland fired off another shot. The second one went wild, presumably somewhere into the wall by the window.

Sally ran into the bathroom and brought Minola a towel with which to wrap her shoulder. Bleeding profusely, it looked like a tiny faucet had been turned on. Sally sat her down on the bed, and dialed Robert, then Peter.

I've been shot. Her shoulder ached as the blood continued to seep through the towel. *I won't go to the hospital, nor will I let Sally call for an ambulance. I absolutely hate both.*

Sally, believing Minola was in shock, kept talking, frantically waiting for someone to arrive. Robert arrived first. Shaken, Robert pulled Sally into his arms.

Peter moved quickly. Bypassing the elevator, he tore up the stairs. Still on the phone with Sally, he fired questions, trying to ascertain the damage caused by the bullet.

Robert did some damage assessment of his own. He could see Minola was not in any imminent danger, but the bleeding would have to be stopped soon. He made a pressure bandage with a clean bathroom towel to help staunch the flow.

Peter could feel adrenaline coursing through him. He couldn't get to Minola fast enough. He needed to assure himself she was alive. He kept asking Sally how badly she was hurt. "Has an ambulance been called? For God's sake, how is she?"

Sally gave him everything he needed while trying to appease his panic.

"I'm almost there." He ended the call abruptly and called the Police Nationale and Dr. Le Brun.

LeBrun met Peter in the hall. Still in his pajamas, with medical bag in hand, he asked what had happened to warrant such a frantic phone call. Peter did not stop, but explained in short, abrupt sentences while running the length of the hallway. He finally made it to Minola's door, barged in, nearly tripping over the elegantly presented coffee tray Roland had left behind.

"Who the hell ordered coffee?" yelled Peter, his eyes focused on Minola. He looked at the shoulder, then at her, and took a long, haggard breath.

Minola returned his gaze. "Peter, I am fine. Actually, Sally ordered the coffee. We were going to have a morning coffee klatch, something we used to do frequently. Roland delivered it, and a little bit extra. I'm not badly hurt, but I really, really could use a cup now."

Staring at Minola and ignoring her plea, Peter led LeBrun to Minola's side. "Doctor, the police are on the way, but I would rather you took care of this right now. I do not believe Miss Grey is in any more danger at the moment, unless we let everyone know the attempt on her life has failed."

Sally, still shaken, watched the drama unfold. Wrapped in Robert's arms and sitting on his lap, she followed the coiled tension in Peter's movements, noting his gaze lingered on the red towel covering Minola's shoulder. His face was unreadable, but she noticed his shaking hands as he lowered her onto the pillows. The pressure pad seemed to have stemmed the blood flow. He went to the bathroom, grabbed a clean towel, and replaced the blood-soaked towel.

Dr. LeBrun prepared his medical paraphernalia on the table. Sally heard him tell Peter to relax, she was in good hands, as he prepared to examine the damage done to the shoulder. He removed the towel, took a look at the wound, saw it was a deep flesh wound, but appeared to have missed anything vital. From the size of the wound, the bullet came from a small-caliber revolver. He applied a topical anesthetic and proceeded to quickly remove the bullet, then stitched the wound closed to stop the slow trickle of blood.

Minola continued to plead her case. "So, can I have the coffee? I've had no coffee, nothing. That's not a good thing."

Peter couldn't help but smile at her resolve. *God, how I love her. While LeBrun is patching up her shoulder, she is trying to finagle a cup of coffee.*

Peter waited for the doctor to respond. He was ready to pour the moment the doctor agreed with this bizarre request. She most definitely was an unusual woman, and she had to be his.

Lips twitching, Dr. LeBrun continued to work on her shoulder.

Peter blamed himself for not protecting Minola better. The thought that he had come so close to losing her was untenable. He was astounded at the turn this investigation had taken. Without even realizing it, he had issued orders for the apprehension of Roland, not waiting for the Police Nationale to react. He wanted that man caught. Now.

A loud knock at the door brought Peter to his feet, gun drawn. The police had arrived in force, to begin the interrogation process. Peter opened the door and let them in.

"Lanier, I did not expect you to come. Thank you." Peter was grateful Lanier had taken charge.

"It is nothing, my friend. I was in the office when the call came in. My sergeant notified me." He nodded toward Minola and continued, "Miss Grey, I am sorry you have been hurt. Are you capable of answering a few questions? I promise we will not tire you out."

"I will help in any way I can. I can identify the shooter. It was Roland, the bellman at the hotel. Other than that, there is not much to tell. It happened so quickly." Her voice dwindled to a whisper.

The police photographer took pictures of everything. The usual dusting for fingerprints progressed quickly. One bullet was removed from the wall and processed; the bullet removed from Minola was handled the same way.

Peter asked, "Can you think of any reason at all why Roland would want to shoot you? Anything at all?"

"Peter, he looked right at me, pointed the gun, and shot me. If Sally had not screamed, I would be dead right now. I ducked behind the door just in time. He meant to kill me, but why? I barely knew him. We exchanged the usual civilities, certainly nothing that would give him a reason to kill me."

Since the shooter had been identified, there were not many questions. Sally and Minola couldn't offer anything else.

The police worked quickly and, shortly Lanier thanked Minola and Sally for their help and told Peter they would talk later. The officials packed up the equipment and departed, leaving only a few telltale signs of their presence.

Visibly upset and unable to sit still, Peter stomped back to the window. The view somewhat alleviated the bleak sense of despair inside. *Minola means everything to me. I did not protect her. I failed her. Good God, I almost lost her.* The raw fear he felt inside needed an outlet.

Abruptly, he turned and faced Sally. "Do you remember what he was wearing? Did he have gloves on? Did he often deliver room service?"

The words jolted her out of the safe cocoon of Robert's arms. Sally replied in a dazed monotone, "Peter, there was nothing unusual in his appearance. He didn't wear gloves. He was delivering coffee. It was his job. No one would question his fingerprints on the door, or the coffee service." The shock and violence had shaken her memory of the incident. All she remembered was the hissing sound the bullet made and the blood on Minola's shoulder. "Besides, Minola mentioned once that Roland was always very diligent–he frequently worked where needed," she added.

Wryly smiling, Peter responded, "You are absolutely right, Sally. There would be no reason for him to take any precautions. He was where he was expected to be. I was not thinking."

His focus shifted to Dr. LeBrun. "Minola must go to the hospital."

"Why? I removed the bullet. The bleeding has stopped. She is safe."

"She could develop an infection. Anything could happen." Peter had stopped thinking like a cop the moment he heard she had been shot.

"Chief Inspector, if a fever develops, she'll go to the hospital. She is secure in her own surroundings. I'll monitor her progress. She is safe."

Minola focused on Peter. "I don't want to go the hospital. You are here. I want to stay in my own bed. I'm not going anywhere."

She thought his face was the color of her charcoal grey paint. She watched as he walked over to the other side of her bed. He bent down and tenderly caressed her face with a trembling hand.

"Peter, I am fine." She touched his hand.

"I was not here to protect you. I...please, please be careful, and don't make any sudden movements. Your shoulder may start to bleed again." He took her hand and kissed the inside of her wrist. He felt her shiver, but whether it was from his touch or her pain, he was not sure.

Dr. Le Brun spoke up. "All right, Chief Inspector, who is the doctor here? She will be fine. It is a deep flesh wound, but not dangerous. Miss Grey was very lucky."

While LeBrun chided Peter, Minola returned to her quest for coffee. "Doctor, that was not a rhetorical question. Coffee relaxes me, and I still have one good hand with which to drink it."

"All right, Miss Grey, you can have some coffee, as long as you realize that coffee is a stimulant. You would be better off with some herbal tea with lots of sugar. The shock to your system emotionally and physically might not support the coffee."

"Are you telling me I might throw up?"

"That is indeed what I am telling you," the doctor replied with a grin.

"Doctor LeBrun, I have never, ever, thrown up coffee."

"I give up. Give the lady what she wants, Chief Inspector, but have something handy–extra towels, anything, just in case."

The doctor hummed to himself as he cleaned and packed his case.

Minola seemed satisfied with his response, and looked

expectantly at Peter. Peter poured the now cold coffee, offered a cup to Sally as well, but Robert shook his head. He wanted to continue to hold Sally, who still visibly shook. He covered her with the blanket Peter had used last night.

The sergeant, meanwhile, came up to the room and was ready to offer his assistance. Unobtrusively, he stood in a corner, waiting for Peter to give him instructions. He reported the hunt for Roland was well under way.

The irony of the situation was not lost on Peter. The morning phone call from Welsey had been about Roland. The sergeant had been going over reports, taking a closer look at the hotel staff, trying to pinpoint inconsistencies he had found.

Roland had served Yardleigh well. He was a student, but not a very good one. He liked expensive women and he liked to gamble, neither of which he could possibly afford on a bellman's salary. His activities did not show up in the initial investigation of the hotel staff. Cash has a way of not leaving a trail until it is too late. Finally the authorities had found the connection. Yardleigh had paid Roland to be his errand boy.

The Sergeant felt helpless and guilty. He looked at the blood-soaked towel, and then at Minola.

Peter wanted action fast. "Sergeant, we have a new player in the pool. I want the ballistics report as soon as it is available. I suspect it will match the gun used to kill Yardleigh. Work with the local police. Find him," he said tartly.

"Sir, all that is being done. Is Miss Grey alright? Shouldn't she be in the hospital?"

"No, Sergeant she is not alright. She has been shot," Peter said brutally. "Fortunately, it is a flesh wound. She will be in some pain, but Dr. LeBrun assures me she is in no danger. Right now, the hospital is not a safe place for her–another attempt could be made."

"Should we post a man by the elevator? I assume you will remain here. We'll find a lead–Roland could not have gone far."

Peter, once more focused on the investigation, considered the situation. "He had ample time to blend in with the workforce and disappear. I'm assuming he is not going to show up for work any time soon. Let us check him out more thoroughly. How often did he visit Yardleigh? Where has he been going? Whom had he been meeting? I want to know what he has done every second of his life since Yardleigh's murder. Also, Sergeant, get someone in here to act as a bellman. We need to know who is coming into the hotel. Have the service area watched as well."

"Yes, sir." The sergeant looked toward the bed and saw Minola smiling at him.

"I will be fine, Sergeant. Don't worry. But I think the Chief Inspector needs some support."

Sergeant Welsey, not quite sure what to say, wished her a speedy recovery. "I will follow up every lead, Sir. We will find him." He quietly let himself out.

Peter locked the door.

Minola saw Sally huddled in Robert's arms. She couldn't bear her distress. "Sally, if you hadn't been here, I would be dead now. I just froze, and he would have had a clear shot. I am fine."

That didn't seem to console Sally. The shock of the morning had not yet worn off–she had come so incredibly close to losing her dearest friend. Robert kept reminding her how quickly she had reacted.

Peter's gut tightened as he listened to Minola. *I would have lost her, just like that.* He clenched his hands. *I need something to do.* He ran his hand through his hair and walked over to the window.

Minola took note of his every reaction. She needed to ease his guilt–he was hurting more than she was. "Peter, I am not in any pain, the topical anesthetic is working. My shoulder has been numbed. I am fine. Please, it was not your fault. But I must have seen or heard something at this disastrous dinner. I just, for the life of me, can't think what."

Peter was unsure whether to question her further or allow her to rest. However, since she was looking at him expectantly, waiting for his response, he decided to plunge right in.

"I had the same thought. Since Sally is already here, we could try to place into perspective all movements during the dinner in the restaurant as well as the lobby."

"I don't want anyone to know the attempt on your life failed. Roland knows he missed. He may have to try again, and I can protect you better here. I will not chance your life again, do you understand me?" he said firmly. Seeing his expression, Minola subsided.

"Who are 'they'? It was just Roland."

"Whoever they are, Roland did not act on his own initiative, he was following orders. If they find out he failed, he becomes a liability. I want him found alive. You need to stay in seclusion for the time being."

Dr. LeBrun glanced at Minola and gravely said, "I think he means business, Mademoiselle Grey."

"It is Minola, Dr. LeBrun."

"D'accord, je m'appelle Henri."

"Henri and Minola it is. I know he means business. I did a very foolish thing, but I have been very well taken care of. Thank you, Henri."

"Now pay attention to what I am about to tell you," the doctor continued. "Do not move that shoulder for the next forty-eight hours. It could start to bleed again, and that we do not want. It could mean a visit to the hospital. Also, I will leave a couple of stronger pills if the pain becomes too great. Listen to that man over there." He pointed to Peter.

"I can do all that."

"I am not finished yet. If a fever develops, go immediately to the hospital. Now, my last request, if you please. I am familiar with your work, Minola. If it would not be an imposition, may I see some of it?" He finished impishly.

"Thank you, Henri. Yes, of course, I will show you some of the finished pieces. I am getting ready for a showing in two weeks."

Sally instantly jumped up and walked to the studio, Dr. LeBrun following behind her. She needed to focus on something other than almost losing Minola.

At the sound of a knock on the door, Peter drew his gun, keeping it down next to his leg, and opened the door slightly

Minola couldn't get used to the idea of Peter with a gun.

She knew it should not surprise her how adept and comfortable he was with the weapon, but the sight of it made her anxious.

She saw, through the partially opened door, someone from Housekeeping had brought new linens. *Peter must have called for them.* Peter inspected the packed linens carefully before taking them, then he closed and locked the door.

Peter walked over and leaned against the door to the studio, watched as Sally showed LeBrun all the paintings save the one on the easel. He knew enough of her foibles to realize that one easel, completely covered, was not for public viewing.

Peter marveled at her talent. There were a few pieces from her favorite gardens and sketches of faces that had seen a lot of life, perhaps not always kind, but still full of animation and even joy. Hers was an unparalleled generosity of spirit.

LeBrun eagerly inspected everything shown to him. "Minola, I am at a loss for words. Your work is exceptional, excellent. Thank you for showing it to me." After requesting the date and location of her show, he shyly asked for an invitation before Peter escorted him to the door.

Looking at his pale wife, Robert said firmly, "Minola needs to rest, and I want Sally to take a nap. Peter, I assume you will not leave Minola's side?"

"I'm not going anywhere," he replied tersely. He locked the door after their departure, and started pacing.

Minola watched him pace, her mind working. "Peter, if you would rather not go with me to the gallery, I do understand." She assumed he wanted to get out of the invitation and he was here because he felt responsible.

"Where the bloody hell did that come from? You invited me, and I am going with you. Don't even think about changing your mind." Peter stopped pacing, tasted bitterness in his mouth. *She is running from me...I can't lose her...*

He tried a more formal approach. "I should be delighted to go with you, Miss Grey." *Hell, that didn't sound any better, it was too stilted.* When she did not respond, he continued, "I think you are probably getting tired. Why don't you sit on the couch for a bit? "

"Peter, I am fine. I can go downstairs. They will find out I am not dead, one way or another. I am not hiding in here. For God's sake, Housekeeping was just here, and rumors are going to fly. Why do we have to cancel breakfast? Couldn't we just say I fell or something? I was looking forward to breakfast."

"Minola, my love, we are going to cancel breakfast. Sally will be back later, and together all of we are going to rehash that blasted dinner till we figure something out or you become too tired. We are not going anywhere." His attention once more turned to the bed and the linens that had been delivered.

Minola recognized a losing argument when she heard one. It was not lost on her that he had gone back to calling her his love. He made a few more phone calls, settled everything, then returned to the couch and realized Minola was watching him. He returned the gaze.

"All right, Miss Grey, what is on your mind?"

"Why, predominantly you, Chief Inspector," replied

Minola as she made herself more comfortable on the couch.

"Indeed, that is a good thing. It is, is it not? When did we become so formal?"

She did not respond to Peter's query. She felt restless, so she got up from the couch, started to walk back to her bed, then decided she needed to freshen up. She wondered what sort of shower she could take without getting her bandages wet. Peter kept glancing at her bandages; he wanted to make sure she was not in too much pain or discomfort.

She watched him pacing around. He suddenly froze in mid-step. He stared at the bed, then walked over, reached out to touch the red stains. With sudden fury that shocked her, he ripped the sheets off. She could not bear to see him so torn by her stupidity. She should have been more careful, but it was just Roland, after all.

"Peter, it is not your fault. We need to get beyond this shooting. I promise I will not let any strange men with guns in this room again."

Upon hearing her voice, he regained his composure and responded, "You didn't know Roland had a gun. You should amend that statement to say no men in this room at all, except of course for me. Before you say anything else, I am here to make sure the rules are followed," he spoke, his voice tight with anger.

"Peter, you can't stay here and guard me indefinitely."

"Would that be such a bad thing?"

"You have a life outside this hotel. I don't want you…" Minola stopped and searched for words to express her feelings. Cutting in, he said, "You are going to finish that sentence, I trust, with something more agreeable."

"I was, but you cut me off. As I was saying, I don't want you to feel obligated to guard me because you feel responsible for the shooting."

"What the hell are you talking about? I do not feel obligated to do anything. You were under my protection. I failed miserably, but it will not happen again. I am here, and I am staying. End of discussion. No one will hurt or touch you again."

She looked at him to see if the statement had a double meaning. He returned her gaze with amazing steadfastness. Something in his intense scrutiny made her blush, but she assumed it was all her imagination. It was his job, to protect her. The kisses were just sex. *I have to remember that, or I will fall apart.* She lowered her head.

"Peter, I am fine. You did not fail. You can't be with me all the time. You could have been in the bathroom, and I would have behaved the same way. I knew Roland, and I had no reason to be suspicious. He was where he was supposed to be. Since it was me he aimed for, the answer lies with last night's dinner. I must have seen or heard something. We just need to go over the events. We arrived at about the same time, before most of the guests. We all milled about. People were at the bar, walking around, just generally getting acquainted. We need to find out what happened during dinner, the break, and right after dinner. The answer has to be there."

"Later this afternoon, we will discuss everything. Right now I will make up your bed, and I fully expect you to take a nap."

"I am tired, but I am too wound up to sleep. I need to shower and change. I still have blood on what is left of my top. Henri cut it to pieces." She watched as he methodically made her bed, asked what she wanted to wear and where she kept it. He pulled out her lacy cinnamon front-buttoned set from the armoire, and reminded her not to get her shoulder wet.

When he heard the water running, he thought back over the day's happenings, waiting patiently until she needed him again. So far it had been one hell of a day–the woman he loved almost got killed, she didn't trust him, she felt betrayed by him, and she suspected him of involvement with another woman.

The police had rummaged through Minola's room and collected blood samples, a useless exercise since the blood was all Minola's, but procedures had to be followed. They wiped the door for fingerprints and found Roland's, which had every right to be there. Had he succeeded, he would have been beyond suspicion, an accustomed face, he had nearly flown beneath the radar. All this, and it was still morning.

Peter sat on the couch and kept going over the events. In the distance he heard the water turn off and called out, "Do you need help with anything?" He knew she was out of the bathroom before he saw her; he could smell her perfume. The only fragrance she ever wore, Patou's Joy. "That scent becomes you, Miss Grey." He did not approach her, terrified she would withdraw, and he couldn't handle the rejection.

"Thank you, Chief Inspector. I feel human now, and I

am thirsty and hungry."

She was eager to continue and pick up the thread of the conversation, but Peter wanted her to relax and take a nap. "You need to rest."

She would have none of it. "No, I need to do something. I will not be a prisoner in this room. I want to know why he tried to kill me."

"So do I. So do I," Peter muttered. Giving in, he dialed Robert's and Sally's room number.

Robert answered, "How is she?"

"Restless. She wants coffee and food. In that order. Care to join us for breakfast?"

"We'll be there as soon as Sally is finished in the shower. Peter, she wouldn't take a nap. She just sat there on the bed, Minola's blood on her shirt, not moving. I finally convinced her to go take a shower. Seeing Minola will be great for her. By the way, I extended our stay here. For both their sakes."

Peter agreed, and gratefully acknowledged the gesture. "I do understand. Minola will need the support. She is just as obstinate, didn't nap, just showered." He knew Minola would feel better having them close. He placed an order for a late breakfast for four, along with fresh coffee.

While Peter arranged the breakfast, Minola sat in bed.

Peter started to pace again.

She watched him, mesmerized. He looked like a caged animal. Minola was afraid he felt trapped and stuck with her. "Peter, you look like you have been ensnared somehow. You don't have to stay. I can get a private security agency to do the job. They will report to you if that would make you feel better."

"Have we not had this discussion already? I'm staying."

"Then stop pacing. It's driving me crazy."

He stopped in his tracks and fully focused on her. "You do understand that you came very close to being killed, and that another attempt might be made?" His terror for her came through his words.

"I realize I was very lucky, but at the risk of repeating myself, I am not going to sit here and be a prisoner."

"Then we have to find out what happened last night. You absolutely must think about everything. In the meantime, we are going to take some action of our own."

"Yes, I understand, and I also understand you have a job to do. But I can't find the missing link. What kind of action?"

"We are going to get the word out on the street that you remembered something, and you are cooperating fully. This may take some of the pressure off. If they think you have given us the information, they might assume another attack is futile. It is just a gamble, and you still need protection. That means me, and only me."

"How are you going to do this? What is the procedure for this kind of game plan?"

"There are no set procedures. We have not had a set procedure for any of this–from the beginning, nothing has been by the book."

"So what are you going to do?"

Peter explained, "Tomorrow, they will question LeClerque about his relationship with Edwards. The same with Giselle and the rest of LeClerque's staff. We'll make sure everyone hears about Roland's participation in the debacle. I will clear it all with Lanier."

Breakfast arrived while Peter explained his strategy. Minola got up, making a beeline for the coffee. "Sit down," he barked. "I will get your coffee. I know how you like it, steamed milk from the carafe. Everything is here."

He dialed the Jones' room. "Robert, breakfast is here."

Soon, they knocked on the door. Sally still looked a bit wan, but seeing Minola cleaned up and smiling restored her spirits.

Robert took Peter aside and whispered, "Ian called me this morning. He was upset that he couldn't see Minola because you called him to cancel. He is quite fond of her. They are friends, have been for a long time, and he is worried about her. I told him she was fine, but..." He could sense Peter's jealousy.

"She is tired. She won't admit it, but she is. I know he is a close friend. I have to–I need to protect her. I want to be with her, alone. There are issues between us that have to be resolved, but they won't be until this is finished." Peter paused. "Robert, I need to be with her."

Robert looked at Peter's haggard face and understood perfectly. "Peter, she may be afraid to face it, for whatever reason, but she cares, deeply. I have known her for many years. She will bolt rather than face a relationship she feels isn't complete, or is one-sided."

"Thank you, Robert. She is not going anywhere, and neither am I. That cheating bastard really did a number on her," Peter swore under his breath. Serving breakfast was a welcome distraction.

Once everyone was served, Peter started the process rolling.

"Minola is still in danger, make no mistake about that. If not because of what she might know, then in revenge for spoiling their plan."

While they ate their meal, Peter questioned Minola. Although he wanted her comfortable, he tried to focus her on visualizing her surroundings on Saturday. "Minola, concentrate on the evening. You are an acutely observant person. You must have seen something, like the anomalies of Yardleigh's Avenue Foch office."

"I have thought about that evening. It all seemed so normal."

"Could it be what people were wearing? Was something stained, dirty, replaced, missing? Anything that you remember, anything at all? Was there a meeting in the lobby that aroused your suspicions? Was anyone there who should not have been at the dinner? Something that struck you as odd?"

"I remember the frenzied gust of wind when we were in the lobby during the break. I was standing near the bar; Jacques was letting someone in, and the wind almost knocked them down."

Sally, listening intently, asked, "Why is that significant? Was it because of the people coming in? Do you remember who they were?"

Minola tried to think back to that moment and replied. "No, they were heading to the restaurant, not familiar at all. But I remember that LeClerque's tie was blowing up into his face. He was at the bar, and I must have been staring at him.

He quickly smoothed the tie back down, and glared at me, then picked up his drink and went back to his table."

"Why is that significant?" Peter thought they were on to something, and didn't want to let go.

Minola thought for a moment, then suddenly looked up. "When we first came downstairs, I watched people coming in. The weather outside was calm and no one entering the hotel was disheveled. I saw LeClerque go to the bar, and he was impeccably dressed. Why do I remember the calm and then the wind?"

Peter pressed on. "Where are the notes and drawings from your session last night? Remember when you met with Sally?"

She had to think for a minute–so much had happened since yesterday. "I think they are in the studio, on the little table."

Peter moved swiftly and returned with a small sketchpad and a notebook. He gave them to her, hoping they would jar her memory.

Minola focused on her sketchpad. "I remember. Look at this!" She pointed to the sketch.

Peter looked. The sketch was of LeClerque. Minola had concentrated on the tie clasp he wore. It was large and exquisite, with beautiful vivid colors. She had drawn it as if it were alive with a blazing rainbow of colors.

"I saw the colors. The light was just right, and it was magnificent. The intensity of the colors caught my eye. Peter, look…the gust of wind. In this sketch, I drew LeClerque without the clasp. It was gone, and the tie was in his face. What happened to the clasp?"

Peter moved off the bed so suddenly he startled her. "I know exactly what happened. He damaged it while struggling with Edwards. We found small sparkling stones near the body. He probably thought that the missing stones would attract more attention, so he took the clasp off. He didn't count on your artistic eye, Miss Grey."

"He saw me staring at him. He must have suspected I had noticed something. That is so obvious, why did it take me so long?"

"Everything is obvious once you become aware of it. I know Roland was working last night. While we were at the bar, I saw him talking to Jacques."

"Oh, my God." Sally suddenly came to life, realizing the chain of events. "Roland was working the night of the party. LeClerque killed Edwards, and then told Roland to eliminate Minola."

"So, was Roland working for Yardleigh or LeClerque?" Robert found the process incredible.

Peter continued trying to piece the puzzle together. "We have no proof, but my guess is that he worked for both. He has proven to be a greedy bastard–he got paid by Yardleigh, then he probably reported to LeClerque and got paid by him as well. Once we get the ballistics results, we'll know for sure whether the same gun was used on Yardleigh and Minola."

Chapter 18

Peter's mind focused on Monday, when he planned to provoke a reaction from LeClerque by using Minola's memories of the dinner. His gaze frequently settled on Minola.

Robert's attention focused on her as well. "Peter, I think Minola is exhausted. We are going to leave. I'll insist Sally nap too. Call if you need anything."

Peter put out the 'Do Not Disturb' sign, closed, and locked the door, then turned toward the bed. "All right, Miss Grey. You need to rest." He did not go near her.

"Are you going to stay?" she asked very quietly.

"I'm not going anywhere. Not without you, never without you," he whispered. He still did not go near her, but stood and waited until she fell asleep. He went to the bed, lightly kissed her forehead, and tucked her in, then walked to the couch and watched her sleep. *When did she become so important to me?* He didn't want to think about his life without her. He wanted and needed her on every level. *I have never felt like this before. Never like this, never with anyone else.* Peter shook his head and began to plan his Monday itinerary.

He went over his notes, and diagrammed the fateful events of Saturday: Edwards was killed between six-thirty and eight. Peter saw him about six-thirty loitering around the restaurant, and they found the body at eight-ten. Roland was working that evening, helping Jacques. The focus was on Roland, LeClerque, and Edwards. Thanks to Minola, he had the 'who'. All he needed now was proof of the 'why'.

He was certain Giselle Armand knew what was going on, but did not commit the murder. She was reasonably successful as an artist and was able to support her lifestyle. Further investigation indicated she lived within her means, and greed was not an issue.

How closely did Roland figure into the actual business dealings? Was he a deliveryman? If so, how, and of what? Drugs, dirty money? How were the deliveries made if the police were watching the offices? There had to be an established routine. All he had to do was find the key.

He picked up the drawings and looked again at what Minola had done, not as a policeman, but as a man deeply in love with the artist. He glanced toward the bed; she was still asleep. His gaze traveled over her face and down to her wounded shoulder, where it lingered as he watched her sleep. With an acute sense of longing, he shuddered and returned to the drawings.

He got up, stretched, and walked over to her studio. As he looked at the finished pieces, he noticed a new grittiness to her work–fresh harshness that dominated the drawings.

He was saddened, yet at the same time exalted. Saddened because he was the one who showed her the dark side of humanity, exalted because she had reached a new depth in her artistry. With the additional perception, her canvases were now gut-wrenching. He wondered if she was aware of the intensity showing in her most recent work.

Once more he returned to the task at hand. The missing link that had bothered Minola so much was the clasp. The big question became whether the scuffle had turned into homicide, or did Roland go in and finish the job. Finding Roland was vital.

He again played with the pieces on the table. The homeless landscape painting and the codes Minola had found in the desk drawer all pointed to a deliveryman. Peter outlined everything. Roland could be the point man. He could pick up and deliver, and no one would ever be the wiser. Peter's considerable frustration began to affect his thinking. He found himself rearranging the pieces, and frequently glancing at Minola's sleeping form.

Roland was the obvious center, the common link in the two murders. In touch with all concerned, he had unquestioned access to Yardleigh's affairs. What about mail delivery? Mailmen were expected to make daily deliveries—everyday people doing their everyday jobs could easily earn a little extra cash in their pocket simply by making an added delivery.

He thought about the painting on the wall. Was that the signal? Two Yardleigh offices, the East and West locations, were involved, but what about the third, the South location? Could the hotel be the central business center from which everything originated? Was that possible? It seemed very contrived, but plausible.

Suddenly exhausted, he checked his watch on the table-already past nine in the evening. He checked once more on Minola then, bone-weary, he curled up on the couch and fell into a fitful slumber.

Dawn arrived all too quickly. Peter awakened with a start and saw Minola was not in bed. Panic-stricken, he frantically looked around and noticed a light in the studio. He found her calmly sitting on the windowsill happily painting.

"Why didn't you wake me? Why aren't you asleep?" he demanded crossly.

"Good morning to you too, Peter. You are grumpy this morning." Glancing up at him, she noticed the dark smudges under his eyes. Turning back to her work, she said, "You look like you could either use a few more hours of sleep or perhaps some coffee."

"You need rest, not work. How is your shoulder?" His concern for her well-being was obvious, but she looked perfectly relaxed and rested.

"I am fine. I have to paint. It's therapy. Besides, I need to be ready for the show. Did you make any progress yesterday?"

"No…well, yes. At least I think so. Everything is a bit hazy this morning." He shifted gears. "All right, my love, what would you like to do today?"

She raised her head and their eyes locked. She felt hot under his intense scrutiny. "I would enjoy spending the day here, with you if possible. I also need to finish this painting, maybe go downstairs for meals. I want to get as much done as possible." Detecting his apprehension, she quickly added, "Peter, I feel fine. Really."

"With me, Miss Grey?" As delighted as he was with her response, he was not convinced that she was fine.

"Yes, Chief Inspector, with you, just the two of us."

"I shall be delighted."

Peter shifted his Monday schedule. He asked Lanier to visit the LeClerque offices and let him do the warm-up interrogation. Peter thanked him, grateful that Lanier had taken a personal interest in this investigation.

They did manage to spend the day together. He was intimately aware of her presence. There were no visits from Robert and Sally. No one bothered them.

For Minola, it was enough to have Peter with her. She made no other demands.

Everyone at the hotel knew what had happened. Privacy was an issue during breakfast, but Minola didn't mind. She knew the staff was concerned, they meant well and, of course, the gossip lines had to be satisfied.

By late evening, she was reasonably well prepared for her show. Once she finished her last piece, her portfolio was complete. She had decided to simply put forth her best effort, and leave the rest to fate.

They sat on the couch eating dinner. Room service had delivered a French version of hot dogs and *pommes frites.* Peter watched as she obviously enjoyed her hot dog. "I am really looking forward to your show, Miss Grey."

"So am I. To say I am nervous is an understatement. Peter, what happens now?"

"While you were sleeping yesterday, I put some of the pieces together and Lanier is working out the details. We absolutely have to find Roland. He is the key."

"Do you think he is still in Paris?"

"We started looking for him right after he shot you. I don't think he had prepared an escape plan–he fully expected to complete his task and blend in." Peter's eyes darkened, a muscle flicked angrily at his jaw.

Minola reached out, and touched his cheek. "Peter, look at me. I'm fine. My shoulder is healing. Maybe I do look at things differently now. I see dedicated people taking personal risks to protect others, but I have never seen greed become so twisted it destroys lives. Oh, of course, I have read about it, but I have never seen it in the form of a corpse lying on the floor. Peter, what you do is amazing. I would never have the courage. I-" She stopped when she saw the blood drain from his face, and the pain in his eyes.

"Peter, are you alright?"

"Is that what I have shown you? Is that what I did to you?" He attempted to move away from her.

She wouldn't let him. With both hands, she cupped his face. "Peter, I grew up because of you. My art has changed because of you. I'm a better painter because of you. I admit that, when I first met you, I wondered how you could do this day in and day out and still keep your integrity intact. No one forced me-I decided to get involved. You showed me what a decent man you are. I soon realized that for you law and justice fight chaos. I learned that you care about people. Peter, I have the utmost respect for you. I don't often say that."

The touch of her hands on his face made him burn with desire. Turning his head, he kissed the inside of one wrist and sensed her tense. He was humbled by her response. She dropped her hands to her lap. Before she had a chance to withdraw, he drew her close and kissed her. It was a slow, poignant kiss. Her mouth was so warm, and he needed that warmth from her. Tilting his head slightly, he touched his forehead to hers. "You take my breath away, Miss Grey."

He knew their personal relationship was on hold. He did not apply any pressure, not yet. He knew she cared, and that was enough for now. It would have to hold him.

Never in her life would she have dreamed someone would shoot her. She meant every word she had said to Peter. Life for some people was meaningless if it stood in the way of whatever it was they wanted. She wondered if they held their own lives in such low esteem. Life could end in seconds.

She loved Peter because and in spite of his chosen profession. It was not a difficult concept for her to accept, not anymore.

The assumption that he still loved Alexis was never far from her mind, but today she decided just to relax, enjoy his company, and accept the inevitable. *I am collecting moments for my own life canvas.*

Chapter 19

The investigation continued, but now on two fronts.

Sergeant Welsey and the local police continued their search for Roland, thoroughly checking the hotel, searching his home and the school. Now they knew the association between Yardleigh and Roland, the sergeant requested another search in the now shuttered Yardleigh offices.

Sergeant Welsey got to know Roland a bit more through the ongoing intensive investigation. On his own time, Welsey had been watching the offices on the outskirts of Paris, continuously asking probing questions of the area residents.

Since he couldn't be in all places at the same time, he had made it a point to talk personally to local residents. The Sergeant was there so often that he had become a familiar face in the neighborhood. People expected to see him. He realized that Roland could have gained the same level of acceptance. It was a perfect hiding place. The local shops could provide everything Roland needed to survive. Sergeant Welsey surmised Roland would most likely feel safe, especially if he kept on the move, since the police had already been in, and gone from, the area.

Roland lived in fear. He was terrified of being found by

both the police and the man paying him to kill. He hid in the closed Yardleigh office, with little food, no bath, no clean clothes. He lived in squalor. His days of easy money were gone. When venturing out to buy a loaf of bread, continuously on watch, he suspected everyone he saw on the street of gunning after him.

What do I do now? What happens now? Instead of the overwhelming fear, arrogance now took its place. *I need to think.* He realized he knew enough about the business to be dangerous, but not enough to be useful. If he went to the police, he would be charged with murder, or attempted murder at best. Minola Grey had recognized him, and by now the police probably knew his gun had been used to shoot Grey and kill Yardleigh. *I have no place to go, I need money. The bastard owes me. Why should I be afraid?* What did he have to lose? He already had at least one murder hanging over his head. Roland was young and naïve, and believed he would be paid to disappear. He used a public phone to make his appeal, dialing the memorized number. He had no idea where he would go once he had the funds, but money in his pocket always made him feel better.

Once the call was answered, Roland started talking quickly before his nerves got the better of him. "I need money. I won't bother you again, I will disappear. You owe me."

The voice on the other end was glacial. "You will need to finish the job. I pay for completed tasks, not failed ones."

"So, she's still alive." Roland gulped. Sweating and frantic, he responded, "Why? What purpose would it serve? They know it was me. I can just escape. They won't find me, and you will be safe and in the clear."

"Finish the job," came the answer. "I don't like loose ends. She is a loose end." Roland quietly hung up the phone.

"So are you," whispered the voice.

Lanier's investigation of LeClerque served as a second front. LeClerque apparently hadn't expected another visit from the police and seemed to believe he was beyond reproach.

"M. LeClerque, you were seen entering the bathroom around the time of the murder. You were also the accountant of record for Yardleigh Enterprises. We have records that show your financial dealings with the business. We have…"

"You have nothing. No proof. You have Miss Grey staring at me, that is what you have," LeClerque interrupted. His relentless icy stare began to show cracks.

Lanier saw the man was visibly shaken. "I do not remember bringing Miss Grey into this conversation, M. LeClerque. You would be well advised to tread carefully in that direction. Good day to you, sir."

Once outside, Lanier reached for his cell phone and dialed Peter. "I think we need to put some security around the hotel. I just left LeClerque. I believe I made him jittery, too jittery. He mentioned Miss Grey staring at him." Lanier heard Peter swear. A brief, tense silence ensued.

"Lanier, can you get a couple of the local gendarmes to watch the front and side entrances? He must have felt threatened to let himself slip like that." Peter's stomach twisted in knots.

"Already done, my friend."

"Thank you." Peter ended the call and took a long, haggard breath.

Standing in the doorway between her studio and the bedroom, Minola watched Peter finish his conversation.

"What happened?"

"I think Lanier put the fear of God into LeClerque. He made a veiled threat in your direction. Needless to say, you will not be going anywhere in the near future,"

"That is absurd. I have a show coming up. I won't be stuck in this room. You are here, what could possibly happen?"

"You forget, I was here a few days ago, and you still got shot. Minola, will you listen to me?"

"All right, Peter, I will stay put. Can I help in any way, maybe as bait somehow?"

"Don't even think about it." He walked over to her, tilted her head with a finger under her chin, and kissed her. Speaking quietly, he said, "There have been two murders and one attempted murder. Yours. I cannot and will not risk your life. It will be over soon, I promise." He captured her mouth, drinking in her sweetness.

At the first sign of her response, he deepened the kiss and felt her tremble as she tangled her hand in his unruly hair and pressed herself closer to him. He could not let go of her. The thought was the only tangible hold on his sanity "Minola, my love" he groaned, "We need to talk, and soon."

"I know. Alexis…" Minola stopped as a knock on the door interrupted her.

"Damn it to hell," Peter swore as he headed to answer the door.

Through the peephole, he saw a weary Sergeant Welsey leaning against the door. He let him in. "Sergeant, you seem tired. Sit down, please."

"Thank you, sir." Welsey sat on the couch. "Sir, I believe Miss Grey should stay in her room. There might be another attempt."

"Yes, she has agreed to do just that for the time being." Peter took his cell phone and dialed Lanier's number.

After a few rings, Lanier picked up the line. "*Bonjour*, Peter."

"*Bonjour*, Yves. Thanks for the earlier heads up. I think they will try the hotel again. She has been in seclusion, more or less."

"I think you are right. I can probably get two or three men to watch inside the hotel. I think we should probably set them up in appropriate hotel uniforms. However, Peter, it cannot be for any great length of time. I have manpower problems as it is. Since this is such a high-profile case, I can rationalize most of the expenditures to my superiors, but as the Americans say, I do not wish to push my luck. I will do all I can, my friend. How is Miss Grey?"

Peter glanced at Minola's resolute expression and said, "Let's not delay. I can't keep her locked up for too long. Thank you, Lanier."

Hotel activities continued to function normally, despite the addition of gendarmes posing as bellboys and porters. Nothing untoward happened for three days. Peter kept a close eye on Minola. She was safe for the time being.

Chapter 20

Thursday night Sergeant Welsey was enjoying his dinner when his cell phone rang. He heard a gurgling sound and then nothing. Recognizing the sound, he shot out of the restaurant while dialing for an ambulance. His second call went to the local police department and the third to Peter. "Sir, I have called for an ambulance, the police are on the way. The front is secure. It had to have been an attack in the back."

"See what is going on and call me back. I will wait to hear from you." He turned toward Minola and tried to explain in a calm and rational voice what was happening. He didn't get a chance. His cell phone beeped incessantly.

"Sergeant, what is happening?"

"Sir, one of Lanier's men is down. It's messy. Lanier could use your company."

"I will meet you downstairs. I just want to make sure we post someone outside this room." Turning to Minola, he asked her not to leave the room under any circumstances. "I beg you, don't open the door to anyone. There has been a shooting. I must see Lanier."

"Go. I'll be fine." She was going to ask for details, but his expression was so dejected she decided not to. She didn't want to burden him. "Peter, please do be careful." She tasted fear, but would not allow it to dictate her actions.

"I won't be gone long." His fingers stroked her cheek. "Please stay in your room, love."

Peter waited for the cop to arrive, then hurried down the stairs. Bursting out of the back door he saw Wesley on his knee bending over a man. The man had been shot in the neck. The anguish on Lanier's face told Peter it was one of his men. "Yves, I am so sorry."

Lanier spoke in a hushed tone. "He was a good and seasoned man. I don't understand what happened. This should not be. At least he alerted Welsey. He must have been surprised somehow. There are no bruises on his body, no defensive wounds. Just one shot." He began shouting into the eerie silence that now permeated the alley. "I want to know what happened here tonight, and I want to know *now*. Where the hell is the coroner?"

While Lanier knelt by his fallen man, Peter looked around and saw another body, a few feet away at the back entrance of the hotel.

He recognized Roland. Peter looked up and saw where Roland's head had been bashed against the brick wall; splashes of crimson painted the dull, sooty brick.

The hotel gossip mill was in full swing. Jacques, still working, called Minola to let her know a policeman had been shot and that Peter was involved.

Jumping to the wrong conclusion, Minola flew out the door, a cop running behind her, down the stairs, and out into the street. She had to know it was not Peter. As she fought her way through the crowd, she ignored the police, who had surrounded the hotel, until one policeman finally restrained her. By then she was at the scene. Seeing the two covered bodies, she gasped, terrified what might lie beneath the tarps.

Looking about, she spied Peter and Lanier, and began to breathe again.

Walking with Lanier, Peter caught sight of Minola. She was an ethereal vision in the pale moonlight, her eyes huge and lustrous. He realized why she was there, and what had terrified her. He needed to get to her. The alley had not yet been cleared by the police. Peter watched as she slipped away to the park. *Damn it to hell. I have to get to her.*

"Lanier, Minola is heading to the park. Please have a couple of your men follow me at a safe distance." He plowed through the throng of police, following her at a running pace. What he found seemed to freeze the blood in his body. He positioned himself at striking distance and waited for a safe opportunity.

Thankful that Peter was not hurt, Minola decided she needed some quiet to examine her feelings for him. Reaching the park, she started down a silent path towards a favorite bench. The sight of a man, stepping out of the shadows, gun in hand brought her to a stumbling halt. The small pistol, held delicately, as though he held a fragile teacup, in LeClerque's hand, stopped her breath in her throat. *What an absurd analogy. What on earth do I do now?*

"I might as well finish you off right now. I have nothing left. You ruined everything. Everything." LeClerque spoke as if he were standing in a nightmare. Terror gripped his eyes.

"Why? How have I ruined everything?" she asked quietly, not shifting her focus away from the weapon.

"You interfered, that is why. For the obvious reasons–money, power, and more money–I lived very well. This was not your affair, not your business." He seemed to have regained some of the coldness in his demeanor, as though ice flowed through his veins.

"What will killing me accomplish, M. LeClerque?" She used his name purposefully; it became more personal that way. "Four people have already died. The police will hunt you down. You have a chance now to give yourself up. Don't make it five deaths. I can try to help you–I can plead for a lesser sentence." Although shaking, Minola forced her voice to remain calm. *Don't show fear. He will feed on it. Keep talking.*

"It will avenge my failure," he replied.

"It will still be a failure. You cannot guarantee your own survival. You have destroyed yourself. There is no going back." Out of the corner of her eye, she saw a moving shadow behind the trees. *Keep him talking. It is your only hope.* "Do you have a family, M. LeClerque?" She saw a bitter smile line his mouth.

"I have a wife who could teach Alexis Yardleigh a few things about avarice."

"I am sorry," she murmured.

"Why are you sorry? You destroyed me."

"No, M. LeClerque, I did not. You did that by yourself. You precipitated your own destruction." Her voice was quiet, even-toned, and resolute.

Without moving, LeClerque calmly said, "Chief

Inspector, please come and stand beside Miss Grey." As if he felt Peter hesitate, he emphasized his demand. "Now, Chief Inspector, or I will shoot her."

Peter stepped out of the shadows and positioned himself in front of Minola. Her safety was paramount to him. "I am here, LeClerque. You cannot possibly escape. There are two dead bodies across the street. One of them was a cop." Peter's tone was even, giving no hint of the thoughts behind his eyes.

Minola stepped up to stand beside Peter. Furious, he tried to push her back. She did not budge.

"Stand still. Don't move. I did not shoot the man."

"No, most likely not, but you did kill Roland. The gun you hold, I assume was used to kill the officer and Yardleigh, not to mention the attempt on Miss Grey's life. Everything points to you, LeClerque." Peter needed to keep him talking.

"Roland killed the cop. He was out of control. I did not mean to kill Edwards. He demanded more money, and he was afraid. It was an accident. Everything began falling apart," LeClerque wailed. The gun in his hand did not waver.

"Just as you did not mean to kill Roland, yet both men are quite dead. Edwards was hit twice. You meant to kill him. Roland's head was bashed against the alley wall more than twice. You meant to kill him as well."

"Edwards was stealing from me. He even told me how much. He kept that damned black book. The fool itemized everything. It was perfect. In the beginning, no one was hurt, it was just money. Normal mail deliveries. Yardleigh liked the money. He was losing Euro trade–he didn't understand. I helped him, but he became frightened and he called you. He had to be silenced." LeClerque babbled.

"Yes, I can see how easy it was for you." Peter knew Lanier's men were watching and waiting. He needed to get Minola out of the way.

Peter felt Minola start to step forward and grabbed her arm, trying to stop her. At the same time, Peter saw LeClerque's hand move. Peter wrapped his arms around Minola and pushed her to the ground, falling on top of her. He heard the bullet whistle above them, missing them both.

Lanier's men leaped out of the shelter of the trees, grabbed LeClerque, and carted him off. As they took him away, he broke down, becoming a weeping, pathetic figure.

Peter rose, helped Minola up, then helped her brush dirt off of her. "What the bloody *hell* were you thinking? You just took a decade off my life. Don't you realize you could have been killed? That was a gun. Don't you ever, *ever* do anything that stupid again! Your shoulder…are you alright?" He crushed her to his chest and held her hard, waiting for his gut-wrenching fear to subside.

Still numb, she said nothing. She felt safe in his arms and he was safe in hers. Neither was willing to let go.

Chapter 21

Minola sat on her bed, legs tucked under her, a fresh bandage around her shoulder. Peter stood near the window, leaning against the wall, seemingly composed, watching her. Robert and Sally huddled together on the couch. *"This is such a delightful, peaceful tableau for a painting, if only I could edit out all the violence."*

Peter saw Sally's eyes fill with tears. "Minola, we missed our...maybe tomorrow after breakfast, the four of us could go to the Rodin Museum for a short visit."

Shocked out of her musings, Minola said, "That would be wonderful. Peter, I want to thank you for giving Ian his headline. I finished the Yardleigh portrait, and he is delighted with the whole package. Breakfast and Rodin sound terrific."

Sally and Robert finally broke the oppressing atmosphere in the room. "So, why was Yardleigh killed?" Sally asked.

"For the most basic of reasons–greed and self-preservation. Yardleigh came to us, making LeClerque feel threatened. Based on what LeClerque had said to him, Yardleigh told Roland about Interpol, and Roland reported back to LeClerque. By double-crossing Yardleigh, Roland caused not only his own destruction, but that of the others. LeClerque started talking, even before his arrest. It was as if the floodgates opened. He blamed Yardleigh, he blamed everyone. They were laundering drug money, and Roland and a courier made the deliveries."

Wondering at the sums that would rationalize murder, Robert queried, "Peter, just what kind of profits are we talking about?"

"In the millions. The accountants are still poring over the books and codes. Minola was right, the painting did signify the locations, centering on Yardleigh's two offices. The deliveries and pickups from the LeClerque office were done at various times during the week, by a courier. Nothing was consistent."

"After Yardleigh's death Edwards handled the process, but he cheated LeClerque." Peter looked at Minola. "The money was picked up as routine mail deliveries. In each office, Roland acted as courier and general gofer. Edwards knew what was going on. When Yardleigh decided to talk, he became expendable and had to be eliminated. LeClerque took care of the rest. Once Edwards was put in charge, he helped himself to some extra funds–he deemed it an increase in his salary. He decided he was dealing with more risk and so deserved more money–the criminal theory of economics."

"It all seems so easy, now that it is over." Minola sounded drained.

Peter continued. "LeClerque, a greedy man by nature, didn't like the shortfall. He was also concerned that things would surface during the investigation, and he wanted to pull out. Edwards, on the other hand, wanted to expand the business. They arranged to meet during the dinner, a seemingly perfect venue, but LeClerque got scared and a brawl ensued. The first hit on the head was an accident, but LeClerque realized Edwards was on the verge of panic and decided to limit his losses. He hit him again, finishing the job. I think I must have made Edwards nervous. He was the contradiction, the weak link. He wanted more, but he frightened easily. The rest of the tale fits in with your observations, Minola. You became a liability, and Roland was hired to silence you." Even to himself, he sounded exhausted. He had come so close to losing her, but finally it was over. She was safe. *Where do I go from here?*

Chapter 22

Minola's shoulder had not completely healed by the gallery opening, but the bandage covering her wound was minimal. She wore a long-sleeved black silk dress, along with black sling-backs, and no jewelry. She felt uncomfortable wearing the opal, but couldn't bear to put anything else on. Her pale complexion, along with the austere clothing, gave her an appearance of desolate luminescence.

Peter was still with her, although their relationship was strained. He didn't advance. She didn't retreat. He noticed the missing opal, but said nothing. It just added to his already dark and gloomy mood.

As the taxi took them to the gallery, Minola was subdued. This should have been a very exciting time for her, yet she was miserable. She loved her art, but it no longer fulfilled her. She realized her time with Peter was ending, but thought of life without him left her feeling empty and depressed.

The gala reception was held in an old well-known gallery that had ventured toward combining classic and contemporary art. Minola's work was the first attempt in fusing the modern and the old, established venue. She received accolades, and even sold three pieces. The evening went smoothly, although she became increasingly aware of Peter's deepening bleak and somber mood.

After the show, everyone met back in Minola's room for coffee, cognac, and dessert. The discussion revolved around the art show. Peter no longer participated in the conversations, completely withdrawing. *Now the murder is solved, he only stays out of politeness. He must want to get back to Alexis. I need to go home-I can't stay in Paris any longer.* Minola managed to continue acting the perfect hostess while wishing for and dreading the end of the evening. Finally, it was just the two of them in the room.

It was very late. Room service had finished picking up the remains of the party. Minola stood near the window watching the Paris lights. She heard Peter walk over and stand near her.

"Peter are you still in love with Alexis? I thought you would be going back to her now that the case is finished." She couldn't bear to look at him.

He turned her around, looked at her, pushed some hair out of her face, "No, I am not. I have been trying to tell you that for a while. Why?"

She decided she would override her scruples and make this one request. "I have a favor to ask of you." If he agreed, she would have this one memory to keep for the rest of her life, and he would never suspect how much she cared for him.

"Please–I doubt I can refuse you anything." He waited, appearing calm and comfortable, but he was afraid what her request might be. If she asked him to leave her, he wasn't sure if he could live with never seeing her again.

She gathered all her courage and looked straight at him. "Make love with me tonight?" She saw astonishment, and a hint of anger. He glared at her. *He can't be angry. This is what he's wanted.*

His curt voice lashed out. "Are you asking me to have sex with you? A one-night stand? Do you want to see if Alexis' boast holds merit?"

She stepped back under the onslaught of his fury, saw the pain and disappointment in his eyes. *Strange. I know his face so well.*

"Peter, I…have sex? I asked if we could make love. I am so sorry, Peter, please forgive me," she stammered.

She turned away from him, tears stinging her eyes. She tried to hold them in so he would not see the pain he caused her. Suddenly, she realized how he would see her request. She loved him, but he didn't know that. He would assume that she was just…what? Exactly what was she doing? She had told him once that she made a distinction between having sex and making love. She sighed, her plan evaporating. She knew she could not do this.

Peter turned her around once again and searched for any sign to give him hope. He saw her eyes were filled with tears, and watched as she took a deep breath. Her face drained of color under his intense scrutiny, as he recalled her stated distinction between making love and having sex. His stance softened. He wanted her to tell him, he needed to hear it from her. Peter stroked her cheek with a finger, forcing her to look at him.

"Why, Minola? Why do you want to make love tonight?" Peter knew how much this request cost her. He wanted more than one night with her–he wanted a lifetime. What could he tell her? Should he tell her that he loved her beyond reason, that one night with her would never do? Was she ready for that kind of emotional and physical commitment?

He knew he had to make a choice, too. He needed to get back to England, but given the chance he would follow her anywhere. The murder case was closed. His time was severely limited by his responsibilities at home.

"Minola, I'm deeply and passionately in love…I couldn't possibly make love to you just for one night," he whispered hoarsely. "I am so deeply into you, I can't see straight. I want a lifetime of love with you. I don't bloody want a one-night stand."

Minola heard he was passionately in love and closed her mind to the rest of his words. She shut her eyes and accepted the pain seeping into her heart. She interrupted him immediately. "Stop, Peter, please. I am so sorry. That was unforgivable on my part."

Minola turned back toward the windows so he wouldn't see her face. "I am leaving next week." She desperately needed to go home. She couldn't bear to remain here any longer. She took a deep breath, resolving to end this now.

"It went well tonight, quite successful in fact. We have reached an agreement to show more of my work at the gallery. I thought this would be a lovely way to celebrate. Peter, other than finding out if you loved Alexis, I had no other agenda. I'm so sorry, I didn't think beyond Alexis. I didn't think there was anyone else in your life; I wouldn't want you to betray anyone." She bowed her head, defeated and desperately unhappy.

Her sudden plan to leave caught him by surprise. He saw she was crying, no longer trying to conceal her tears. He reached out, drawing her close, and tried to get her to look at him, but she closed her eyes. "Bloody hell, Minola. Look at me," he said in a harsh, raw voice. She tried to move away from him, but his grip on her was solid, although he was careful not to hurt her.

Forced to look at him, she saw his gaze on her was steadfast and so very gentle. "Alexis be damned. What do you mean, you are leaving? Didn't you hear what I just said? Minola, listen to me. I love you. It has always been you, ever since we met. I'm deeply and passionately in love with *you*. There is no one else. I have never loved as I love you. It is lust, passion, desire, and everything else rolled into this incredible sensation. You are my world." He watched as her tears continued to flow. He bent his head and felt her shudder as he slowly kissed them away.

"Me?" she asked, astonished. Still unsure, she felt a warm glow start in her chest and begin to flow outward. "I thought it was just sex on your part. You responded to me, but I thought…God, Peter, what is the matter with me? What a fool I've been. Are you sure? Me?" She still could not believe him.

"You, Miss Grey. You are the only woman in my life, and have been since we met. How could you not know? I tried to tell you and show you. Now, why did you request my services tonight?" He kept his tone lighthearted, but he desperately hoped she would be generous enough to give him some hope for a future together.

"When I saw Alexis greet you, I thought you wanted

her. She kissed you. She claimed you, and you did not withdraw."

He gathered her into his arms and held her. "I will be blunt here, my love. Alexis and I had a good physical relationship. The only way I could show her that it was truly over was not to respond, so I didn't. There was no reaction, Miss Grey. None. Nowhere on my body. Do you understand?" He pressed her closer still, so she could feel his reaction to her.

"I do." She put her arms around his neck. "Peter, I love you so very much. I didn't want my love to be a burden to you, yet I desperately wanted a memory of us together. I knew our time together was limited, so I asked you to be my lover for the night. I wanted to make love with you." She barely finished that last sentence before he enveloped her in his arms.

He lifted her chin and thoroughly kissed her, exploring her mouth hungrily, taking care not to strain her shoulder. She responded just as passionately. She hugged him closer and was left in no doubt abut his love and desire for her.

Elated that she had finally admitted her feelings, Peter nevertheless was cautious. He still held her, reluctant to let go even for a minute. "My love, I absolutely adore you. It's not a question of your leaving. I will relocate. I am willing to do anything that will keep us together, on any continent."

She was thrilled he saw a future for them, amazed he was willing to give up everything to be with her, but she couldn't allow such a sacrifice. She could paint anywhere. A gallery in England would work just as well as one in America. He had family and his profession in England. She would be happy in England.

"Peter, you can't relocate. You belong in England. I'm

the vagabond here. I could be anywhere, but where I want to be is with you. Are you sure that you want–"

This time Peter interrupted. "I'm so very sure, my love. We belong together." He held her with the utmost tenderness. She had just given him the greatest gift he had ever hoped to receive. Wordlessly, they clung to each other.

Peter released her and went over to the desk, chose a CD, and inserted it into the CD player. "May I have this dance, Miss Grey?"

"Here? Now?"

"Here. Now."

"Certainly, Chief Inspector. What–" Before she could finish, she heard Tom Jones singing 'You're My World'.

"This is our song. He says it better than I ever could. You are my life, my world, Minola," he murmured. "To say I love you just doesn't seem adequate." He tilted her face up. Her eyes were huge luminous pools of liquid bronze.

"When I came to Paris, I never expected my life would change with such force. I wanted to be a better painter. I wanted to share my love of art with others. I think I have accomplished both, but it is meaningless without you. You are my life, Peter, my world, now and forever."

Peter kissed her with a sense of passion he did not know was possible. He devoured her. Her solemn promise reached his very soul. "I want you so very much." He pressed her closer to him. "Do you feel what you do to me?" he whispered. His arousal was total.

Minola responded to him as she always did, fully and completely. She took the initiative, and started unbuttoning his shirt. She continued one button at a time, one drugging kiss at a time, her hands shaking. Peter groaned.

Peter captured her hands in his. His lips brushed against

hers as he spoke. "Before we continue, I'm going to put the 'Do Not Disturb' sign outside the door. Nothing and no one is going to interrupt us tonight. I cannot wait any longer to make you completely mine," he whispered into her hair.

He came back to her outstretched arms. She was ready for him. He took her to peaks she had never reached nor imagined before as he slowly and sensuously undressed her, caressing her skin with his mouth and hands. His lips seared her back as he took off her bra and reached out to capture her full breasts. With his eyes and hands, he feasted on her body then, back to her mouth, making it throb from his kisses.

Passion drove away any shyness she felt. Totally naked, she wrapped her arms around him. This was right. It was Peter, his whispers hot against her neck.

He moved down to her breasts, and his lips claimed first one, then the other. His hands and lips laid claim to her body. It was a slow, raw act of possession. He moved slowly, deliberately across her body. She responded, her hands touching him with equal fire. He heard a moan and realized it was his. He knew she was ready, she was wet with desire, and he couldn't wait any longer.

As he slowly slid inside, he felt tightness, a slight barrier. He pushed through, burying himself in her. Her gasp of pain stopped him. "Why didn't you tell me? Don't move, my love. I…" He tried to slow down for her comfort, and not rush so.

"Peter, don't stop now, please. It's alright, I'm fine." She moved her hips underneath him, and he was lost. Her passion igniting once more, she felt him move inside her and his hardness excited her beyond reason. She couldn't get enough.

They were lost in each other. He waited until she reached her peak, and then surrendered to his own ecstasy.

Drained, he lay on top of her, still inside her, not moving. She was finally his, completely. He couldn't bear to break the intimacy. "Why didn't you tell me? I could have been gentler. Are you alright?" He caressed her arms, trying to soothe away any discomfort; as his hands seared a path down to her thighs, he realized he wanted her again.

"I didn't think it was important. I told you I didn't believe in casual sex, and there was nothing casual about my feelings for you. I am glad I waited–you made it perfect." She reached out to him, felt him grow inside her, and hungry desire spiraled through her. She reached for his mouth. "Peter, could we try this again?"

She smiled as she felt his response. "*Hmm*...that's perfect. I do need the practice," she whispered against his heart. He had finally unlocked hers, heart, body, and soul.

"I think I can manage, my love. All the practice that you want, anytime that you want." He nibbled her ear, and felt her melt against him. "I have waited so long to make you mine. 'I love you' doesn't begin to describe what I feel for you." He trembled as he felt her respond, gave her a hard, driving kiss, and took her again. This time, neither had the patience for tenderness–it was a combined act of possession.

Together, they moved in perfect unison. She had given him an incredible gift, one he would treasure forever. She was his, and only his. He was shocked to feel this possessive, primitive sense of joy at being the only man to have her. Exhausted, they slept, wrapped in each other.

Chapter 23

Paris is a romantic city. Peter kissed the tip of Minola's nose. With a twinkle in his eye, he elegantly inquired if she would be interested in visiting London.

"I would love to show you my home, Miss Grey."

"Is that anything like showing me your etchings, Chief Inspector?"

"It might be. It just might be, my love."

"Well, in that case I accept. I would never refuse to see your etchings. I should be delighted to see your home, Chief Inspector."

"Then London it is." A sheepish grin crossed his face.

"You look a bit apprehensive. Is there something you are not telling me?"

"You know me too well. I know I said things would move at a nice slow pace; however, there is a small catch to this request. My mother never has had much patience. She wants to meet you as soon as we arrive. In fact, she wants to meet us at the airport."

"So soon? Couldn't we wait for a bit? I'm not quite ready. What should I do? If I bring a particularly good likeness of you as a gift, do you think that should ease that first dreaded meeting? I can do that. I have one, you know. Only, it's mine. I finally finished it, and it's my best work I believe. You haven't seen it yet. I cannot bear to give it away. Peter, I'm babbling. Peter, are you sure you want to do this?"

"Yes, you are, and yes, I am very sure, my love. Everything will be fine. Is that the piece that you have kept under wraps on the easel?"

"Yes, it is. Would you mind if I just did a quick sketch of you for your mother?"

"You can do anything you like with this face, I have no objections. I would like to know, though, why you don't want to give the finished product to my mother."

"It's a very emotional, personal portrait and I cannot bear to part with it. It was going to be my second memory of you. Do you want to see it?"

"What was going to be your first, memory?" He still couldn't believe she was his.

"You know perfectly well-my one night with you. I don't think I would have had enough strength to walk away from you. After we made love, I didn't want you to move away from me. I love you so very much, it terrifies me." She reached up and gave him a quick, possessive kiss. "So, do you want to see it or not?"

He held her, he could do nothing else. "Your love is fully reciprocated. I wouldn't have let you go—I couldn't, and survive. Let's see that painting." His lips traced a sensuous path down her neck.

She returned his caress, then led him to the study. The easel held an incredible likeness of Peter. All his intensity of purpose, commitment, and passion were reflected in his eyes. It was an honest portrayal of the man, an intimate portrayal, done by a woman who obviously deeply loved and respected him.

It was the culmination of the progression of the earlier sketches she had done of him. As her knowledge of him deepened, so had the portrait. Done over a few weeks, it reflected the man as she had come to know him. A man of integrity, a deep, abiding love of life. Now, a new softness and gentleness was visible around the eyes and mouth. His previous sardonic, jaded look had been replaced by a new vulnerability.

So involved was she in her own emotions, she had completely missed the reflection of a returning passion. His stance was relaxed, casually leaning against the window frame looking to the street below. She captured him as if she were sitting on the windowsill painting his likeness. The proximity of the artist and her subject was profound and revealing.

The painting took Peter's breath away. It showed the true depth of her love. He knew it had to remain private for them alone. It was the only work of hers he had seen that bared all. Sensual and very intimate, she had intended it to be a secluded and lasting memory for her of their time together, as she had come to know and love him.

Peter did not know what to say. She always was able to shift his focus. He reached for her. "I love you, Minola. The painting absolutely will not be going anywhere. It is ours, and stays with us. It's remarkable. My love, am I seeing too much here? Is it wishful thinking on my part? Do you really care so much?" Peter could not tell her he saw his own feelings for her reflected in the portrait. It was so much more significant to him that she painted what she believed to be her own ardent emotions. She was no longer afraid to admit to them.

"Yes, I do. Everything you see there, I feel. I no longer wanted to conceal my love for you and so I reflected everything on the canvas. This was going to be completely mine, and absolutely private. I just painted what I felt. This is the first painting I have ever done purely from an emotional perspective—it was, and still is, new to me. I love you so deeply, Peter, and it does terrify me. When we made love and you were inside me, I felt so vulnerable, yet so complete. You are the other half of me."

"I've been so very much in love with you, and I didn't want to frighten you. I'm humbled and exhilarated at the same time. I know I've said it before, but you take my breath away." Peter caressed her face, wrapped his hand in her loosened hair, and held her as if he would never let her go.

She whispered how much she loved and wanted him. He slightly released his hold on her so he could look at her face and respond in kind. She touched his lips with her fingertips. He kissed them and continued to hold her. Her emotions were raw.

"I am nervous about the trip. Right now, things are still too new. I know it's cowardice on my part. I just need a bit more time to get used to our relationship, and to the fact that you love me."

"Loving you is easy. Making love to you just for one night would have been intolerable. We will move slowly at your pace. I may have mentioned once or twice that I am a patient man. You, my love, are worth everything I have in me to give. Take all the time that you need. The one thing you are not is an emotional coward."

Minola reached up and gently brushed her lips against his. It was a light sensual kiss that aroused his senses beyond reason. He returned the caress and tempered his desire for her, covered the painting, and guided her back to the bedroom.

They stood by the window, gazing into the street below, his arm around her waist. Minola turned to Peter, and kissed him with a force that shocked her. She whispered, "Please make love to me. I want you so very much." Her hands explored his back.

Peter deepened her searing kiss, dragged his mouth away, and stilled her hands. "My pleasure, my love. Are you ready for me?" he asked hoarsely.

"Yes." She moaned, totally lost in her passion.

Peter did not need to be asked again. Even though the intensity of their desire drove them to distraction, they made love slowly. They lingered and seduced each other.

Minola appreciated him well enough by now to understand the implications of going home with Peter. He was moving slowly for her sake, yet her commitment to him was total. She returned his sentiment with complete honesty and joy.

New adventures awaited them both. Minola knew this was going to be a significant journey. She knew that by accepting Peter's offer to visit his home, she relinquished her personal freedom. She understood what he asked. He promised her the pace would be slow, but Minola had already made her decision. She could not imagine her life without Peter.

Somewhere along her journey, Minola realized she had become a true artist. She no longer portrayed the niceties. She had seen depraved behavior in people firsthand, and she no longer disguised her feelings to be kind. She had seen anguish, greed, desperation, isolation, and all the other elements that make up our existence. She painted what she saw. Her color choices became bolder, her shadows were darker, she had evolved, no longer afraid to experiment. Her memories of Paris were her palette, sometimes light, airy, and cheerful, sometimes dark, moody, and foreboding, but always, always exciting.

Peter had taught her never to take life for granted. Life is precious, and it can end suddenly and senselessly. He taught her to feel a passion for life and, somewhere along the line, a passion for him. She was ready for whatever came next. With Peter at her side she knew it would be an exciting adventure.

For Peter, this was coming home, in more than just the physical sense. She was his haven. Through her, he could glean the beautiful, serene side of humanity rather than the vile side. She made his life palatable, and accepted it without question. She understood that he was a cop and openly acknowledged his commitment to law. He was able to be himself, and through her eyes, a better man. He understood the tenuous hold that people have on decency and how quickly it can slip away.

With her, he felt complete.

The End

Born in Poland, Margot Justes has lived in some of the world's most wonderful places, including Israel, France, and South Africa. Currently living in the Midwestern United States, she has taken her love of art and travel and cultivated it into unique settings and stories for her writing. *A Hotel in Paris* is her first novel.

A Member of Romance Writers of America and Sisters in Crime, she serves on the local board of both organizations.

In her spare time she enjoys travel, museums, summer art fairs, reading, gardening, music, and the occasional shopping spree. She is now working on her second novel, *A Hotel in Bath*.

You can visit Margot's website at
www.mjustes.com